THE GHOST OF AN IDEA

Karo watched the specter flick his riding crop against his boots. "Objectivity and objectifying are not the same things."

"But you want . . ."

The notion should have been repulsive. It was repulsive at an intellectual level, especially if participation wasn't voluntary. But wouldn't it be fun, just once, to be completely and utterly in control of one's partner? Or, okay, maybe to sometimes be relieved of the burdens of self-determination and guilt and all that twenty-first century politically-correct garbage women were supposed to be masters of, to become more submissive than usual? Free will was great. It was everything—almost. And while political and economic equality were to be striven for, did the battle for feminine equality have to come into the bedroom? She wanted to be in control sometimes but not thought unfeminine. She wanted to be overpowered sexually and not thought weak. Was this her chance . . . ?

Other books by Melanie Jackson:

THE SELKIE BRIDE
THE NIGHT SIDE
DIVINE FANTASY
A CURIOUS AFFAIR
DIVINE NIGHT
WRIT ON WATER
DIVINE MADNESS
THE SAINT
THE MASTER
DIVINE FIRE
STILL LIFE
THE COURIER
OUTSIDERS
TRAVELER
THE SELKIE
DOMINION
BELLE
AMARANTHA
NIGHT VISITOR
MANON
IONA

MELANIE JACKSON

The Ghost and Miss Demure

LOVE SPELL NEW YORK CITY

In fond memory of Becky and Max and Goldie,
Gone over the Rainbow Bridge—
Rest In Peace

LOVE SPELL®

July 2010

Published by

Dorchester Publishing Co., Inc.
200 Madison Avenue
New York, NY 10016

ISBN 10: 0-505-52835-5
ISBN 13: 978-0-505-52835-3
E-ISBN: 978-1-4285-0900-9

The name "Love Spell" and its logo are trademarks of Dorchester Publishing Co., Inc.

Printed in the United States of America.

10 9 8 7 6 5 4 3 2 1

Visit us online at www.dorchesterpub.com.

The Ghost and Miss Demure

*There is no ghost so difficult to lay as the ghost
of injury.*
—Alexander Smith

Chapter One

"Oh, geez! I'm being haunted." Karo blinked several times and tried to refocus her eyes on the wet pavement that was whipping by at a good twenty miles over the advised speed limit. Her involuntary shuddering at her ex-boss's image had nearly shaken the Honda off the road and into a stand of fall-blooming hollyhocks that hadn't yet blossomed but whose buds were almost bursting off the stem with the promise of new color. Such happiness did not suit her mood.

"Post-traumatic stress disorder," she announced to the universe, though she suspected that the starry vastness was uncaring. Karo had been alone so much lately that she had taken to talking to herself. She had no one else; she was avoiding her family and being reluctantly shunned by her wage-slave peers. And deservedly so. Her hysterical catharsis at the faculty welcome dinner had been a summary example of professional hari-kari carried out in full view of the entire documents department. It had been momentarily satisfying, seeing F. Christian Merriweather fall on his chauvinistic butt, blinded with potato salad, but the public act of rage had left others with no choice but to quarantine her the moment word of it spread—and it had spread, with a speed that shamed a pandemic. She was now a leper, as welcome as flu or cold sores. To be seen with her was like being in contact with a highly contagious venereal disease, but far more damaging to one's career. Which was why she was on a waterlogged back road in the middle of a torrential storm trying to find some old plantation in Bumble-fart, Virginia: she was fleeing the consequences of her dramatic and extremely public resignation from the historical society and seeking asylum in a new world.

Until that Armageddonous day when she attacked her employer, Karo had considered it an interesting but irrelevant bit of trivia that the average working woman reached job burn-out somewhere in her late thirties, when, typically, she hit a glass ceiling in her career or her biological clock started chirping its insistent wake-up call. Irrelevant, because it didn't seem to have anything to do with her life. She was barely thirty and had no urge for children, though the notion of getting a dog had growing appeal: they were loyal and true and asked for no more than some pats and kibble. Of course, she had always realized that every human had a breaking point, a time of potential personal and professional midlife calamity when an emotional critical mass could be reached, but she'd had her zero hour scheduled for years in the future—say, around forty, when she would have the financial means of coping with it in some societally approved manner.

The traditional methods for dealing with breakdown varied with gender, of course. Men bought sports cars and took up with young bimbos; women had babies or went for face-lifts at spas in foreign countries. Given a choice, Karo planned to cross gender lines and go for the car. That seemed a better investment. But it wasn't cheap to go nuts, and it would have worked out better if she'd had a couple or ten years more to plan for her madness—or if she had a better credit rating.

Unfortunately, fate was ready to destroy her before her savings account was secure. Statistically, Karo was too young to go nova, so she wasn't prepared. She wasn't vested in her pension plan. She didn't have a stock portfolio. She hadn't even gotten around to planning for a maternity leave. As a part-time employee, she didn't have a health plan, so there was no option even of COBRA payments while she found another job. All she had was a liberal arts degree, and they didn't shell out big bucks for that in this economy.

But, her emotions hadn't cared about finances or statistics. They'd seen another person's name at the top of the magazine article, claiming all the research she had submitted to her supposed mentor and boss for evaluation, and made an intuitive but accurate leap of understanding that she had again been used—just like in college, when her professor had stolen her term paper and published it under his own name. Years of pent up frustrations were vented on her ex-boss in one ballistic explosion. She had been possessed by a demon, had spoken in tongues. She had actually resorted to violence, a thing anathema to her family. That was bad, of course, but it gave Karo some small comfort to think that, like the lucky victim of a classical bloodthirsty Valkyrie, she had gone out in a blaze of emotional and untenured glory.

Glory. Maybe its afterglow would keep her warm in the winters ahead when she couldn't afford utilities or rent, because jobs were going to be scarce. Even if the economy ever got back on its feet, from here on out she would be viewed as a loose cannon. Never mind that everyone knew F. Christian was a shit-heel who couldn't think his way out of a jar of slime; assistants were supposed to be like ministers' wives and suffer in devoted silence no matter how assholish their bosses—at least until they were tenured and could start being cruel to *their* interns, who would in turn suffer in silence.

Karo frowned direfully at the golden boughs whipping by the edge of the aging chariot carrying her to paradise or hell. It was going to need a new paint job. The '78 green Honda Civic was older and wiser than she, but it was beginning to show two-tone camouflage, changing from green to rust. She and the Honda had been going steady since her second year of high school, and it was symptomatic of what was wrong with her: an inability to let go of things, even when she should. Her few trade-ins never led to trade-ups. Because, at heart, she was a social coward, a good girl. She'd never had the guts to go for the gusto, though she was far smarter than most of the people for whom she worked.

Actually, though she would rather be tortured than admit it, Karo had always been vaguely displeased with being bright. In her experience, bright girls were lonely ones, and lonely girls got pestered by their mothers about dating and had bosses take advantage of their awkwardness with the opposite sex and their empty social calendars. They also drove cruddy cars. Of course, the only thing worse than being smart was pretending to be dumb. Such a ruse was exhausting, and she hadn't possessed the courage as a child to face her devoted and very bright parents, standing in the principal's office with a sheaf of astonishing placement tests in their hands, and deny that she was gifted. She hadn't said she didn't belong in that advanced placement class, which would make other children hate and mock her, and now it was too late. She was known for having a brain. Her parents had expectations.

But, why should she play dumb, damn it? What use was the woman's movement if she couldn't admit to having more than two thoughts to rub together and could actually balance her checkbook on the rare occasion when there was anything in her account? She just needed some guts to back up her IQ. Perhaps she'd join a support group for doormats with genius IQs. Maybe take a little assertiveness training.

"I'm turnin' over a new leaf, starting a fresh page. If it's dog eat dog out there, then I'm gonna be the head wiener." She started to make a snarling noise but stopped when she heard herself. It was a bit too convincing.

Of course, she still had a ways to go. In spite of

her heroic beginning, Karo's brain had seized up as soon as she'd staggered up the stairs of the front porch of her tiny rental home. She still couldn't recall how she'd gotten there. Unaccustomed to participating in public brawls, she had reverted to her native jellyfish form and barely made it through her front door before collapsing in a shaking bundle of calico petticoats, the historically correct outfit the historical society insisted their female employees wear in public. Rage, Karo decided, took practice. So did handling prolonged stress. She would get better in time.

But she hadn't gotten better right away. Crisis levels rose in town for days as rumor of her action spread through the society rank and file. Tales of her transgressions expanded exponentially as they went, as did the assessed damage to F. Christian's bruised butt and ego. She hadn't just dumped potato salad on him; she had brained him with the bowl and concussed him. For half a day it had been rumored that F. Christian Junior was actually in a coma brought on by massive brain trauma, but he had fortunately come back from Boston before that bit of gossip made it into the local rag-sheet. Of course, the idiot liar then had to brag that he had slept with her. Karo had taken her vengeance by starting a rumor that F. Christian wet the bed. The story caught on. Too bad that making up the tale felt both too mean and not mean enough.

The phone had rung ceaselessly as her coworkers grew more avidly curious to hear the truth of the incident, until Karo had finally plugged in the answering machine her parents gave her for Christmas and begun screening calls. Her recorded message said that she was in Brazil and couldn't be reached by any means known to man. She'd also quit opening her door unless the visitor knew the secret knock: *shave-and-haircut-six-bits*. It was usually the delivery man from Forget-Me-Not Florist with another bouquet and some more witticisms about the wages of sin being pretty good. The only other human she saw was her friend, Diane, who kept her informed of the gossip in the tavern where she worked.

The floral tributes from her anonymous admirers got embarrassing, and they made her living room look like a funeral parlor—or, more horrible, a Hindu suttee, since the flower arrangements were divided equally between twenty-nine dollar Thinking-of-You bouquets and the more expensive funeral wreaths with the black satin RIP banner. Under cover of darkness, Karo had hauled all the offerings outside to the curb, hoping that some enterprising thief would steal them. But, no. No one wanted free flowers for Grandma's grave or a twenty-nine dollar arrangement of leather-leaf fern and sunny yellow carnations to take home to their wife or mother. Instead, Karo was cited for violating city landscape ordinances—something F. Christian had probably put his friends in city government up to when he heard about the funeral sprays. In a show of solidarity, one of the women in her office talked to her tour guide boyfriend, and suddenly tours from his company began running buses by her house and pointing her porch out as a landmark. She was touted as a modern-day David going up against an institutional Goliath.

A reporter from *The Capitol* heard the story and called for an interview. A local ambulance chaser left a message urging her to sue. Karo knew something had to be done, but she'd burst an emotional aneurism and couldn't get her brain working. She didn't want to be a poster child for the underpaid masses of Williamstown who detested the bigoted, sexist, soul-eating Merriweathers. All she wanted to do was eat chocolate sorbet and hide under the Saint Anthony's Thift Shop coffee table until it all went away.

She might have gone on cowering for weeks, but two things happened within days of one another. On Monday, she was served with an eviction notice. *Want to see time fly?* Karo had said to her friend, Becky. *Don't have fun. Just get an eviction notice.* And then something more terrifying flushed her from the hole where she'd been hiding. It was her mother's dreaded second Saturday of the month phone call reminding her that her parents were coming for a visit at the end of the week and were expecting a tour of her workplace, so she'd best be back from Brazil.

Their visit alone would have been enough to force her into action, but the voice of maternal concern, coming at the end of the fourth day of the worst week of Karo's life, reached ears even more attentive than usual. Karo actually heard her mother's hidden message through the flow of superfluous, maternal verbiage. Mother was saying that she had been "wasting her life on a poor paying career," and on men who wouldn't commit to any woman they couldn't dominate because they were afraid their penises weren't big enough. (Well, her mother hadn't said that last part, but Karo could read between the lines.) The real message was: Karo needed to make a change. Perhaps a new hairstyle and some fall clothes? Skirts were shorter this year.

Discounting the fashion advice, Karo had to admit that her mom was right. She needed a new Karo Follett, a new life. Especially after the fiasco in the faculty dining room. No matter how hard both she and her boss tried to smother the flames of gossip, she had to face facts. Her job was dead, even if no one had officially buried her. No amount of sackcloth and ashes would change it. Her days in historic Williamstown were over.

No, there was no defending what F. Christian had done, the rat fink, but no one in power was going to sympathize with her feelings. After all, Karo wasn't the publicly wronged party, the one with potato salad in her face. She was the ungrateful intern who hadn't been appreciative of her mentor's advice and guidance. It did no good to protest that she'd had her work stolen—again— that her track record as an ostrich was complete where F—*F for "Fucking rodent"*—Christian was concerned. The powers that be would not listen to her appeal, even had she cared to admit to such stupidity as handing over work for which she had no back-up copies because she thought she was talking to a potential boyfriend who was offering to edit her work and not her thieving boss who, it turns out, had a history of pulling stunts like this.

Resolved to change her life, Karo had spent the rest of her weekend networking by phone and considering her limited options. In spite of her underground popularity with the working grunts at the historical society, there seemed to be only three choices open to her: suicide, homicide of every employee the rank of department chair and above, or leaving town before she was run out on a rail by F. Christian Senior, or by his perverted younger brother who happened to be an attorney. Never slow to act—at least, not once circumstances forced her hand—Karo had a five minute telephone interview with a friend of a friend who knew some guy, and decided that she preferred the sound of working on a quasi-historical restoration project at the ass end of nowhere to learning how to spin dough at a pizza parlor.

She'd called her mother back with the news on a Monday afternoon, when she knew both parents would be having lunch at the Senior Center. She would have avoided all contact if she could, but she felt that she had to give them the new address in case an emergency—like Mom's long-threatened nervous breakdown—ever actually happened. She had frowned as she hung up the phone and finally admitted that it was an act of craven cowardice to hide behind an answering machine, but an outright confession to her parents that she was changing jobs again, after letting some man use her, also again, was beyond her that week. So what if her message had been deliberately vague about her reasons for vacating her old corner of Virginia? So what if she had recommended strongly that her parents delay their vacation for a few weeks while she settled into her new job? It wasn't like she had told any actual lies. Honor thy father and thy

mother, the Bible said, but who would blame her
for this one slightly cowardly action? Wasn't it self-
defense, considering her extraordinary circumstances? And they would be happier not knowing
the truth.

A disconcerting clatter from the back of the
car intruded abruptly on Karo's brooding. Her
left rear tire had flattened something large in the
road. She checked her side-view mirror but the
mud was too thick to be certain of what she was
leaving behind. Whatever it was, it was long and
tubular.

Damn! She should stop and pick it up. This was
littering, and spare parts were so expensive, even
for cars as old as hers. On the other hand, the car
was still running and it might not stay that way if
she took her foot off the gas, especially with the
battery being as old as it was. And, there was nowhere to turn around. And it couldn't be anything
important, like the transmission or engine, or the
car wouldn't still be working. She'd check the
muffler later. Her father was always warning her
about that.

Karo felt a different sting of guilt as she sped
away. Dad loved this old Honda. He would die
when he saw the way it had deteriorated. Maybe
she could get it to a paint shop before he came to
visit. It was only money, right? And how much
could a coat of cheap paint be? But Dad would
never be fooled by paint, no more than either of
her parents were fooled by her carefully worded
answering machine message. Mother had called
back immediately, and her recorded sigh, captured by Karo's machine, said all too clearly that

she did not believe her youngest daughter's explanation about an exciting career opportunity. If Karo truly needed to dress up in costumes in order to enjoy her work, at least Williamstown had maintained a certain cache. If she wanted a change, why didn't she just come home? They had jobs in California where she could wear a costume, like Sam's Lobster House, where she had worked her last year of high school.

"Go home? When pigs ice skate," Karo muttered, wiping at the window. Her defogger was on the fritz again. She'd promised to get it fixed last March but never got around to it.

Dad had called, too. As he did whenever he was concerned with one of his children, he gave detailed instructions on auto maintenance and road safety. He was discussing the muffler when time ran out, and now Karo felt doubly guilty for her car abuse and for worrying him enough to fill twenty minutes of recording time.

Well, why shouldn't he worry? Karo asked herself as she swerved around a chunk of road detritus and scraped some more paint from the bottom of her passenger door. She was a little worried, herself, but this job was one of those gift-horse things. A job in her field, more or less, that she was qualified for? That was a rare thing indeed. Who could refuse, even if the pay was minimal? At least she got room and board while mending her very sketchy resume. She might be a while, waiting for the Smithsonian to call with a real job offer now that she was notorious. Besides, Tristam English sounded like a very nice, very calm, very British, very honest employer. Everyone knew that the

English—in general, and hopefully in specific—were trustworthy, unemotional people. That was just what she needed.

After all, hadn't she had enough of the romantic delusion that love in the form of a tall, handsome man with a reasonable degree of intelligence would come sweeping into her life and conquer all? Wasn't her present predicament proof of the damage brought on by trusting someone because they had lovely eyes and were flirting with you and there was hope they might be able to fix your computer? Career and romance didn't mix! That two-in-one economy pack was usually as bad as a sexually transmitted disease, and a hundred times more disastrous to the heart and wallet.

It didn't matter that she had meant well by dating F. Christian, or that he'd spun her a sad tale about being so wrapped up in work that he had no time to meet interesting women. He never dated people in his office, he'd said; he was doing it just this once, because she was so smart and fascinating. She hadn't suspected a thing when, after discussing the piece she was working on for an architectural magazine, F. Christian had volunteered to edit it. Add some impulsive screwups, and you had a slippery slope that never led to the kind of everlasting love her parents had found . . . or even to any kind of reasonable mental, financial or physical well-being. Why, the sound of his voice—the mere *memory* of the sound of his voice—made her want to do mean and mostly illegal things. She clearly had given F. Christian too much control over her emotions.

But that was all in the past. She'd had enough

of being low woman on the romantic and professional food chains. She was taking charge of her destiny. No man was ever going to screw with her life again.

Karo let up on the gas pedal as she went glissading around a blind curve in something approaching a true hydroplane, leaving a little more of her precious paint behind on the roadside bushes. She exhaled a shaky breath and wiped the film of sweat from her brow, knowing she had to get a grip. She couldn't afford to go into a rage every time she thought about F.-fucking Christian. She had already broken her eyetooth bridge by grinding her jaw, and she couldn't afford another nine hundred bucks for dental repairs. After all, her new employer hadn't said anything about dental insurance. Did such a perk come with a guide/curator/secretarial-dogsbody job?

Still, it was hard to keep her temper as she thought about what a fool she'd made of herself. Did her IQ simply drop twenty—fifty!—points every time she got involved with a man who claimed to like smart women? Did the occasional red rose left on her desk destroy her reason? Why had she been the only person in Williamstown unaware of F.-fucking Merriweather's reputation, and that he had his job only because his father bought it for him with huge annual grants to the society?

She unconsciously pushed down on the accelerator and fled another memory of the day she committed professional suicide; the Kodak-moment flashbacks seemed never ending. F. Christian *deserved* his bruised butt and bump on the noggin! If only the entire board hadn't been standing behind the buffet when she'd upended the potato salad on his head, it would have been grand. She could have had her revenge and no one would have ever known, because F. Christian wouldn't have brought it up.

"Well, hell!" Karo beat her hands on the steering wheel. She had to stop reliving that awful moment. It would be the rubber room for sure if she continued to dwell on the fact that she was this decade's main entrant for the Williamstown Hall of Infamy. It didn't help her mental state that she felt belated shame about what she had done. Violence was never the answer, not even to snakes like F. Christian. Public executions had been banned for a century, at least, and she shouldn't have ruined that party. Especially not if she wanted to be assigned to the visitors' project, which had been her plan before she'd lost her mind.

Things weren't a complete loss, though, Karo reminded herself grimly; she understood now why the Williamstown Historical Society wanted its employees to change clothes before leaving work. Real clothes could save a person a wealth of embarrassment out in the real world. She'd remember the lesson for the rest of her life. No one took the shrieking chambermaid seriously as she'd stomped through the lobby, raving; they had laughed uneasily at the slapstick routine instead of calling the police. The visiting professors had been very polite, too. Karo had to give them credit. Standing calmly in the ruins of the buffet, they had managed to pretend that it was an accident Karo had thrown the potato salad at her boss. Of course, what else could they do—laugh at the man whose father patronized the foundation they were hoping would provide some financial backing for their latest project?

"That'll be the day." Karo aimed for a puddle, pretending it was F. Christian himself. She still couldn't believe the rat fink had actually tried convincing her that they could continue their relationship—if she was willing to finish editing his crummy paper for the *Quarterly Historical Review,* and if she kept her mouth shut about him stealing her work. After all, wasn't he her official supervisor? Most of her thoughts had only come to fruition because of his expert guidance, he'd insisted. She should be grateful that he was providing her with this learning experience.

The pain she'd felt was not in her heart, but in her head. Years of blinding scales had been scraped from her eyes like barnacles off a hull. The painful therapy had worked, too. She finally saw the reason for the emotional pressure F. Christian had been applying for the last six weeks. Those long-stemmed roses and dinner invitations weren't the result of a late-blooming, soul-searing passion for his scholarly assistant; no, his daddy, F.-fucking Christian Merriweather Senior, had again started leaning on his son and heir to publish something, to start making a name for himself that wasn't purchased with family money. Junior soul sucker had chosen her to be his savior.

He'd been using her for her research. The thought was disheartening. Karo felt emasculated, or whatever it was they did to women to take away their femaleness. She was unsexed. Didn't anyone want to use her for her body? Why was it always for her brains? She supposed she should be down on her knees that very instant, thanking the Lord that she had noticed the hair plugs and hidden emotional insecurity and hadn't completely succumbed to F. Christian's fine wine and blandishments when the pressure got intense, but she was stuck in her worn seat for another ten miles and would have to content herself with simply reminding herself of the bright side of the situation until she reached some place suitable for kneeling.

There was little of anything bright in the torrent outside, she saw, cracking her window a bit more, hoping to clear the fog from her windows. This storm was very weird. If she didn't know such a thing was impossible, she would swear that she was being deliberately herded toward the woods. But that was just silly. Yes, she'd had some bad luck lately, but that didn't mean the forces of nature were arrayed against her. Okay, so she'd imagine something bright and shiny until something real came along.

Well . . . there always was the shining fact that even if she'd stayed in the apprentice program, she would never have been promoted out of it. After all, a move to get rid of an assistant who could actually write when he, himself, couldn't string two coherent sentences together would hardly benefit F. Christian—and he was the only one who could recommend her promotion. But that wasn't much of a silver lining. In fact, the thought made her angrier than anything else about the situation. Trifling with her affections was bad. Trifling with her job was . . . Words failed. Her parents hadn't taught her enough vile terminology to cover a situation like this.

Driving Route 5 through a bad storm was a semi-insane act, but escaping the city limits cheered Karo considerably. On some level, she was actually enjoying her rage. Her perkiness quotient was nowhere near her mother's natural level, but she was feeling better with every mile she put behind her and those burned bridges. So what if the wind was screaming like damned souls denied the joys of paradise? It seemed reasonable to her that the storm would howl with sympathy.

Yes, she had made the right decision. There was no reason why working at this new job couldn't be an exciting if somewhat lonely opportunity. And as for the lack of company on the job . . . well, if she got lonesome and felt her IQ begin to slip around her new boss, she would go out and buy a hamster or a dog. Animals were very loving, and they didn't care if you had brains instead of big blonde hair and bigger boobs. And even with vet bills, they couldn't possibly be as expensive as changing careers.

Also, maybe, if she could keep a job for six or eight months, she'd finally be able to trade up to a newer, single color car with all the extras—like a muffler and a working defogger.

"It is required of every man," the ghost returned, *"that the spirit within him should walk abroad among his fellow men, and travel far and wide; and if that spirit goes not forth in life, it is condemned to do so after death."*
—Charles Dickens from *A Christmas Carol*

Chapter Two

Tristam English looked up from his desk and re-alized that the impossible East Coast weather had actually grown worse in the last hour.

"Bloody hell!" He hit the red power switch on his desk radio and listened to the update. The broadcaster's message, though delivered with relish, was unnecessary; Tristam could hear more than enough proof that a strong storm was racing by at seventy miles per.

At first Hurricane Paula had been only a faint flicker to the west of the Chesapeake, and the rumble that followed was barely louder than the wind tossing the boughs of the tattered birches against the garret windows. But the autumn storm that should have passed to the south had unex-pectedly changed its destination. Instead, she had defied all predictions of staying below the Caroli-nas and had veered north where she was rolling ruthlessly toward the Virginia interior.

Tristam first heard about Paula's change of plans

on the noon news: a special edition lasting two hours, all of it talking about the murderous storm and the billions of dollars of damage she could do. The litany of disaster to the south had been impressive. The hurricane may have been officially downgraded to a mere tropical storm, but she didn't seem to realize that she was supposed to be losing her fortitude as she headed in over land. Whatever the weather boffins chose to call this meteorological disruption, the lightning strikes that followed in Paula's wake were managing to take Virginia's wooden giants, the chestnuts and birches and oaks, and blast them out of existence in the blinking of an eye. As an added oddity, several cemeteries had also been hit, causing damage to large mausoleums and splitting head-stones into rubble.

Unfortunately for Tristam, the James River and the Belle Ange plantation were currently in the way of Paula's meteorological whimsy. He could only be grateful that the estate was located on inferior real estate that was far from the rising river's angry water; the official opening date did not allow for repairing flood damage.

He put down the odd whip he'd been examining and walked over to the balcony. The suicide doors were opened to the rain and wind. Welcoming weather indoors was not a practice he often followed back home, but with temperatures on the third floor in the high eighties and the humidity near one hundred percent, the thought of closing off the only ventilation was unbearable. He didn't know how his American cousins endured this bloody climate. England and Germany saw temperatures in the eighties on rare occasion, but not when it was about to begin raining like a flood at the end of the world.

He glanced down at his watch and frowned. His new assistant hadn't arrived yet, and he didn't have a cell phone number for her. Normally he would not be concerned at the lack of punctuality. They hadn't set an exact time—just "around noon"—and the drive from old Williamstown was a lovely one that encouraged dawdling and gawking at the splendid scarlet and gold colors of the area's strangely premature fall. But the weather had worsened considerably since he had last spoken with the clear-voiced Karo Follett, and he couldn't imagine that she was dallying for sightseeing purposes on such an unpleasant afternoon. The roads to Belle Ange were narrow and twisting, and the birch trees offered only intermittent protection from the buffeting winds. Nor did he care for the look of the advancing pyrotechnics that were lighting up the four o'clock sky and limning the trees with white fire. It was going to be quite a show, and he would feel better if his employee saw it from indoors.

No sooner was that thought conceived than Paula obliged by upending an ocean over the house. The rain went rapidly from autumnal shower to biblical deluge, the sort of downpour that must have stampeded Noah and his beasts into their ark. Visibility would be down to nothing on the roads, and there might even be flooding in the streams that crisscrossed it at intervals. He sincerely hoped that Karo Follett had the good sense to pull off on some high ground and wait

out the storm. It seemed wrong that he was resting on a velvet settee—albeit a somewhat moth-
eaten one—when the young woman belonging to
that soft, sexy voice was lost in the stormy confusion outside.

Karo searched the gloomy woods and was finally
rewarded with the sight of a carriage drive. Even
in the downpour, it would have been hard to miss
the twin Gothic pillars topped with squatting gargoyles; they flanked the wrought-iron gate someone had thoughtfully left open for her now very
late arrival.

As the intensity of the rain diminished, Karo
was able to make out her surroundings in the per-
vasive gray light of the stormy afternoon. Things
were definitely looking up. She had lost some
more of her paint and a bumper about forty minutes and ten miles back when a newborn stream
had sluiced past directly in front of the Honda
and nearly taken her on an unscheduled cruise
down the James. The trip had been stopped only
by an old oak tree, which had also relieved her of
her fender and her side-view mirror. But now she
was in the home stretch and she was surprised—
and thrilled, frankly—by the sight of the two stone
urns lying in the deep, shadowed niches carved
in the ancient gateposts.

She was prepared to swear that the pyxis were
originals and not cement copies. And that they
were Italian, not Greek, though they looked to be
decorated with blind muses of Greek mythology
who wept eternally for the death of art and beauty
and for whoever was inside the urn. They were

ridiculously out of place on the abandoned, over-grown road . . . but what a welcome portent! If Belle Ange could afford to put real antiques at the carriage gate, there was no telling what treasures might be waiting inside the house. The urge to burn rubber all the way to the mansion and seek shelter in a sturdy, rain-proof house was tempting. But, those pyxis! Could they be real, or were they just more of fate's recent cruel tricks?

Come out, come out, wherever you are, a little voice whispered in her head. It was scary because the voice sounded masculine. Was her inner voice a male?

Too intrigued by the funeral urns to simply drive past, Karo obeyed her sudden mad compulsion to stop and leave the car. Forgetting about the crotchety battery, she stopped the Honda and climbed out into the drizzle. Just one little peek, she promised herself as she unfolded her cell phone and prepared to take a picture, and then she'd head for the house. She was already very late for her meeting with her new boss; another minute wouldn't matter. And she really wanted to know if the urns were a cheat or a promise of great things to come.

Closer, closer, you're almost there.

Her footsteps were loud in the cracked shells that paved the drive around the ornate fortifications as she carelessly crunched across the sea's old bones in her delicate loafers. The smell of electricity was strong in the air. It made her skin prickle and stirred the fine hairs on her nape. The damp heat was straight from the tropics, but she would only be in the wet for a moment. Just long enough to see if the pyxis were really Italian, and then the barely functioning air conditioner could have its way with her clothes and hair.

She was within an arm's length of the elaborate wrought-iron fence when the storm let go with a final barrage. The light and sound of the strike were simultaneous, and Karo's short scream was drowned out by the thunderclap that tore the atmosphere in twain. She was hurled to the ground by a giant white hand, too stunned to move though her face was in a puddle of water. She had taken a picture, but whether it was of the urn or of trees rushing by, she did not know.

Through the blackness in her eyes, she sensed movement in the harsh vibration of the road under her as the lethal shockwave passed beneath her prone body, and something large fell to the ground with a resounding thump. Her eyes were open, she was sure, but she was unable to see or hear anything. The lightning strike had left her blind, deaf and numbed, a helpless target for the renewed rain falling around her in a thousand stinging drops. All she could do was cover her face and cower under the onslaught until the world stopped spinning. Her phone was clutched tight in her hand.

Eventually the world stilled, more of her senses returned and she was able to roll over and stagger to her feet. She put her phone in her pants pocket. The nerve endings in her fingertips tingled violently as she clasped them to her still sightless eyes. Her cheeks were caked with grit and her eyelids burned with sudden, scalding tears as they tried to dislodge the dust paste in and around them.

"Oh, God! Am I dead?"

She clutched blindly at her chest. Her heart was still beating, wasn't it? Yes, there it was, pumping like an insufflator on an old engine. But her eyes! Why couldn't she see? Hadn't she read somewhere that a lightning strike was five times hotter than the surface of the sun?

Before she could begin to truly panic, her baby blues had worked up a good cry, and they began to wash the dirt and calcium away. Karo hung her dizzy head and let her tear ducts have their way, and her vision slowly cleared enough to see that her shoes had more chalk on them than Minnesota Fats's favorite pool cue. One of them even had a hole punched through the toe like a summer sandal! Another pair of Italy's second finest had bitten the dust, literally. She looked like she'd been wading in wet cement.

She cried harder. So much for that old chestnut about the benefits of dressing for success! What was the point in investing in expensive footwear if Mother Nature was going to spit on it? Wasn't she in enough trouble already? Now she had to face her boss looking like a dirty snowman.

A good cry for her loafers' destruction drove back her panic to bearable levels and she began to feel more competent. Karo wiped her face on a clean bit of sleeve and began to consider other important things.

"Well, hell," she muttered, looking beyond the end of her white feet.

It soon became evident what had happened. Lighting had struck at the old dogwood that leaned on the gatepost and snapped it like kindling. The charred remains lay shattered and smoking only a few feet away. The tree trunk was toast. The road around her looked like the aftermath of an explosion from a howitzer round. Seashells were blown yards clear from the fresh red scar plowed in the topsoil.

Karo stood utterly still, her damaged shoes forgotten. She was numbly grateful that the lightning hadn't actually struck her, as she had assumed in those first blinding moments, but holy moley and all the apostles! It had been close. Of course, getting crispy-crittered would only have been what she deserved for being such a moron as to be caught standing by an iron gate in a lightning storm.

She took a shaky breath. When she felt a little better, she would kick herself for being volatile and frivolous—and treasure hungry—during a hurricane. At the moment she was too cold and tired to punish herself further.

Taking a minute to inventory her tender body, she was relieved to see only minor scrapes and bruises. She hadn't even torn her clothes, although they were now very wet and dirty. No osteoporosis for her jeans, she thought wryly; they'd just absorbed enough calcium to stave off brittle bones forever.

Except for the ringing in her ears and the odd painful tingling in her hands and feet, she was back on her feet and ready to roll—this time at a reasonable speed. If she could get past the poor blasted tree that was blocking the drive.

Karo stared at the burned offering with growing consternation. It was still smoking, and it looked awfully big and flammable to try moving on her own. She could try nudging it with the car, but what if it wedged under the engine and the fuel lines caught fire? She didn't need her dad to tell her that she might not survive a second explosion.

She wiped her hands carefully on the sides of her pants, frowned at the new white smears on the palms and tried to decide what to do. Fact number one: The road was completely blocked by the smoldering remains, and she couldn't move them without some extra muscles and asbestos gloves. Fact number two: She was shaking like the proverbial leaf, and cognizant enough to realize that she was shivering because she was suffering from shock and cold. Which was an important fact. What had they said in her CPR class about treating shock? Get the victim warm and elevate the feet. That was it. The day's temperatures were in the high eighties, but she needed to get warmer. It seemed scarcely feasible, but she had to try.

Karo walked slowly back to the Honda and climbed in through the open door. The seat was wet on the left side and the old sheepskin smelled like a barnyard. Had she left the door unlatched and maybe the wind had blown it open? Surely she hadn't been so careless as to walk off into the rain and leave it standing wide. . . .

What was she doing? Oh, yeah. Getting warm.

She started the engine without any trouble and turned the heater up to high and only then remembered to close the door. Soon the interior was warmer than the outside, and Karo began to dry out. As the cold receded from her quivering limbs, she was able to let go her grip on the steering wheel and to think more clearly about what should be done.

The only option that she could see was to walk up the carriage drive. Belle Ange couldn't be that far away now, and even it was, there was certainly nothing on the road behind her for at least eight miles. She should also be safe from lightning once she was away from the gate. How could the storm find one lone Yankee down among all these trees? There were plenty of other things to draw Paula's fire if she was still hanging around looking for a target. The thing to do was to get away from her car and the gates. All that metal was just asking for trouble.

Despite her pep talk, Karo sat unmoving for several more minutes, staring at the path beyond the smoking dogwood, feeling oddly reluctant to travel any farther up the gloomy tunnel of foliage. She hadn't noticed before, because of her excitement with the urns, but it was dark down there, with a premature twilight that belonged in a monster movie, and badly overgrown with clawing bushes that probably hosted spines and spiders. It was, in a word, spooky. Which was to be expected, she supposed, at this time year. Though Virginia had a kinder and slower onrush of winter than the north, Fall was still the season of dying and haunted things.

A belated sense of concern that had been lacking for the last twenty miles, due mostly to her inability to give attention to anything beyond skiing down the slick road with her bald tires, now prompted her to think carefully about the air of desertion along this path. She was pretty certain that this was the road to the plantation, but . . .

If you go into the woods today, better not go alone.

"Shut up," she said to the taunting singsong voice in her head. Of all the times to think of that tune! But Karo still looked about cautiously to see if there was any proof that she was truly on the drive for Belle Ange. There were no conveniently placed signs. The urns and gate were suggestive, but she would have preferred a note from her employer, or a nice brass plaque announcing the plantation by name—unless these were hidden under the vines, which were pretending to be ivy but which were actually some parasitic plant whose roots were trying to tear the gates down.

"Well, hell."

A moment's examination showed that the dark shrubs were actually carefully maintained by human hands. The narrow tunnel of birch and quickthorn disappearing into the distance was deliberately trimmed from a living canopy that blotted out the sun. The path would be colorful in the spring when bursting with new leaves and blossoms, but just now it was rather rank, and she did not care for serpentine undulations moving through the foliage, especially those right near the soggy ground.

"Wild hares. Birds. The wind," she told herself. But she didn't believe it, not all the way down in her bones where she was still shaking. Could the rain have driven out snakes and forced them to search for higher ground?

Karo's eyes moved higher in the gloom, searching for any bit of sky. She forced herself to be reasonable in her reaction. The fear pinching her shoulders was not precognition; it was just shock and nerves. Anyone would be upset after such a close call as she had suffered, and there was no need to be hysterical. The sky was still there, even if she couldn't see it.

"Everything is going to be fine." But the ranks of whiplike saplings above and to the side, which danced so eerily in the blanched light of afternoon, were certainly an odd choice of roadside landscape for a tourist attraction—unless it was a Halloween haunted mansion.

There were probably plans to change this path before the plantation was opened to the public. The owner would have to do something, she thought with a flash of comforting common sense, because this was strictly a one-lane road and he couldn't risk the sorts of accidents that could happen with gawking tourists who always end up driving the wrong way. So everything was okay, right?

Karo took a deep breath and made herself stop listening to the frightened voice in her head that was urging her to find some other way out of this predicament. No, there wasn't any other option but walking this dark path. Ominous or not, she would have to trot up the road to the house and find someone with oven mitts or fireplace tongs and large shoulders to help her with the Honda. It would be stupid to risk a long drive back to the highway in the rain and growing twilight just because a pair of funeral urns and a close call with a freak lightning strike had shaken her nerves. The trees weren't really shuffling closer together, lac-

ing their branches into a tight cocoon to prevent
her escape. That was nonsense, freak optics and
the result of reading too much of the wrong kind
of fiction.

"Don't be such a coward." Karo shut off the car
engine and thrust open her door. Water attacked
her. The sticky dribble burned, perhaps having
picked up some toxins from the local noxious
plants as it passed through the trees.

If you go into the woods today . . .

She slammed her door resolutely and stepped
around the smoking birch tree's burly bulk, trying
to blot out the sickening smell of charred honey
that rose surprisingly from the exploded oyster
and clam shells. Drizzle fell from the gold trees in
a thin drooling veil.

Karo jogged quickly through the shadowed
wood, looking neither right nor left in case there
were indeed trolls or wolves hiding in the shrubbery; if they were there, she didn't want to know
about them. It was enough to watch for poison ivy
and copperheads; thoughts of bigger beasties she
couldn't handle.

If you go into the woods today, better not go alone. . . .

What gruesome tunes her brain was playing!
What moron had ever sung that song to her as a
child? Still, it had a good galloping rhythm and
Karo used it to set her pace. Eventually the tunnel
widened and she stepped onto a lawn riddled with
tree roots from a giant oak that grew in its middle.
Something moved overhead, and she dropped to
her knees gasping in fear. For one horrible moment she thought she saw bodies swaying in the

ancient limbs, soldiers dressed in Yankee uniforms, but a second terror-stricken look showed her it was only Spanish moss being tossed about by the wind. Feeling foolish, she regained her feet and trotted double-time toward the clearing where the light was somewhat brighter.

At last the main house came into view. It grew and grew with every step. It was an enormous thing that defied the usual rule of symmetry that was the passion of the early American architects. It was almost Romanesque Revival, mated with Gothic and loco rococo. Arched windows, iron railings and flying buttresses were grafted on at random to the asymmetrical turrets and gables. The river stone walls faded into deep shadows as they disappeared into the restless, golden trees. Up and up the house went, like a Gothic Jack's beanstalk.

"Holy spit." Karo's footsteps slowed. This hybrid mongrel was looking very familiar. A small Hearst's Castle. Only, more sinister. This was not a gracious, sprawling mansion where Ashley Wilkes would live. Frankenstein's monster, maybe, but not a southern gentleman.

Karo craned her neck further. The round rocks gleamed damply in a stray bit of light that had found its way through the haze and gold leaves, and pointed to the diamond panes of glass with a bright finger. She was pleasantly surprised by a lovely tangle of roses that were rampaging up the south side of the mansion in sprawling abandon. The storm had stripped it of many blooms and hurled them to the ground, but others still clung tenaciously.

No, there wasn't a single sign of the expected early eighteenth or even seventeenth century architectural order here. No courteous Georgian windows lined up in neat rows, no symmetrical Greek Revival columns holding up an Athenian temple. It was plain to see that Belle Ange—if this was indeed the Vellacourt family plantation and not some other unknown mansion she had found while driving lost in the rain—was totally unexpected.

She failed to see any sign of life or light inside the strange house, or any vehicles in the drive. But, perhaps the power was out. That would be a comfortable reason for the place to be dark and silent. She liked that explanation much better than the idea that she was alone in an abandoned wood with a rather creepy house that wasn't Belle Ange, because that would mean another walk down the wriggling green maw behind her. Not good. Her stores of courage were depleted.

Karo stood for a long minute absorbing the neo-Gothic splendor that sprawled before her. The disquieting feeling grew that it was, in spite of the scarlet roses and quaintly crazy roofline, a less-than-welcoming abode. Still, in the sunshine it would have a certain storybook appeal that tourists might like and that would make her job easier. . . .

As if sensing her qualified praise and wishing to deter her from any comforting thoughts, all stray sunbeams were snuffed by roiling clouds, and the damp twilight and lonely silence settled back around her in a cheerless shade. Soon there was only the gentle drizzle of rain on stone, and the sly, sighing wind for company. The whole scene put her in mind of some of the more sinister fairy tales in her mother's antique books, the ones that hadn't been cleaned up for children. Sleeping Beauty, perhaps. Or Cinderella. No, she had it now! It was the cover of every gothic horror novel she'd ever read! And wasn't that a cheery thought with darkness coming on?

As she wrestled with her nerves, trying to work up the courage to actually walk up the flight of shallow stairs that led to the imposing front doors and use the knocker, Karo finally noticed that a faint light was burning high up in a north end gable, nearly hidden by the towering trees that leaned against the wall. It was steady, like a weak, guiding star, and was just as comforting to see, for it meant that someone was home after all besides the vampires she was imagining. She was not the only living being in this dangerous forest.

If you go into the woods today . . . watch out for ghosties and ghoulies, and long-legged beasties, and things that go bump in the night.

"What? Shut up." The voice wasn't even getting the lyrics right, and her consciousness chided her cowardice now that a light was plainly seen.

It's just one *light.*

"Yeah, but one is enough for me." Her voice was barely audible over the droning buzz, the aural remnant of the lightning strike that continued to assault her ears.

Feeling foolish for talking to herself, Karo pushed forward. She arrived at the top of the stone steps and took a moment to smooth her blouse and finger comb her hair. It was a wasted effort at respectability, but it had again occurred to her, now that her incipient panic had died, that filthy and hysterical and very late was not the best way to present herself to a new employer. Everyone knew that the British were neat and punctual. They probably appreciated those features in their staff.

The iron-studded door was an impressive specimen that some desecrater had stolen from a thirteenth-century Spanish fortress and then shaved down to fit this smaller doorway. The family was obviously not bothered by anachronisms or adaptation of historical artifacts.

She raised her hand to an inappropriate Victorian knocker affixed by a tarnished spike ala Martin Luther. Karo hesitated a moment. It seemed pretentious in the extreme to use this shiny klaxon that would undoubtedly sound like a Civil War cannonade inside the house, and yet there was no doorbell, and she had no desire to further damage her hands or shoes by pounding on the heavy wood with bare fists and poorly protected feet.

If you go into the woods today, better not go alone. . . .

"Just shut up with the singing already."

She picked up the gargoyle's lolling tongue between finger and thumb. But, before she could let the heavy brass fall, the east wind, in another of its irregular fits and starts, snatched the knocker from her hand and hurled the entire door open—just like, she supposed, it had done with the Honda. Unlatched doors seemed to be the order of the day, and this one slammed against the interior wall with casual brutality. Karo winced as violent echoes receded into the darkness beyond the wide entry.

The crash should have brought someone running posthaste to see which army had invaded, but not a soul appeared to demand that she be more careful of the priceless, fine oak paneling that filled the dark and no doubt haunted hall beyond. She looked about uneasily and ventured a tentative hello.

"Please come in," a voice replied from the hollow house. "Enter freely and of your own will."

Karo gasped at the quiet whisper, which sounded rather a lot like Bella Lugosi in his most famous role, not sure that she had actually heard the voice through the continued ringing in her ears. She waited anxiously for some other sign of a person within, but as she hesitated on the polite side of the wide threshold, there was nothing more than the patter of renewed rain behind her and the strong wind pressing at her back.

"Come in, girl! Come in and know me better!" breathed the impatient voice, the bad Carpathian accent forgotten.

Karo looked about quickly, but no one was there. It was a fortunate circumstance that no one in her family—well, besides Mom—was given to nervous breakdowns, because if one was predisposed in that direction this situation would definitely send you there.

If you go into this house today, better not go alone. . . .

Karo took what was left of her sniveling courage in hand and stepped over the threshold. The wind died abruptly as she walked down the hall, much as if she had closed the heavy door upon it.

But she hadn't shut the portcullis yet, and had no plans to. Not until she knew who had called

her inside. After all, there hadn't been a nice little
sign on the door saying: BELLE ANGE—VISITORS
WELCOME.

She walked slowly over the gloomy stone floor,
letting her eyes grow used to the dusk. Once past
the inevitable suit of rusting armor standing at
the entrance like a hostile sentinel ready to cleave
and chop with its corroded battle ax, Karo could
see a dim light coming from a short, arched passage to the right. A thin, stooped opening at the
end seemed to lengthen and waver as if lit by firelight or a flaring torch.

"Oh, goody. A troll hole," she muttered. "Let's
hope he's not hungry."

Karo walked forward cautiously, resisting the
urge to duck under the low ceiling that pressed
far too close overhead. She halted at the dwarf-
sized door at the end of the corridor and rested a
hand against it. Her breath echoed down the tiny
tunnel behind her as she stood watching feathery
shadows dance around the edge of the partially
closed portal.

"Hello," she said again, though this time it took
more effort to force the words out. She breathed
in hot air and felt like she was going under seda-
tion, floating at the edge of consciousness. There
still came no answer.

If you go into a house today, better not go alone. . . .

Though she half expected the door to slam shut
against her, Karo pushed it wide with tingling fingers and stared into a library. Her relief was immediate and out of all proportion. A small fire
had been kindled in the hearth of an enormous
fireplace constructed of the local river stone. The

tiny blaze gave off unbelievable heat and set her clothes to steaming like dry ice in coffee. It was only then that Karo realized how cold she still was. With her coating of shell dust dripping off her drenched coat, she must look like a snowman who had blundered indoors and was beginning to melt.

She thought she saw a small movement by the heavily draped windows and turned expectantly, peering through the clouds of vapor that plagued her still stinging eyes. "Hello." She spoke into the deep, unlit corner. There was no reply.

She took a small step closer to the corner of the room and then waited for her boss to come forward into the light and introduce himself. Any polite Englishman would. Even in the gothic horror novels they did that, didn't they?

Nibble, nibble, little mouse. Who's that nibbling at my house?

"I'm right here," she said helpfully, in case he was napping in one of the chairs whose large winged backs faced her. Tristam English hadn't sounded elderly on the phone, but perhaps he was. "Come out, come out, wherever you are," she added and then frowned at her silliness.

Nothing.

"Well, hell." She slid off her right loafer and wiggled her toes. They felt numb. Cold as freezer pops. It was because of that blasted hole in the toe. The rain had gotten in. "Guess I'm all by my lonesome." She began to carol: "Ollie-ollie-oxen-fr—Eek!"

Something took her up on her childish dare. It was large and bristled up like a frightened cat,

and a terrified Karo froze in place with one foot
still lifted above her shoe. A long, spiked shadow
unfolded itself from behind the stalwart desk and
then glided out into the murky firelight. The room
grew colder, though her face and the part of her
body facing the shadow felt like they were too
close to an open fire.

Karo's breath wedged in her throat as the disjointed creature reassembled itself, extruding
into full height, the limbs filling out like meat
poured into sausage casings. Her brain blanked
out most of the image, unable to comprehend what
it was seeing for the next several seconds. She
didn't doubt that he was there, though. The displaced air kissed her skin with fevered lips and
made her shudder.

He was a tall man, gaunt and pale. Though not
old, his hair was pure white and floated about his
face like fine cobweb caught in an updraft. He
stood with utter inhuman stillness. No breath
or movement disturbed the strange, theatrical
clothing thrown carelessly onto his wiry frame.
He looked like a courtier turned torturer. Or a
seventeenth-century executioner with a taste for
finery. The final bizarre touch was the red velvet
hood tucked into his thick, black belt, along with
calfskin gloves, a tapestry purse and a thick length
of ribbon.

She noted the pallor of the skin where it showed
at the cuffs and above the high black collar that
framed his face in a small ruff. Rice powder,
right? Cadmium white theatrical makeup, maybe.
The only sign of life or color was the eerie gold

eyes that studied her like a hungry cat from across the dusky room.

For a moment he lost substance. His face seemed to flatten and indent into a weird chiaroscuro. He might have been a painting, Karo thought, for all the life he showed. Except for those eyes! Those were wickedly alive, and she sensed that they looked upon her with presumptuous familiarity that warranted a sexual harassment complaint—or maybe even a smack of his leering chops, if she could find the courage to move a single quivering muscle.

"Please tell me you're not Tristam English," she whispered, not realizing that she had spoken aloud until she saw the cloud left by her breath. She stuffed her numb foot back into her wet shoe and got ready to run. Her muscles liked the idea and complied with alacrity. Her knees tensed, her calves coiled.

Those liquid yellow irises blazed briefly with what might have been amusement. The figure's mouth opened. The lips peeled back, showing a lot of pointy teeth that looked like they belonged on a vampire. No-no-no-no, Karo thought, her scalp tightening. This was a monster, a manifestation. Ectoplasm shouldn't talk.

Suddenly, light—beautiful, electric and sane light—exploded above and behind her. She heard a noise and whirled at full speed to see what fresh, nerve-shaking menace was coming her way. Another man stood at the top of a short staircase she had failed to notice upon her entrance to the house, descending steeply from off to the right of the library door. The setting, even with the lights on, was pure Dracula, but this man was hardly anyone's idea of gothic peril. Fair and tweedy, and wearing a slight smile, there was nothing scary about him. Her nascent scream aborted itself as she realized that there was no need to throw her body through a window and flee into the twilight.

Though he was unthreatening, the newcomer was staring at her with mild surprise and perhaps vexation. He somehow managed to climb down several stairs without her seeing or hearing him move—more freak optics due to the storm, she told herself. Her ears were still whining, too. That was the problem: shock.

Karo stared hard. The lightbulb above him, though rather dim, did provide enough illumination to reassure her that he couldn't be a figment of her overworked imagination. His clothes were also reassuring twenty-first century, mild-mannered casual. In other words, everything was actually okey-dokey, and she had been about to act like a nitwit with the other old guy in the library. She let out a depleted breath and sucked in some fresh oxygen for her sorry brain. What was wrong with her? She'd worn a costume to work every day for the last three years, and of course that's what she'd seen: a period costume. And she had been ready to scream the house down because it was dark and she was thinking of monster movies. She was losing it big time.

Feeling suddenly embarrassed by her intrusion into the house, Karo looked over her shoulder to ask the scary man in the library to explain that he had called her inside. The room was empty.

She glanced back at the flesh and blood male on the stairs. He was now halfway down, still watching her, but with an expression that was one part relief and three parts amusement as he scanned her battered clothes. She was likely showing a rather spooky complexion, too, if her chalky hands were any guide.

"Hello." The voice was deep and soothing, with just the trace of an accent—an English one this time. "I take it that you are my new assistant. Is that your car parked out by the gate?"

Karo heard herself answer from far away. "Yes. I'm sorry to be so late, but the lightning knocked a tree across the road and I couldn't get by." She looked over her shoulder again, still wondering where the unpleasant man in the library had gone, since she could see no other door. But the sense of his presence, along with the fire's intense heat, was fading quickly from her flesh. Shock certainly did funny things to a person: one moment cold and the next too hot.

"Don't give it a thought. I'm relieved that you are unhurt. What storms you have here in the States! I've been feeling a bit like a toad under a harrow." He'd reached the bottom of the stairs and she realized that he was very tall—well over six feet—but he moved with the grace of a fencing master. "You are frightfully wet. I must say, that was quick work with the fire. I haven't had much luck with that particular fireplace. Wood in it simply refuses to burn for me."

Karo looked over at the hearth and then back

at her new boss. He had moved closer in the blink of an eye. She still hadn't heard his tread on the stairs, but it didn't seem to matter anymore. The tension had gone from the room along with the other man and the intense cold.

He's kind of cute, she thought, smiling. He was like one of Rafael's exquisite fallen angels, studying her soul with dangerous appreciation while he decided what to do with her.

Karo frowned at that idea. It didn't sound very nice at all once articulated. And the longer she gazed at him, the less pleasant she felt. The image of a moth—an embarrassed one—caught fluttering in between twin pools of hammered gold was vivid. And all the while, he was observing her plight with unholy amusement, laughing while he watched her slowly drown in confusion.

Karo blinked twice. What an imagination! He wasn't an angel at all, and he wasn't laughing. That was the other man. This one was just very . . . cute and tweedy.

Feeling more discomfited than ever for gaping at her host, she glanced hurriedly away from that chiseled face and tried to remember what he had just said. Oh, yes. It was something about the fireplace not working.

"I didn't light the fire. I went to knock, but the door was open. Then the man said to come in. . . ." She trailed off, no longer certain that she had actually seen or heard anyone. She'd thought she'd seen bodies swaying up in the trees twice while walking, but they hadn't been real. Maybe she had imagined the old man as well.

A stray drop of water ran between her breasts,

and a fast look down showed her linen blouse plastered against her slender frame in a nearly transparent layer. She could count the daisies embroidered on her bra and her employer probably could, too. So much for wearing nice lingerie because it gave you confidence. Karo felt fresh color burning in her cheeks but resisted the urge to cover herself.

"If someone could help me move the tree . . ." She looked up again. Her employer was only inches from her now. His left eyebrow had quirked upward, the expression on his aristocratic face still amused. "Perhaps after the rain has stopped we could . . ."

"I almost hate to ask this, but . . . what other man?"

The electric light glittered in his soft gold hair. What was it she had been thinking about gold hair? Or was it gold eyes?

Karo swallowed and tried not be distracted by his proximity, but she could feel the warmth radiating from his body. In her abnormally chilled state, it seemed reasonable to want close contact with this hot-blooded stranger. He also smelled deliciously of vanilla and coconut, and she was suddenly very tired.

"The man in the library," she managed to say, gesturing vaguely to the shadowed corner where the leering man had stood. "With the ruff and those teeth. He sure fooled me. I thought for a minute that he was the real thing."

Her golden-haired visitor stepped past her into the dim room. Their arms brushed, and she followed him like iron filings after a magnet, or a hungry dog after a meaty bone.

"There's no one here."

"I . . . I know. He's gone now."

The man turned her way again. There was a faint movement of a curving brow and a small, bemused smile at her reply.

He thought she was telling stories, she realized, but he was not upset. No anger or rudeness radiated forth while he waited in royal silence for her to get to the punch line. He had breeding to the nth degree, in both his cheekbones and manners. Not like . . . What was his name? The bastard she'd worked for.

"Since the workmen all went home hours ago, I can only conclude that it was the Vellacourt ghost who welcomed you," her host said at last, when she failed to speak.

"Ghost?" she asked, disturbed and startled that he was also thinking about restless spirits. His tone was easy, though, and she didn't know if he was teasing.

"Can you doubt it?" He gestured at the short open door that led to the entry hall. There was light out there now as well.

She walked back to the door and looked around the entry slowly, really seeing her surroundings for the first time. The house's interior design completely eclipsed the exterior's tasteless Gothic-rococo-Romanesque revival. It did in fact resemble the set of a low budget horror flick. At one side of the room was a massive curved staircase with a wrought-iron banister and worn wooden treads. It

was like some set designer had eaten hallucino-
genic mushrooms, she decided. The walls were
paneled in more of the dark oak that would have
been pretty in moderation, but which had been
used to cover every last inch of wall, all the way
from the second-story gallery to the dusty black
and gray marble floor.

The room's vertical surfaces were decorated
with ancient weaponry and what looked like—
what probably *was*—standard sixteenth-century
Spanish Inquisition–issue devices for torturing
heretics in the New World: witch prickers, shackles,
thumbscrews. There were also several glassy-eyed,
moth-eaten badger masks interspersed among
rusty bear traps and cooking accoutrements, and
rack after rack of deer and moose antlers stacked
on the floor like cord wood awaiting a bonfire.
This prickly bone hedge was half hiding the fireplace, which would have stalled a fair-sized pony
and cart with room left over, but was instead being used as a temporary home for a worn Queen
Anne settee and a broken grandfather clock.
These were both coated with ash. If this was a
fairy tale, it was a dark one.

The overall effect was more than morbid or
tasteless. It was bizarre in the extreme. "Maybe
lightning did hit me," Karo murmured to herself,
again feeling very uneasy. "This doesn't look like
enchantment; it feels like a hex."

Her host came to her swiftly, concern replacing
amusement as he drew her into the pool of artifi-
cial light at the base of the stairs. He picked up
her right hand and stared at the long scrape

along the edge of her thumb and the mud on her cuff and palm.

"You fell?" A careful finger wiped some of the red earth away. Her hands were still tingling violently but she appreciated the tender touch.

"The lightning strike was close. It knocked me down. I thought I was fine, but I guess I'm seeing things because I was sure that someone was in the library."

"You're rather chilled and mussed." Her companion looked thoughtful. He dropped her fingers and again gestured to her. This time he indicated the hearth in the library.

"I feel cold," she agreed.

"And you didn't light the fire?"

"No. At least . . . I don't think so." She looked up at him, no longer embarrassed but still mildly confused. She felt thickheaded, like when she had a cold. "You are Tristam English, aren't you?"

"Yes. Sorry, should have mentioned that straight off."

"That's okay. I'm glad you're here. I didn't like the other man. Do you have some rope?" Her mouth asked the question without permission from her brain, and her voice seemed to come from down a long tunnel. It was like that other time with what's-his-name. The one she had assaulted with potato salad.

"I don't know."

The reply was perfectly sensible, but Karo didn't think that he'd understood her request. He continued to stare at her, as if she had said something strange. "If I had a rope, I could use the car to move the tree. I still have one bumper," she explained, wishing to demonstrate to her new boss that she had ability to cope competently with an unexpected crisis. "It's too hot to touch."

"I see. Let's worry about that later, shall we?"

Obedient to the pressure on her arm, Karo allowed herself to be guided to an overstuffed, wing back chair and thrust into its generous seat. Her employer walked over to a sideboard—a fine one made of rosewood, probably seventeenth-century French, her brain noted—and turned on a small lamp. It chased away the last of the creepy shadows behind what turned out to actually be a rococo desk. No one was hiding in the corner, not even a cat.

She watched Tristam pour out a generous snifter of brandy from a crystal decanter—cut glass, Venetian this time, so someone was very inconsistent with their decorating theme—and returned to her side. "Drink this." The voice was kind but firm. She accepted the pewter goblet—early colonial—but didn't taste the contents right away.

"Is this really Belle Ange?" She heard the disbelief in her tone and flushed again. She would never impress this man with her mental skills if she kept asking stupid questions! The humidity must be rusting her brain.

"Yes. This really is Belle Ange."

"That's good, I guess." She leaned forward. "I wasn't certain. One professional to another, this place isn't anything like Berkeley or Westover or . . . well, any plantation I've ever seen."

"No, it's not," he agreed. Walking back over to the sideboard, he poured a drink for himself.

"Whoever decorated must have had a bad drug habit. Quaaludes and acid, I think. Or did they just have opium back then?" Karo was aware that she was being less than politic in her observations, but couldn't seem to stop the tactless phrases from tripping out as she stared into Tristam's lynxlike eyes that were again on her face. "I know about this stuff because I put together an exhibit of druggies' paintings in SF when I was still in school. We called it Opium Dreams, but it was still just twisted art. Put me off ever taking drugs, let me tell you."

"Twisted art. Well, we all start somewhere." The voice was polite. "Not too appropriate for stuffy old Williamstown, though."

Had she gone as red as mulled wine? She certainly felt so. Maybe she should just shut up for a while. Karo leaned back in the old chair and sipped from the fake Revere goblet. The brandy went down like razor blades until it hit her stomach. There it stopped slicing and turned into a pleasant fire easing away some of the chill and her nerves.

"So, what do we do now?" her mouth demanded, without paying any attention to her brain's call for quiet reflection.

Tristam topped off his brandy and didn't answer for a moment. He replaced the bottle's stopper and then returned to the shrinking fire, pulling a worn velvet hassock around to the front of her chair. He looked at her intently, no longer smiling.

"You know, I haven't the faintest idea what to do with you," he confessed. "Did you bring your purse with you? I feel like I should ask for some ID in case you are really Alice gone seriously astray through the wrong looking glass."

Karo frowned while she thought. "No. I left my purse in the car." Then she brightened. "That's what we should do. We'll get a rope and rescue my car. Then I can show you my purse. It matches—well, used to match—my shoes."

"Maybe later."

She didn't feel as discouraged by his answer as she should have. The brandy had knocked out the few props that had been maintaining her alarmed alertness, and she was feeling quite comfortable and secure in her fluffy chair. Even the auditory ripples and clangs that were remnants of the lightning strike were fading into a gentle surflike shushing.

Besides, this handsome man was her boss. If he didn't want to get her car now, she wasn't going to worry about it. She had the doors shut tight this time, so no more rain would get inside. Everything was fine.

"Is this a dream? You sound like a caricature of an Englishman. Or an actor. I like it," she heard somebody say, and then watched with deep interest as her employer began to frown. It was a minimal expression, just a slight tightening of those perfect lips. Well-bred people could do that. She'd read about it in a book once.

"I am a caricature. It meets expectations and it's good for business to sound English. Did you hit your head when you fell?"

"I don't think so. It doesn't hurt." She wasn't alarmed when Tristam leaned forward and ran his long fingers over her scalp. Karo shivered, but it was not with cold. His hands were very warm and . . . nice. She leaned into them like a dog asking to be petted.

"No bumps," he murmured.

"That feels wonderful." She wasn't certain that she had spoken aloud, but her employer's mouth was at eye level and his amused lips said that she had.

Karo felt happy again, because she had made him smile. It was important that he be happy. She wanted them to have a long, productive relationship so she wouldn't have to get another job right away.

"There's no sign of injury. What am I to do with you, Karo Follett?" The question was rhetorical. He took another sip of brandy, apparently as bemused as she.

"We have to move my car," she reminded him, clinging to her one practical thought. "It's in the road. Someone might need to get by."

He tilted his head a little to one side and continued to study her. "I don't suppose that you've been drinking. . . ."

"Certainly not!" She was indignant. "I don't drink . . . often. I like ice cream better. Butter pecan. With peanut butter sauce. That's what I have when I'm troubled."

"Well, I certainly can't leave you alone to wander this house of horrors while I fetch some help. And I can't take you out to the guest cottage because it's likely flooding as we speak," he went on, obviously not heeding her gastronomic observation.

Karo opened her mouth to tell him that she

wasn't going to wander anywhere by herself while it was raining and there were ghosts about, even if she wanted her purse, but he beat her to the punch.

"Yes, your car and your purse. But I don't think that we can do anything about that this evening. Anyway, it's doubtful that anyone will be out in this storm."

"No? I just don't want you to think that I'm a sluggard. It's bad enough that my clothes are messy. And look at my shoes! They were my best pair," she said sadly.

"I don't think that you're a sluggard. Only a very determined person would have kept on in that rain. You must be boiling with impatience to start this job—though I can't imagine why."

"Well, yes, I was. I *am*. I really wanted to come here. You have no idea. But can I—uh—can I have another drink first? Or should we make tea, hot tea? I make very good tea, you'll be glad to know."

"Actually, I think it would be best if I put you to bed." His tone was meditative. He seemed to have given up on conversation.

Karo wasn't offended. She vaguely comprehended that she wasn't quite herself just now. The brandy had made her very sleepy and she was having trouble focusing her eyes. "Okay. Here?" She looked around the library with the highest degree of alarm that the brandy would allow. It was a sad effort, but she still protested. "I don't like it here when the lights are off. There's a bad shadow in the corner that gets very hot and then very cold."

"No, not here. This room would give anyone a *cauld grue*. Come along."

He helped her up with brisk efficiency. His hands burned on her arms. It felt like her muscles were melting. First her arm, then her back and then her legs. He was better than a heating pad.

She followed him back out into the entry hall—the one laid out for a Frankenstein revival. They walked over to the main staircase. It spiraled like an infinite corkscrew, punching its way up through the center of the stone house.

"The beanstalk," she breathed. "I knew there had to be one."

"Can you manage these? The other stair is almost impassable as yet."

"Yes." But she made no effort to climb. Instead, she looked up at the gallery that ran along the second floor of the house. After a slow inspection failed to turn up the strange vampirelike creature or any man-eating giant peering down at them, she turned back to Tristam and asked again: "Am I dreaming?"

He shook his head in a gesture more of sorrow than of negation and then scooped her up in his arms. Karo uttered a faint protest about being picked up like a load of dirty laundry, though she was quite filthy enough to fit the bill, and then relaxed in his embrace when he didn't throw her over his shoulder like a sack of grain. He carried her easily against his chest just like an angel or hero should.

"Take me—I'm yours!" She giggled daringly. "Where are we going?"

"To bed. After I tuck you in, I'm going to call the doctor. He lives just down the road."

They were walking down a long hall. Karo couldn't make out any details, but the walls were obviously embellished with myriad long, lumpy things. Muskets perhaps? Or flails.

"He can't come," she reminded him. "There's a tree in the road and my car is in the way."

Tristam English remained patient. "There's another road to Doctor Monroe's house."

"Oh, then I can go get my car," she pointed out.

"Yes, but not just yet. I want the doctor to have a look at you."

"I'm not hurt. It's just scratches." She glanced down at her shirt and was relieved to see that it was again opaque. "The daisies are gone. I'm all dry now."

Tristam just smiled at her and shook his head.

They arrived at a set of double doors. Karo looked closely at the intricate carving six inches from her face. The indelicate relief looked a little bit like satyrs chasing naked, Rubensesque women, but that couldn't be right. Belle Ange was a historic building. All historic buildings in Virginia were dignified and beautiful. Knowing this fact, she squinted harder, trying to make the figures change into cherubs or fruit.

Nope. They were definitely satyrs chasing—and sometimes catching—impossibly big-breasted women.

"These doors are ugly and tasteless. Do you think they were made that way on purpose?" she asked, no longer bothered by her own disjointed conversation.

"Yes, I'm afraid so."

"Why?"

Her host crossed the semidarkened room and deposited her on the double bed without answering. She sank into the satin duvet. Karo stared up at the silk canopy in big-top colors of purple and red, and momentarily forgot her question about the carvings on the door. "Wow! It's like the circus."

"More like a bordello. I've come to the conclusion that the Vellacourts all have what I will generously call 'eclectic taste,'" Tristam answered. He knelt while he slipped off her shoes, pausing to study the small hole in the right one and then peeling down her torn wet sock with great care. Karo decided to allow the familiarity since he wasn't leering like that strange man in the library.

And his hair was so lovely—like an angel's, she thought, her concentration fracturing yet again.

"Are you really British?" she asked his bent head. "You sound British, and I've been hoping that you really are. I want to work for a real Englishman."

"Yes, I'm all 'Rule, Britannia,' tea and scones and the Union Jack. But I've lived in the States for a number of years. I hope you don't mind the defection. After all, my ancestors did their part in the crusades and all. And I was born there."

"No. Me, too." She giggled, aware that her answer sounded strange. She tried to explain. "I used to live in Europe with my parents. My dad's a historian. I am, too. Sort of. Art."

"I know. That's why I hired you. Let's see. Your father would be Alex Follett."

"You know my dad?" Karo was pleased.

"I've read some of his work in the *Journal of Military History*. I'm also a bit of an airplane buff."

"He likes to write about war planes. Plenty of war in Europe. Plenty of war back here, too, but the wrong era. No planes. Just soldiers. I thought I saw some hanging in the tree out front, but it was just Spanish moss. Only, Spanish moss isn't technically a moss," she observed. Then politely: "Do you like Virginia?"

"Love it, except for the weather. Stand up, please." He set her on feet long enough to pull down the covers on the bed. The lovely duvet slipped off onto the floor with a soft puff. She wanted to slide after it. It looked so soft and nest-like as it puddled on the rug.

"In you go now. I'd undress you, but I think we'd best wait for the doctor in case . . . Try and rest, Karo. I'm going to call Doctor Monroe but then I'll come right back. I have to use the land-line. My cell gets no reception inside the house. I might as well be on the far side of the sun."

"I'm really not hurt," she told him again. "Tell the doctor I don't want a shot."

"Be a good girl," was all he said before turning out the light and half closing the ugly, obscene door. His footsteps grew soft and distant and then disappeared.

Karo shut her eyes and slid immediately into a deep sleep that was haunted by strange yellow eyes and wicked satyrs that ravished her under a sky filled with weeping birch trees and a moon that looked like a bloodshot eye. She was, some-where in the recesses of her convoluted brain, quite surprised to find that she was enjoying herself. This might have been because the faun that finally caught her looked a lot like Tristam English. He even tasted like a coconut macaroon when she bit him on the shoulder.

An idea, like a ghost, must be spoken to a little
before it will explain itself.
—Charles Dickens

Chapter Three

Dawn on the morning after was a gray-green malevolence. It bulled its way through the lace sheers on the second floor of windows seeking someone to molest, and an ancient birch, stripped by the storm of all sheltering foliage except a stubborn green creeper that clung to its host like grim death, did little to impede the sun behind the light lace. The intrusive glow finally reached Karo's goose down pillow, and then, apparently satisfied with its location, remained unmoving until Karo felt compelled to open an unappreciative eye and face the smug new day.

She groaned. She knew exactly where she was and had a painfully clear recollection of her appalling behavior the evening before. She was little comforted by the fact that her new boss had been unfailingly courteous, or that bizarre circumstances had contributed to her inexplicable behavior. Karo, more like her mother than she would ever admit, almost always practiced good manners. Massive shock was not an adequate excuse for behaving like an all-around nitwit, as Karo was certain she had.

She had a dim but utterly realistic vision of trying to sink her teeth into Tristam's strong shoulder and making yummy noises. This had happened when he returned with the white-haired stranger and helped her to sit up in bed. She had been dreaming of a Bacchanalia where guests consumed enormous desserts instead of wine, and she had gotten confused. That last thought alone was worth a second moan. Being rude wasn't good; mistaking your boss for a cream puff was probably unforgivable.

Thank heavens Tristam was nimble. He had even appeared to understand and forgive her confusion.

"Well, hell. This is as bad as Williamstown." But it wasn't. And after thirty seconds of self-mockery, her natural buoyancy brought her spirits upright and Karo let her waking eyes look around the bedroom in which she had slept.

She was mildly pleased by what she saw. The faded opulence that had repelled her the night before was still present in the tattered canopy overhead, but seen by the light of day, even if it was rather tacky, the open space still felt like a room where someone actually lived rather than a cluttered B-movie set or a museum's Renaissance display. Searching farther, Karo cautiously rolled her head to the side and peeped around the scarlet bed curtain.

The open armoire in the corner provided the first clue as to why there seemed some relief from the previous oppressive grandeur. Someone of the male persuasion with contemporary and subdued taste in clothing had been living here. Someone who favored thick cotton shirts and sensible woolen slacks. Someone other than a Vellacourt, and someone who must have removed all extra furnishings. The knacky tweed slacks within practically shouted Town and Country.

Karo suffered another moment of embarrassment as she realized that she was using her boss's room. Sleeping in his bed. She had to be; he would never have put her in some other person's private quarters without asking permission—and anyway, as far as she knew, there wasn't any other person whose bedroom she could commandeer. They were, as he had explained over the phone, on a very tight budget. He worked on a profit-sharing basis, preferring a steady inflow of earnings over the next decade to lump sum fees.

If he hadn't stayed in this tiny, quasi-normal haven inside Castle Frankenstein, then heaven only knew where—or under what conditions—he had slept last night. It was one more thing she was going to have to apologize for.

Deciding that there was no avoiding the morning, Karo threw back the thin sheet and rolled out of bed. Her feet felt solid on the bare wood floor. Her body was back under control, and minus yesterday's prickings and tingles. She was glad that her extremities no longer felt like an overloaded transformer. Maybe her brain would be up to average performance, too, and if Tristam was merciful—or too desperate to fire her—perhaps she would have a chance to prove her competence.

On the down side, her pants were missing and the buttons of her blouse were undone to the

waist. She remembered uneasily that the white-
haired stranger had woken her last night with a
request for her to undress, something she hadn't
been able to do without help. If there had been
any formal introductions, Karo had missed them,
but there was little doubt that the other man was
poor Dr. Monroe, dragged away from his hearth
and home so that he could check to see if Belle
Ange's new employee was concussed or had forgotten to take her lithium treatments before wandering away from the asylum.

Boy! She had just staggered from strength to
strength. It was embarrassing to think that there
was a second witness to her fall from grace. Soon
she wouldn't just be banned from Williamstown;
it would be the whole state. Not that she really
could blame Tristam for asking the doctor to come.
Her behavior must have seemed nearly mad, what
with talking about bodies in trees and ghosts
lighting fires. She just hoped that she hadn't bitten the physician, too.

"Well, hell." Her disgust echoed from the
vaulted ceiling.

The door to a modern bathroom had been left
ajar. Karo was relieved to find that there was a
bathtub installed, complete with contemporary
plumbing, and that a stack of clean towels was
waiting by the granite pedestal sink. Someone,
again probably Tristam, had brought in her purse
and overnight case and thoughtfully set out her
toothbrush and comb.

Karo bathed quickly in mercifully warm water
using the rather masculine-smelling soap in the
porcelain dish at the side of the tub. Then she

ventured back into the bedroom still wrapped in a towel, hoping to find her suitcase so that she wouldn't have to face her new boss in a wrinkled linen shirt and calcium starched pants.

The battered luggage was waiting for her at the end of the bed beyond the pile of the red satin comforter. The vanilla smell clinging to the sheets was a constant reminder of whose territory she had blundered into, and she firmly denied herself the pleasure of burying her face in his pillow and gulping up all the delicious air. Instead she quickly unsnapped the straining locks and stood back while the leather case burst open, the taut hinges giving a nearly human gasp of relief as they were freed from their duty.

She hesitated only a moment over her many heavily creased selections, and then chose a clean pair of jeans and a navy blue pullover of knit silk. Hopefully Tristam would forgive the informality; her office clothes were about three years out of date—unless you counted her tavern wench ensemble, and aside from the fact that she never wanted to wear the thing again, it was also badly crumpled from her hurried packing job.

Karo dressed hastily and retrieved her shoes from under the bed. A few quick claps over the bathtub dislodged the worst of the gunk, but this also revealed the hole in the right toe. Perhaps a bit of home repair could save—No. She stiffened her resolve. She was going for trade-ups these days. No more settling. Into the trash they went. Karo went digging for another pair, praying that these would last rather longer than the first set. Good shoes were expensive, and there was every indication that she might be needing her money to pay off years of therapy for mental problems.

She pulled open her purse for a bit of titivation material—she needed the added courage of a power lip color that wouldn't fade or feather— and then, with her ablutions done, she felt as prepared to face her employer as she was ever going to be.

Returning her lipstick to her bag, she spotted her cell phone. Someone had wiped it clean, but there were bits of calcified shell embedded in the tiny dents that covered it. A quick check showed that she had no signal. Curious, she looked through her pictures, hoping to see if she had gotten a clear shot on the urn at the gate. There was nothing that showed the urns, but she had miraculously captured the lightning.

Karo shuddered. It was a reminder of how close death had come. Also, maybe it was just some weird trick of light, but the white thing rushing at her seemed to have eyes.

"No. Stop it." She put her phone away. It was time to face the music.

She delayed only long enough to absorb the unusual view from the bedroom window. Because of the dense growth of the trees and creepers that stretched from the turnoff on Route 5 to the front of the mansion, it was impossible to see more than a small clearing at the plantation gate. It actually was a little like being Jack at the top of the beanstalk, or looking out from the world's largest tree house. It was not an entirely pleasing sensation for someone who suffered from mild vertigo.

Even with the recent storm, Karo could see that the treetops boasted an impressive collection of cluttered webs that throbbed slowly in the warm morning air; they were doubtless inhabited by an impressive collection of spiders and their six-legged prey. But there were no bodies, corporeal or otherwise. Whatever she'd thought she'd seen yesterday night, it had to have been a hallucination. Shuddering at the memory, she stepped back from the rippled glass, letting the sheers again cover the window.

It was a good thing she didn't take after her mother. Her mom was a world-class housekeeper and inclined to view cobwebs the way most people viewed incest or infanticide. The disorder of this house and garden would make her crazy.

Karo pulled open the double doors—still ugly and obscene—and walked out onto the landing where she turned right and headed for the main stairs. Facing the scene of her crimes on an empty stomach was not the way she would have chosen to start the morning, but it wouldn't do to get lost in the house her first day on the job and have the boss thinking that she was half-witted—at least, no more of a half-wit than he already thought her.

She didn't hear anyone moving about below stairs, filling the smoky rafters with jolly laughter or cussing out the weather or any of the things workmen were inclined to do as they started their morning routines, which only confirmed the hypothesis that she and Tristam were alone in this great maze of a house. The tempting smell of coffee left an obvious trail to explore, and Karo decided that perhaps it was best that they were alone. If she was for the sack, she'd rather it be done without an audience watching her beg for caffeine before being thrown out bag and baggage into the muddy yard.

Karo shut her eyes against the dusty abattoir in the hall where glass-eyed trophies stared, but opened them again when she passed through the mansion's picture gallery. Most of the portraits needed cleaning, but Karo secretly felt that it might be best to leave them dirty. The paintings were mostly executed by artists not overburdened with talent, and a few that should have been made to apologize for their work. There was one picture that was especially hideous, but not because the artist lacked talent. On the contrary, the likeness was nearly lifelike; the somehow familiar, life-sized portrait followed her with a malevolent gaze as she crossed the room. One didn't achieve a face like that by leading a life of benevolent kindness. Such furrows were created only by years of sneering and dissipation. Or maybe by actually being evil.

She was relieved to finally escape its scrutiny. Hurrying down a tight corridor that had to violate all contemporary fire codes, heading toward the back of the house from whence the delicious odor of coffee was emanating, she discovered her polite boss at a badly scarred work table in the middle of an incongruously modern—and pleasant—kitchen. No way could it be an original room; servants and slaves were not pampered with luxuries like windows that looked out over formal gardens, or real slate on the floor. Karo sniffed. Her nose confirmed her theory; this room didn't smell old and mouse-ridden like the rest of the house.

Tristam was sprawled over a generous quarter of the refectory table, calmly reading the paper as she came in, but he looked up immediately as she entered the room, folding the gazette away and giving her a long stare with his golden eyes. "Good morning." The greeting was cheerful as he rose to his feet. He had certainly been raised a gentleman.

It was a good sign, that smile—or maybe it was just reflexive courtesy. It would be difficult to say until they actually got past the tea and toast and discussions about the weather. Of course, superficial courtesy was better than no courtesy at all.

"Uh-oh. Cat got your tongue?" The question was teasing but those yellow eyes were concerned as they loomed above her. It was heartening that he seemed concerned rather than irritated. Perhaps she wasn't going to be canned before breakfast.

"No, my tongue is still here. More is the pity. So, good morning," she answered at last, allowing him to seat her. The faint smell of vanilla that surrounded him had her appetite stirring.

He chuckled and turned away to prepare something at the professional-sized, sparkling brass espresso maker. Cappuccino. That was what he'd been drinking. If nothing else, her nose was obviously functioning again.

"How do you take it?"

"As strong as possible," she told him. "Make it an Italian two to one."

"Good Italians drink three to one."

"This is an emergency. Hit me hard."

He smiled the same attractive smile that she had seen last night and set the tiny cup in front of her. It was not an antique mug, just rather old. Pure Goodwill bargain basement crockery. Maybe he didn't trust her with the good stuff.

"Thank you," she said as he turned away.

"How do you feel this balmy a.m.?"

"Aces. Not that I was feeling any pain last night," she admitted ruefully. "I want to apologize for crashing in on you that way. I assure you that I don't usually behave like that."

"Apologize? Whatever for?"

"Well . . ." She looked at him, standing there bright-eyed and neat as wax, and felt more than ever that she had been unforgivably discourteous. "I think I recall being very rude. For one thing, I said that your house was hideous."

"It is hideous. And it's not my house. It's just the one I've been hired to turn into a tourist trap— and on an impoverished budget," he said.

Karo snorted into her coffee cup and tried not to laugh. Her other employers had been given to rather loftier goals and higher-flying forms of rhetoric when describing their jobs. Tristam seemed to have no intellectual pretensions about "preserving history" for future generations who couldn't care less about what went on in the "good old days."

"You shouldn't laugh at the truth," he complained. "It's an art, you know. Telling the truth and also turning the useless and hideous into tourist attractions. I belong to a very select guild of skilled craftsmen. We have only three members, and I'm the only one currently working in the States. I'm as rare as an original Holbein. Surely you've heard of my triumph at Lesser Warwick Hall? It contains the most complete display of modern Mediterranean fish skeletons in the United Kingdom, don't you know?"

Karo let herself smile at his claim and slightly exaggerated accent. She was feeling more cheerful now that she knew she wasn't to be fired, and as an added fillip that she probably didn't deserve, it seemed that she was going to be working for a man with a sense of humor. As a contrast to F. Christian, the gods of ironic situations couldn't have done better. Perhaps life was worth living for one more day.

"Okay. But let me get this off of my chest. At the very least I have to apologize for just wandering in and making myself at home in the library. I don't know what to say except that I'm sorry."

"Pure mashed potatoes! I'm glad you did come in. It shows excellent sense that you knew to get out of the rain. Truly, you could have knocked all night and I wouldn't have heard you up in the garret. That room was designed to be . . . private."

"But I chased you out of your bed, too," she said, being thorough in her contrition. "You probably had to sleep in the dungeon, with rack and thumbscrews and giant rats."

Tristam gave her an odd look, then laughed silently. "Sorry, no traditional dungeon. Too much groundwater, I expect. And please, say no more," he finally added, refusing to let her apologize further. "Doctor Monroe agreed that you were wandering around in a daze because of the lightning strike. He says that you may feel some disorientation for the next few days. So, you can hardly blame yourself for anything that happened last night. And I certainly don't blame you for not liking Vellacourt's horror. It would take a certain type of person to appreciate this place's dubious charm. It will be the greatest of feats if we can turn it into something tasteful, and for this I'll need your help."

She had to ask, even though he was being extremely polite. "Um . . . did anything else happen last night while I was wandering in a daze?" Tristam cleared his throat, and Karo braced herself with another swallow of coffee. "Give it to me straight. What else did I do?"

Tristam stared at her, looking entirely too thoughtful for her peace of mind. "Do you remember seeing the man in the library?"

"Well, sort of. I remember thinking that there *was* a man in the library. He was wearing a period costume." She frowned at her cup, trying to recall exactly what she had seen. Everything was very faraway and dreamlike. She remembered feeling like her skin was going to catch fire even when the rest of her was chilled to the bone. "His eyes were gold like yours. I think."

"Don't worry about it, Karo. Doctor Monroe says that it's quite normal to hallucinate after a bad shock. And the good news is that you aren't hurt physically." He leaned forward and stretched his long, lean arms across the table until he was nearly touching her. She could feel the magnetic pull and had to clamp her hands firmly to the table to keep them from crawling his way. She was restored to her wits; there was no excuse for bad behavior this morning.

"Ah. That's good," she said.

"Here, have a doughnut. They are a bit stale but I think still edible. The sugar will give you energy. The carpenter swears by them."

"How old are they?" she asked suspiciously, considering taking one simply to keep her hands busy.

"Old, but the date on the box says they're good for another month. And they don't even need refrigeration! American food is amazing."

"Hm. I think I'll pass. I make it a rule never to eat anything that mold won't consume."

"That's probably sensible, especially around here." He paused, then said, "I moved your car into the carriage house. We've had some flooding out on the road and I didn't want to risk anything happening to it if the creek overran its banks."

"Thank you. You were able to move the tree then?"

Again, he stared at her.

"Someone must have gotten there ahead of me, because the road was clear when I went down this morning. Maybe it got washed away." Her host leaned back in his chair and Karo's pulse settled back to its normal pace. "By the way, your muffler and back bumper are missing."

"Hm? Oh, I know. I lost them yesterday. I should have gone back for them but I was afraid to stop. That battery has been known to take long breaks between uses." Karo drank some more coffee and tried to recall exactly what had happened to her out by the gate, but it was all rather fuzzy and undetailed. She couldn't swear positively that there had actually been a tree in the road.

"Autos. What are we to do with them?" he said agreeably, though she was willing to bet that his car had no such idiosyncratic behaviors.

"You did say last night that you knew my father?" she asked, needing to be reassured that she remembered something of yesterday besides her boss's splendid hair and eyes.

"By repute. I enjoy World War One history and subscribe to some of the journals he writes for. Perhaps I'll get lucky and he'll decide to visit while you're here. Does he still fly that old Feiseler Storch?"

"As often as Mom allows. You said that you were a closet airplane buff? Is that why you hired me?" she asked. She couldn't help feeling a bit disappointed. "You wanted a good excuse to invite my dad out here?"

"How cynical! No, I hired you because I needed someone right away and you were the only remotely qualified applicant that would come anywhere near the place. I was getting desperate." He laughed softly at her expression. "There! Now we're even. I've just been appallingly rude to you, and I didn't even mean it. Your resume is actually quite impressive."

"I bent the truth a bit. Well . . . I omitted a few details."

"That's good. I'm afraid we will need to do a lot of creative lying about this place. Clearly I hired you because it was destiny. I was commanded by angels. Your voice on the phone was a clarion call! Deep calling unto deep—"

"Talk about pure mashed potatoes!" Karo smiled back, not admitting that she had also had some thoughts about his voice, and then said: "I'll get out of your room right away. I can do that much for you. You said that there is a guest cottage?"

"I did and there is, but I don't think that you should move out there just yet." He stopped smiling. "I want to keep an eye on you for a little while longer. You can move out tomorrow if you really want."

The charming buffoon was gone, and the man who had replaced him looked to have formidable potential as a tyrant lordling. His voice was calm and unconsciously edged with a tone of authority. He had said last night that his family was all "Rule, Britannia" and the Union Jack. She believed him; only one born to the manor could be so exquisitely polite while being bossy.

"I can't blame you for thinking that way," she said, feeling color creep into her cheeks.

"Excellent sense."

"But truly, I'm fine now."

"Probably. But I'll feel better if you stay in the main house for another day or two." When Karo didn't answer, he put down his mug and looked at her seriously. "You aren't going to make me pull rank first thing, are you? Be sensible. Right now I'm sorting though the accumulation of junk—I mean, taking an inventory of the main house's contents—and it is filthy work. You have a shower at the cottage, but it has no water pressure and it's cold. Also, I can't swear that I've killed all the mice in the chimney who have spent the last thirty years building a palatial nest. And, flooding always brings out the snakes." He added this last as a clincher.

Karo stared at Tristam English. He wasn't anything like a curator ought to be. Maybe that was because he saw himself as more of a carnival shill than a dedicated academic. Whatever the case, if she was honest with herself, she would have to admit that she didn't mind staying close to this charming, strange man while she sorted through the refuse of Belle Ange looking for treasures. It would be a lot more fun than her old job.

On the other hand, he might not be charming at all. It might just be that he possessed super pheromones that were throttling her higher brain functions; and everyone knew that idle brain waves were the devil's playground. A little caution was in order. Quick pain apparently hadn't been an efficient teacher the first time around, but the prolonged embarrassment she had suffered on the last job was fairly instructive.

"I'm not afraid of mice," she said firmly, trying to read Tristam's expression to see if he was hurt or offended by the show of strength. A thin skin would be a definite minus in their coming relationship.

"But you are sensible—at least, when you haven't been struck by lightning? Or are you afraid of being alone with me, Karo? Do you worry that next time I might bite back?"

The very gentleness of the inquiry was a waving red cape before her wounded ego. Still feeling a bit of the recklessness that had caused her to throw over her old job, she gave in to her baser impulses with a small laugh. "Okay, I'll stay. Why not? I guess we can share. I never liked cold showers anyway," she added, and then blushed at the way that sounded. Should she make it plain that they were sharing a house, not a bedroom? "I'll help you fix up another room," she added firmly.

"Thanks. Herr Frankenstein and I are both grateful. Neither of us is a dab at handling the linens, though he is perhaps slightly better at it than I."

"Wait a minute! Let's not add any sins to my list. I may have implied that the grand entry looked a little like it had been decorated by Edgar Allan Poe on a cocktail of mescaline and acid, but I never said that you were a monster maker."

Tristam laughed. "Certainly not. I was referring to the cat. A spoiled creature, an absolute black hole of neediness and gluttony."

He jerked a thumb to the left. Karo looked over at the sideboard where he was pointing and found herself under observation. A large orange sphere reclining in a pedestal bowl had opened its emerald eyes and was yawning hugely, apparently unimpressed by the guest. The fat tail twitched once, and then the huge head laid itself back down to return to its interrupted nap.

"Spoiled, did you say?"

"Extremely. He'd like it especially if you allow him to share your bed. He was quite put out at being turned away from your door last evening. But we shall both be very glad to have your help with packing up most of Vellacourt's so-called treasures. 'Stein keeps getting his tail caught in the piles of deer antlers he persists in exploring for mice. They are everywhere! The last owner must have had a hunting mania, because the closets were stuffed full of them—antlers, not mice. Though, we have both. I can't believe the junk that has accumulated."

"Poor kitty," Karo sympathized, though Frankenstein didn't notice. "But you know, Tristam, it's not all junk. I mean, some of this stuff is quite hideous, but it isn't garbage."

"I suppose it's all in the eye of the beholder. My job is to preserve the history of Belle Ange as much as possible while making an attraction for the moneyed wanderers who come to Virginia. You're the sop to the local historical society the house's current owner belongs to, and your job is to keep me from burning any treasures when we torch the rubbish heap out back. Uh, those antlers aren't at all historic, are they?"

"Not hardly, but those pyxis at the gates make a great start for the list of true treasures to attract tourists," she told him with renewed fervor. "They're what lured me out of the car yesterday."

"Ah! Well, if you like the funeral urns, wait until you see the cemetery. Pure Southern Gothic, I assure you!" Tristam got up and prepared another cup of coffee with an efficiency that said he and the machine had reached an understanding. Leave it to a man to enjoy fiddling with all those gears and levers first thing in the morning.

"Are you feeling strong enough to take the grand tour?" he asked after a moment, flashing her another killer smile.

"Definitely," she agreed.

"I warn you, this won't be pretty. Better take your coffee with you."

"Of course." Karo stood up. "I'm anxious to see what we'll be working on. There could be just about anything hiding in this house. A few good paintings or some furniture would go a long way to making Belle Ange a starred attraction in the Visitors Center's catalogue of historic sites."

"Then let us be up and doing while you still have some of that enthusiasm."

"That's probably best. 'For by the pricking of my thumbs, something wicked this way comes.'" Karo wasn't sure why she added this.

"You don't know the half of it," Tristam muttered.

After another moment, he asked, "You like our bard of Avon?"

"Of course. We're not all literary heathens out here in the Colonies. Some of us are quite bookish. Of course, more often than not I was assigned to the role of a loyalist when they were passing out costumes at the reenactments where I last worked. I was sent out to die for the British at Yorktown— *twice*. And in one hundred degree heat!"

Tristam chuckled and began their tour. "Perhaps you aren't a godless heathen, but Old Vellacourt certainly was. Well, he certainly wasn't a God-fearing soul. Take a look around." He waved a long-fingered hand at the hall into which they walked, and then around at the room at the end of it. "This is probably the best of the lot, and it is hardly what one would call early American normal. It would, in fact, have been banned in Boston."

The room was huge, large enough to house the Lost Tribes of Israel. It was also determinedly and depressingly medieval—and completely inappropriate in its architecture. What had the space ever been used for? A ballroom?

"I see what you mean. We will have to hope that deficient light will hide the greatest um . . . oddities. If you mean to keep them." Among the strange architectural features were a collection of shallow balconies, each perhaps eighteen inches deep, sprouting like mushrooms randomly on the walls. The lower ones were loaded with maces and morning stars. "How do you get to those?" she asked.

"You don't. Not without a ladder."

"I guess they could be decorated with garlands at Christmas." Karo knew she sounded doubtful. "In the meantime, I don't know what to suggest. Is most of the displayed stuff copies?"

"I don't think anything less than complete blackout will help, but the insurance company says it's too dangerous to have visitors inside without lights. Your point about romantic lighting is well taken, however, and we will restrict this part of the house to the lowest possible wattage of bulbs."

"Good idea."

"And, the pieces are not copies. There were most likely . . . um . . . how shall I say this?"

"Liberated without permission? Maybe when the Protestants were busy killing Catholics?"

"Perish the thought. Though, that might be better than having had them just sitting around the old family home like they were. It isn't reasonable to expect to have bills of sale lying about after all this time, though. Provenance would be difficult to prove, which therefore makes it tricky to sell anything."

Karo shook her head. "The pieces are valuable, but I don't see how we can . . ."

"They're not period. Or, not the *appropriate* period. I know. We'll just put aside the most egregious offenders for storage elsewhere and get them appraised later."

"Do you think the owner will try to sell everything off?"

"I doubt Clarice Vellacourt will sell anything, but the appraisals must be made. For insurance purposes. And there has been no proper inventory in decades."

"Is there a family tree?" Karo asked.

"Yes, but it is badly gnarled in places. If you stick with the matrilineal and patrilineal lines, all is well. But there are many questionable affinal and even fictive relationships to take into account."

"Bastard children?"

"By the busload. And questionable marriages. At least one great-grandson was a bigamist."

Karo signed. It was often the case with families that owned slaves.

"Okay, on to the history lesson. Here is the first thing you might want to know about the house and its builder. Old Vellacourt had had it with Europe's religious wars, plagues and various other persecutions, which reached an exceptionally brisk pace in the sixteen hundreds. He decided that it was time to pack up and move to some locale where he could enjoy life, liberty and the pursuit of degenerate happiness without the constant threat of torture and execution. He chose Virginia since King Charles was handing out land grants and he knew the governor."

Tristam opened a door and gestured her through. They walked back out into the entry hall and Karo braved herself to take a second look at the house's dim interior. It was, if such a thing was possible, even worse by morning light.

" 'I will prepare thee unto blood, and blood shall pursue thee,' " she murmured.

"My sentiments exactly. But how brave you are to be quoting scripture before ten o'clock. I haven't the stomach for it until I've had lunch and two cocktails."

"Sorry. But I stand by my words. It's horrible." She pointed at a portrait on the wall. "That painting can't be original, can it? Stoker didn't popularize vampires until the late eighteen hundreds."

"Isaac Newton said that it is best to shadow as if it were not shadowed. Maybe that was the artist's intent. It is starkly realistic."

"I don't think the artist read any Newton. Did he have a drinking problem?" That seemed like a more likely answer.

"Unknown. She did have an anger problem, though. The slaves were afraid of her insane rages brought on by religious mania. They believed that she saw dead people."

"I believe it, too." Two words the picture would never bring to mind were *kind* and *benevolent*. *Sane* probably wouldn't apply either.

There was a long pause; then Tristam said, "To

continue the unpleasant tale about old Hugh Vellacourt . . . Though sincerely interested in avoiding religious persecution, neither he nor any of his descendants can be found in stories about Pilgrims or later colonial patriots hanging out at Raleigh Tavern with Jefferson, Washington or Patrick Henry. No Vellacourt male ever said 'Give me liberty or give me death.' At least, not considering the liberty of any man but himself. So we won't be able to cash in on that patriotic sort of thing."

They both stared at the next portrait, an unpleasant offering at the base of the stairs. The pictured gargoyle looked as sour as turned wine. Karo was inclined to blame part of the be-ruffed man's satirical expression on his hairstyle, which was not the usual, fluffy wigged headdress favored by the founding fathers, but his own silvery locks scraped back from a pasty face into a band that looked tight as torture. It left one with the impression that his eyebrows were pulled back almost to his ears. The lipless mouth seemed likewise out of scale and unappealing, and the effect of the little edges of pointy teeth was definitely reptilian.

If pets and their owners tended to have strong resemblances, so too did homeowners of certain kinds of houses, Karo decided. Both Vellacourt and his cluttered mansion looked like they were being eaten by termites, moths and rats.

"I really don't know what to say," she confessed. "I don't see any way to make this man likeable. Are there any other likenesses we might use? I don't suppose we can just not mention him?"

"Not likely. And there are no other likenesses

that I've found. This wasn't taken from life," Tristam explained. "It was done by one of Vellacourt's grandchildren, long after the fact. Several of her paintings grace this house. You find them planted at turnings in dark hallways and lying in wait on the backs of bedroom doors. I'd like to think that they were her idea of a joke but . . . Such an odd choice of colors, too. Maybe the paint has turned with time." His tone was wry as he added, "Perhaps tourists will adore the high-camp Dracula touch. No?"

"I guess. There's really no dungeon here? What with everything else . . . I can really picture waxworks figures chained to moldering walls while they wait to be pressed to death," Karo suggested facetiously. "Or maybe something like that church in Italy—the one with all those dead Capuchin monks stacked up like cord wood."

Tristam made a face. "Don't laugh. It's nearly that bad, especially below stairs. There are a few rooms that I don't think will ever go on the tour. They're just not mainstream. I certainly wouldn't use waxworks in them. My reputation would be ruined if word got out."

"Wax would likely melt in summer, anyway," Karo mused. "Unless . . . are you going to put in air-conditioning?"

She was hopeful, but he shook his head in a mildly pitying way. "Recall our impoverished budget. I believe I mentioned it once or twice."

"Well, in a perfect world this room wouldn't be on the tour, either," she said honestly. "It's bound to put people off straightaway. If they haven't paid for their tickets in advance . . . Well, better charge them at the gate before they can change their minds."

"I intend to, and it is nice to know that we think alike." He beamed at her. "However, I don't consider this as one of the problem spots. Furniture and tapestries and proper lighting can hide a multitude of sins. Not all of it is obscene and violent in content. Some is simply sadistic."

Karo was contemplative. "The rooms in this house are strange. Did Hugh Vellacourt entertain? The rooms are certainly large enough."

"Of course. And records suggest his guests played some interesting games."

"Like Pin the Tail on the Devil," Karo muttered, swatting at a cobweb that had drifted down on her shoulder.

"Maybe." Tristam smiled, but it was more wry than happy. "So . . . since you ask, the two worst rooms are the master suite and the garret. I've already stripped most of the pornographic paintings out of the bedroom, but the architectural features are still pretty racy—as I'm sure you saw. We may have to hang curtains everywhere."

"That's where you were yesterday when I arrived, right—in the garret? So, what's wrong with the place? Why does it look like it was designed by someone caught in a nightmare? Did they keep the mad wife up there? Tell me any scandals now. I think I'd like to get the pain over with all at once."

"Yes, well, you've seen the master suite. Pornographic, unquestionably, especially before I cleaned it up. You don't know the half of it. As for the garret . . . I'm afraid that part of the third floor was built as a sort of torture chamber, and I strongly suspect that successive generations of Vellacourts found actual use for it, or it would have been changed. The sadism wasn't a one-off that we can bury, not if we tell any kind of truth."

"A . . . a torture chamber? Still?" Karo blinked, trying to ascribe something other than the obvious meaning to his words. Were she and Tristam having a trans-Atlantic miscommunication? He couldn't mean an *actual* torture chamber.

"Yes. Though, it's not exactly a proper one."

Ah. "A proper one?" she repeated, faintly confused, staring at Tristam's distracted profile as he grimaced at the ceiling. After a moment, she looked upward, too. The old chandelier was gray with dust but might clean up into something rather pretty if they could ever clear the cobwebs.

"I'm afraid it was used for *sexual* fun and games."

Karo made a strangled sound of protest. Tristam's golden eyes turned her way and began to gleam. Her own expression, she was sure, was openly horrified. She had read about things like this but never actually encountered anything like it in the real world.

"Fun and games," she echoed, wondering if he was pulling her leg. Maybe her dream boss had some screws loose after all. It figured that there was some fly in the ointment of her new life. A man with a taste for mixing sex and torture was on par for the kind of week she was having.

"Yes. Fun and games. You know, ala the Marquis de Sade—except the owner of this house was practicing his violent pornographic fantasies long before de Sade was born. I'm afraid that S and M was Vellacourt's hobby and main claim to fame, even if the terminology was yet to be invented. He was rich enough to pull it off—to make an art of it, even. Fortunately for everyone, rich as he was, he never went into politics. There's no telling how it might have changed history if he'd been a governor. After all, there are the quirky, and then there are the true *degenerates*." Tristam English gave a wry laugh.

Karo stared and tried to think of something to say. Tristam shrugged and went on with his lecture.

"Belle Ange is equidistant from Williamstown and Jamestown, and people tend to lump every place in the area together because they were all built in the sixteen hundreds. But there are significant historical, political, architectural and philosophical differences between the three locales. Jamestown was built in tribute to the inefficient King James, Williamstown is named after William of Orange . . . and Belle Ange was built by a man who was loyal to neither. The entire—"

"Please tell me that you're kidding," Karo interrupted as she found her voice.

"About what?"

"About the whole S and M thing. About torture. About that being this place's main claim to fame." She was a trained art historian with some pretense of professionalism, a former assistant curator to a modest but respectable museum of modern art in San Francisco. She had apprenticed under the head honcho at Williamstown and written several articles for the *Journal of American History* on the evolution of female artists in post-colonial government. Her father was considered one of America's foremost authorities of World War I military history. People like her did not get associated with sexual torture chambers, no matter how historical the project!

"I wish I was kidding. Sorry about that. I should have warned you, I suppose, but I was afraid you'd run the other way and I really do need your help. I've been given three months and a tiny budget to whip this place into shape—though there is a bonus if we get things done ahead of schedule. Try and think of this as going off on a holiday where you expect an occasional bit of rain. It may not be fun to slog about in the damp, but it should still have moments of fun. At the very least it will be instructive!"

Karo thought about the Williamstown debacle and the horror of making another call to her parents with another change of address less than a week after the last. It was too humiliating to consider. This job had been a gift without a guarantee, just like the rest of life.

Her spine stiffened, at least metaphorically; the rest of her body was still rather battered for such exercise. "So, they really did this sort of thing in the seventeenth and eighteenth centuries? I thought that it—um, spanking and things like that—was brought on by the repressive Victorian era . . . at least in Britain," she added. She felt entirely out of her depth.

"This sort of behavior is definitely that old. The garret is part of the original house, built in about 1670 and then remodeled in 1812, I think, but the

Vellacourts have a quiet history of unnatural behavior even back in Europe—hence the religious persecution." He paused. "Oh, do you know any of the family history? They were a bit obscure, which is why de Sade steals the spotlight for inventing this sort of thing, but the family manages to show up at some of the battles and in most of the scandals."

"No, I've missed this family entirely. Do I really want to know about them? Aren't they all nuts? Going by this house . . ."

Tristam gave a weary sigh. "That is a judgment you'll have to make yourself. You can do your part of this task without full context, but . . . well, I find it wise to know the enemy. And you can count on at least one clever clog in every historical society who knows something about this house or family. I prefer that it not be me."

Karo sighed. "Okay, let's have it. Give me whatever else you know. Give me the family history."

"The Vellacourts were mostly undistinguished feudal lords until the Protestant Reformation. They did well under Henry the Eighth by sensing which way the ecclesiastical wind was blowing and running before the storm. However, once titled by Henry, and after the family coffers were sufficiently filled with loot from the legal plunder of various monasteries, they wisely switched sides and reverted to Catholicism for the reign of Bloody Mary. They again reversed their political and religious beliefs for the sovereignty of Elizabeth. Things were rougher under James and Charles the First—"

"Also known as Charles the worst," Karo quipped, though she soon realized it was wholly inappropriate. She got frowned at. Apparently Tristam didn't do forced levity before noon.

Her employer continued. "It seems that there was actually a finite number of times that you could swap political horses back then, especially when rumors of bizarre sexual practices and demon-worship begin to circulate at court. Then came the rise of Cromwell. To be fair, I think the devil-worship stuff was fabricated by Vellacourt family enemies. There is no suggestion in any of the diaries that he studied the order of the Left Hand Path."

Karo blinked. "The Left Hand Path? Oh, you mean Satanism. I thought that was all Louis the Fourteenth and in France."

"Yes, it was. But news traveled fast and rumor even faster. In any event, faced with growing scandal and a strong sense that the king was going to lose his argument with parliament and then his head, the Vellacourt family wisely picked up stakes and moved to the New World. Charles gave the Vellacourts a generous land grant in return for a suitable donation to his coffers, and then the doomed monarch waved them off with a somewhat hypocritical 'Satan, get thee behind me'—which didn't impress anyone since he had accepted Satan's bribe. The Vellacourts promptly invested in slaves to build and work this plantation in Virginia, and a sugar cane plantation in Haiti. What these workers thought of Hugh's sexual practices in either place has mercifully not been recorded anywhere, so all that exists are family diaries and journals and letters, and those are largely cryptic. Clarice Vellacourt, the present owner, is not inclined to open the family library to scholars, so perhaps we are safe from outside exposure. If we decide it is to be avoided at all costs."

"If?" Karo repeated.

"Well . . . I have given this matter some thought, and maybe in this era of liberalism we can make a positive feature of the family behavior, as long as we don't go too far or get *too* truthful."

Karo shook her head, baffled. "A positive feature? To the general public? In Virginia? How so? I can't quite picture this: the Disneyworld of S and M, featured in a two-tone brochure, quaint woodcuts of Vellacourt getting flogged. Er . . . or was he the one doing the flogging?"

Tristam laughed. "Both. His mistress was what in the modern parlance is called a 'top.' But Vellacourt liked to change things up from time to time."

"I see." His ease with the subject puzzled her.

He sensed her continued befuddlement. "Well, we couldn't be too obvious in our advertising, and to maximize visitations we would have to offer both X-rated and G-rated tours. But it would be a plus in some circles that the old rogue did what he did. He probably even swung both ways, at least when he was young."

"What! You mean he was bisexual? That's not a plus!" Karo spluttered. "Mention that at all and there goes the Christian audience! Oh, dear. We're going to have to bury this one six feet under.

I just knew the gift horse would have rotten teeth," she muttered to herself.

"Yes. They always do," Tristam said with sympathy. "Pity Vellacourt didn't live in California. They're a lot more understanding of 'reprobates' on your west coast." He turned away from the painting and shoved a set of antlers away from a narrow door tucked under the stair.

"Not *that* understanding, I assure you! In fact, if my parents ever hear one word about . . ." She shuddered. "You're absolutely sure about this? I mean, dead certain?" Karo screwed up her courage to ask the necessary question. Sometimes historical researchers had to be a little bit like priests or doctors when examining a famous personage's delicate—or *in*delicate—past. Probing was always allowed if it was for educational purposes. "He was a man who had a sexual torture chamber. For fun. And he was bisexual." It went against most everything she'd been taught was natural and right.

"Oh, yes." The answer was airy but final.

"How can you tell that the torture was only for fun?" she pressed. "I mean, the *torture*. Some stuff going on in France was horrible. Who was that mass murderer—La Voisin? Maybe Vellacourt liked to mistreat slaves similarly. There's some precedent for that sort of thing. And if that's the case, we really don't want to bring the matter up, especially not in any way that suggests approval or acceptance. The whole monster-vampire thing works in New Orleans, but not here in Virginia. As it shouldn't." The last sounded a little prudish to her ears but she didn't take it back.

Tristam didn't answer. Instead, he pulled the little door open, and a cloud of dust and cobweb billowed into the room on the stale air. It smelled of mice, mold and mushrooms—icky gray ones with little cone hats. He stepped back with a grimace and closed the door, shutting off the unpleasant odors. "Most of the evidence is empirical. Vellacourt is nothing like La Voisin. I have found no impedimenta of witchcraft, though there are devices for hunting and torturing witches. Those aren't in the garret, though. The only suggestion of witchcraft is a vague reference to Vellacourt having read the Grimoire of Pope Honorius."

"A grimoire?"

"Yes, but it isn't here, unfortunately, so we can't see what, if anything, he took from it. No, when I say 'sexual torture chamber,' I think the violence that was done here was mainly . . . Well, there was nothing *horrible* done here, as odd as this man was. He was harmless, I think. The whips I've found are mostly made of velvet. Mostly. There are some leather tawses. Some little golden manacles are lined with beaver pelts, though there are larger ones that would fit a man that are made of iron. Some paddles have illustrated leather. The tooling is actually quite nice on some of them, although still rather, um, limited in theme. There's even a padded rack that can be adjusted for comfort and multiple positions, which is Hugh Vellacourt's own invention. I know this because he left journals complete with bad illustrations to explain it, a sort of owner's manual for the dilettante sadist. All in all, this mansion houses an excellent collection of late seventeenth-century erotic paraphernalia—perhaps the only such set in America," he summed up calmly. Golden eyes twinkling, Tristam asked, "Shall we go up now? Or would you rather face it on a full stomach?"

Well, she'd asked to get the pain over all at once, Karo admitted to herself. Still, this was a lot. "Maybe later," she replied. "I guess I'm still feeling a bit faint from the ideas of whips and chains, sex and witchcraft. No point in facing every challenge at once."

Also, there was something else. It wasn't something she had ever admitted to a living soul—or even a dead one—but a part of her had always been a bit fascinated by the idea of bondage. Here was her chance to actually look it in the face. But she wasn't ready to see this room with Tristam English beside her. No, that would be too much. She would make her first visit alone.

But, the black arts? That had never interested her at all. She didn't believe in the Christian Devil, but she did believe that there was such a thing as evil, and that it could linger. If this house had been used for evil purposes, which was possible, no matter what Tristam claimed, she needed a little while to work up the courage to face the scene of the crimes. A *torture* chamber!

Tristam's brow creased as he studied her. He seemed apologetic for anything he might have said that was beyond the pale and she was annoyed with herself for letting her shock be so apparent. "I quite agree. Let's make sure you are at full strength before we shock your system with any visuals."

"So," Karo said, trying to make some joke to

show that she wasn't entirely upended by this development but drawing a total blank. She often thought of herself as a sophisticate, but she didn't know how to begin rationally discussing Vellacourt's hobbies, much less how to market them to a tourist crowd. She had a sudden image of the gargoylelike man in the portrait parading up and down his torture chamber wearing a red leather waistcoat and a pair of high-heeled shoes with paste buckles and paisley socks. It was pure Monty Python silliness, and the thought made her feel better. Devils got smaller when you laughed at them.

"Yes?" Tristam prompted.

"Are . . . are we certain that this wasn't the summer villa? A hideaway for a mistress would have some tradition behind it, and that could possibly be made into a tourist stop for those with slightly puerile interests if peddled carefully to the right market." She was babbling a bit, but the situation had scattered her wits. She was still trying to figure out reasons this degeneracy could be accepted by normal society.

Tristam didn't seem to mind. "Couldn't it just?" There came a flash of that charming grin and another spray of those invisible pheromones of his that made her insides jump and flutter. "But, no. This was the main residence. Vellacourt wasn't that sophisticated or considerate of his wife, who died shortly after they emigrated. He is especially graphic in his writings about his carryings on. His journals are a disaster in terms of political correctness. He was a competent architect, though. The old house is well constructed and more tasteful than some of these strange later additions would lead you to suspect. And he was a fair farmer, though he did not personally till the soil."

"But still a bisexual lecher sadist," Karo said under her breath, again swept away by morality. "And a rose by any other name."

Tristam shrugged. "Just so. And I always think it's best to look things square on. As I told the current owner, there's nothing to be gained from wincing at cold hard facts, evil ancestors, or even bad grammar." She couldn't tell if there was laughter in his voice.

"Well, one thing is certain," Karo replied.

"Yes?" her employer asked.

"I can't have my parents coming here on vacation. They'll just have to wait for a visit to Williamstown and Jamestown after I'm through. Father might—*might*—understand, but mother is Episcopalian . . . and not the kind who drinks heavily and only goes to church on Easter Sunday."

Tristam began to laugh. "I understand. My own mum is so high church as to verge on Roman Catholic." He pointed up the stairs. "Okay, we won't do the torture chamber, but let's go up anyway. Turn left at the top. I want to show you the ugliest pilasters in North America. Then I'll feed you breakfast."

As they started to climb he asked, "Are you at all attached to the pleasures of the table?"

Karo was glad for the change of subject. "Yeah. Especially if I don't have to cook."

"Are you firm about that?"

His tone was the first sign of worry she'd taken

from him, but she stuck to her guns. "Fairly. It's sexism to think that the woman should always have to cook. It would be more efficient to share responsibilities. Since we'll be sharing our time here."

He sounded somewhat disappointed. "Well, I expect we'll muddle through. I'm a fair hand with the B and E, and I can just manage toast."

She laughed. "Good to know it. And, by the way, I can't stand kipp—Uh, what is that . . . that *thing*?" She pointed, almost outraged.

"Fruit, I think. But, yes, it looks a bit like something else. And that's a snake and a tower, I hope. But the wood is so cracked it's hard to be definite. I felt you needed to get a look at it, so you could ponder it over breakfast. It really has that Vellacourt feel. It's what we'll be selling here."

"It's got to be the ugliest pilaster in North America," she murmured, awed. "And the most pornographic."

"Yes, that Vellacourt feel," Tristam repeated. "Stand over here, actually. See? It looks rather like the south face of the temple of the Kama Sutra. Only, not as artistic."

Karo tilted her head. "No, not by a long shot," she agreed. "That Vellacourt feel. How are we going to sell this?"

Yesterday upon the stair,
I met a man who wasn't there.
He wasn't there again today.
I wish, I wish he'd stay away.
—Hughes Mearns

Chapter Four

If slightly more prudish than himself, his new assistant was correct about many things, among them that Belle Ange was hideous. Tristam simply could not fathom why the abomination of bad taste that was this mansion had been called Beautiful Angel. If Hugh Vellacourt had demonstrated a sense of humor, Tristam would have suspected him of practicing irony, or that he had given in to the whim of his concubine. But Vellacourt's graphic journals were phlegmatic in the extreme and did not suggest that he had developed an interest in anything beyond his libido or purse; humor or affection were right out.

An interest in his libido—a case of the pot calling the kettle black, Tristam admitted, watching Karo's denim-clad legs conquering the maids' backstairs with vigor. But surely he would be forgiven this brief lapse of lasciviousness. It was not every day that a bewildered and utterly delicious nymph wandered in out of the rain to make herself at home in his bed and life. Karo's legs alone made this moldy project worthwhile.

"I don't think we should take tours up this staircase," she called back, a bit breathless. "I mean, think of the cardiac arrests in the over-sixty crowd—especially in the August heat. Though, kids would love it. This is just like a rat maze. And so creepy!" Her enthusiasm was catching.

"You seem to be enjoying it," Tristam observed, lifting his eyes to an acceptable height in case she turned at the top of the stair and caught him gawking.

"Well, it's my first day. I expect my eagerness will wind down some. I'll get a bit more jaded, especially if this search for treasures turns out to be a snipe hunt. I have hopes, though. It is very rare for a house to have actually remained in the same family for so many years. Perhaps they didn't sell off all the good stuff."

Tristam thought about the third floor, packed to the rafters with aged debris, the accumulation of several generations of avid and unchecked collectors who had made it their life work to simply fill the Gothic monstrosity that was this house. From the now nearly drained wine cellars—relocated to an outbuilding some years ago because the basement so frequently flooded—to the steep, grimy garrets added every half century or so, it was everywhere too dusty, too narrow . . . and too *ugly*, as his nymph would say.

Except the torture chamber. That room, original to the house, was remarkably free of dust and surprisingly inviting with minimal clutter. He'd found himself drawn to it, and to thoughts of

Karo . . . But he wouldn't even let that X-rated thought cross his mind.

"How soon will the jading take place?" he asked. "I think the first pall fell over me about twenty minutes in. Miles of endless rat's nest. I'm almost sorry now that I threw out the still."

Karo laughed. He really liked the sound. It was low and soft, utterly delightful.

"It'll happen eventually," she promised. "But I'm a slow cynic. I can't help being a little enchanted with some of what's around. No matter what you say about the designer . . . Well, it's really much better than what I expected last night. Or, some of it is."

"You couldn't have expected much," Tristam retorted.

She turned long enough to give him a strange smile. "I'll have to take the fifth on that. It's a little too soon for total honesty, don't you think?"

Tristam returned her smile. She was right. It was way, way too soon at least for some of the things he was thinking.

"Did you say 'still'?" Karo prompted. "As in, for making moonshine?"

"Yes, they've been producing here the finest grain alcohol that ever blinded man since around sixteen-fifty or thereabouts. Some traditions never die unless you rip them out at the root, raze the shed and threaten the police."

"I see."

Karo glanced out the window. Tristam knew what she was seeing. The meadow had been shorn to a reasonable height but would be freckled with the detritus of the last storm. Beyond that were the ferocious vines with which the gardeners did weekly battle. The damn things did their best to strangle their architectural prey, pulling at the stones from the outbuilding and graveyard, trying to draw them back into the ground from which they'd been quarried.

When she spoke again, his assistant's voice was thoughtful. "Was Vellacourt a gentleman? I mean, I know he was a man of means, but was he considered honorable for his era? I mean, publicly?"

"Yes, but who would judge him otherwise? His peers were few and far between. 'Gentlemen' basically came in two models back then: rapacious or genteel idiots. The idiots didn't last long. Of course, in the very early days no one did. Malaria, understandably hostile natives, starvation . . . Ah! The good old days in early America!"

"All true. But the clothes were pretty. Maybe we'll find some still intact."

"If you were rich they were lovely, I'm sure. Unfortunately, we have found little here worth displaying from the seventeenth or eighteenth centuries. All we have is a few sets of the common man's rough woolens."

"A pity. The slaves and the poor must have suffered in all that wool."

"That was probably the least of their suffering," Tristam pointed out.

"True enough. Eventually I'll have to devote some time to sorting through the papers in the librar—Oh!"

Karo jumped back and landed in his waiting arms, just as he had anticipated at this turn of the hallway. Their embrace was clumsy in the confines of the narrow corridor, but Tristam did his best to appear strong and manly. "Is it a mouse?" he asked, though he knew better. "I'm afraid they are everywhere."

"No, I don't mind mice or even rats. I think I've found another of that granddaughter's paintings."

She stepped from his sheltering arms and gingerly shifted a pile of antlers with her knee. A smallish picture frame leaned against the wall. Tristam had seen it already, had almost shrieked like a girl when it came looming out of the gloom. Karo picked the frame up with her thumb and finger, checking the back carefully to see that she wasn't picking up any pests as well. Tristam had noticed that, while she wasn't afraid of mice or rats, she did not care for spiders at all.

"Valperga." He sighed. "I know her well. She was her own favorite subject. There are even more paintings of her than of Hugh."

"Oh, isn't she a peach? Grandma, what big teeth you have! Was her name really Valperga? How cruel parents can be." Karo sat the frame down on the top of an old trunk. Pushing her hair back from her forehead left a smudge. It also pulled her thin shirt tight enough for him to make out some of the lacy details on her bra, which was different from the floral item she'd been wearing last night.

Tristam began to sweat. The upper floors had grown uncomfortably warm as the day ripened into its full potential, but that wasn't the problem. The real issue was waiting patiently for an answer to his speculations while he stood fantasizing about the lacy flowers under her blouse.

Not that he could be blamed for being distracted, he assured himself. Her dark locks might be dusty and her hands nearly black with grime, but she looked immeasurably pettable in those tight jeans. It was a wonder that the woman could look so good wearing smut and cobwebs, but she did. Obviously, he had been closed up in this house for too long. Or perhaps his brain was addled by the same lightning that had affected his nymph. Whatever ailed him, he wasn't sure if he loved or hated it.

"That's how the old crone referred to herself," he finally managed. "She did not care for her own name, which, according to the only genealogy I've found, was Agartha."

Karo shook her head. "She has only herself to blame. There is nothing wrong with Agartha. I was named after a maternal grandmother, which seemed a good idea at the time, since the parents wanted to please her. And they did, but only for a few months—she died soon after I was born. Her pleasure in the name was short, and my suffering long. It isn't fair, being burdened with a difficult name, but you don't see me changing mine. Especially not to something like Valperga."

"Karo sounds sweet and old-fashioned," Tristam said.

"Yep. Sweet, like the syrup. Would you want to be called after food?" She frowned, changing the subject by glancing again at the painting. "Do you suppose it's an accurate self-portrait? Or was Valperga just burdened with dozens of neuroses?"

Tristam reluctantly turned his attention back to the picture. Hungry black eyes peered out from the cracked canvas, and he frowned with distaste. If the creature in the portrait had ever possessed youth or beauty or kindness, these had fled by the time the painting was done.

Karo shuddered dramatically. "I pity any woman who has *that* as a self-image. Talk about a bad hair day! It reminds me a bit of Poe's degenerative style. You know, the black cat that got more and more abstract each time he drew it?"

Tristam shrugged. "Perhaps it was a familial brain disorder. I think Hugh Vellacourt was slightly mad, though in an English sort of way. He certainly didn't have normal taste in furnishings."

"The library is more or less classic, and *fairly* tasteful."

"Calling the library tasteful is giving it undue praise, but at least the furnishings are less belligerent than in most of the house. They are mostly eighteenth century," he reminded her. Noticing a streak of dust and a bit of cobweb, Tristam brushed at his sleeve. "I do wonder about that low door. Perhaps Hugh felt that people should abase themselves before the temple of knowledge. But, no—that would be giving him too much credit."

Karo laughed. She looked over at her equally dusty companion as he tried to reorder his clothing, and considered again the things he'd told her downstairs. Far from being stuffy or standoffish, Tristam English had proven to be forthright and unflinching—and pleasant company. Though, she was rather baffled by his treatment. On the phone he had sounded distant and formal. Their project was anything but, and today he was behaving very much like an uncle indulging a favorite niece.

Kind. Unhurried. Amused. These weren't characteristics of people she generally met on the job. Bosses tended to take one look at her no-nonsense but eager manner and pointed her at the largest messes they could find. That, or they patted her on the head and called her sweetie. Though she liked to blame her name, she also knew it had a lot to do with her diminutive stature and delicate voice; few people looked beyond packaging.

Tristam was doing neither, and it was confusing—in the nicest possible way.

"What does that mean, anyway?" she asked. "English madness? Insanity with charm?"

"Exactly." Tristam leaned carelessly against a plaster wall. His shirt was already hopelessly begrimed. Some relief would come from bringing in a cleaning crew and exterminator, but he couldn't do that until Karo had found and marked all of the plantation's historical treasures. It wouldn't do to buff the patina off some priceless candlestick.

In the meantime, living in squalor wasn't too terrible now that he had someone to bear him company. He might even survive the beastly late summer weather. Winds could bluster and clouds could threaten; he could just ignore them.

"Instead of just the usual slaves to cater to his whims, he had a defrocked priest." Tristam lowered his voice. "And a tender young bride of wealth and breeding, who died under very mysterious circumstances after providing an heir. Let's see, there was a hunchbacked butler, a French concubine—"

"Really? You're not just saying this to give me hope? I mean, a defrocked priest and a hunchbacked butler would be great in a brochure. Not quite as good as Berkeley—they have two presidents and a signatory of the Declaration of Independence—but it's all still quite usable." She laughed, beginning to have some fun.

"No, really," he promised. "Mad Father Basco, removed from the priesthood before he was twenty and who lived an unnaturally long life. The beauteous Eustacie La Belle—if that was her real name. And S and M master Hugh Vellacourt. These three should be of a great deal of interest to tourists—especially those who are bored blind by the *same old same old* historical plantation tour they usually get," he suggested mildly. "This place is much more exciting than two presidents and a signatory to the Declaration of Independence."

"Well, maybe," Karo allowed. "So, you're really and truly serious about the priest and the concubine?" This bothered her, though she knew it was silly to maintain any illusions about the character of historical personages—especially when she'd been given so much proof already to the contrary. Still, she had always felt that it took a lot of courage and even imagination to pack up one's life and leave everyone and everything you knew behind. If it had been easy, more people would have done it. Hugh had done just that, and she wanted to give him some respect. She didn't say this to Tristam, though, because it sounded naïve. He would probably tell her that most people didn't leave anywhere willingly and were in fact being chased by mobs. He'd say that fleeing for one's life didn't take much courage or imagination.

Tristam's voice called her back. "What sort of

mad-dog Englishman could Vellacourt be without them? He was a favored personage here, you know, one of the privileged gentry. A soul brother—and later a debtor—of John Robinson's. One would have to work hard to be more infamous in these parts."

"John Robinson? Of the House of Burgesses?" Tristam nodded when she gasped. "America's first big-time tax defrauder, who started this nation on the road to revolution?" He nodded again. "Well, that's great! We can really use that. Political corruption is perennially popular," she told him with real enthusiasm. "Very few people have moral prohibitions against tax fraud. In fact, they expect it. Throw in that priest and suggestions of religious persecution and we have a winner. Carter's Grove may be the prettiest of the local plantations, but we'll certainly have the one with the most corrupt past."

"What about the concubine? I think she makes a good part of the story," Tristam suggested. "She really was quite something out of the ordinary, and was definitely corrupt. Not to dress it up in too fine a language: Vellacourt bought her at auction in a bordello in Paris. She was fifteen and already an accomplished . . . businesswoman."

"Well, you're not a historian. And you are a man. I guess I'll have to forgive you for thinking that way," Karo said huffily. Her nose wrinkled. "But a common whore would hardly add tone to the place. At least, not the right kind. Political corruption is fine. Moral corruption is not."

"Um, I don't think she was common. Certainly

she wasn't inexpensive." Karo's hand was back in her hair, pulling her shirt tight. It was perturbing, to a degree, to find such simple gestures on his employee's part to be completely arousing. Tristam cleared his throat and made a stab at gathering his wandering thoughts.

"I bow to your greater experience. The United States does seem to have some distinct regional taboos which must be considered. Had enough dust for one afternoon? I'm ready for some lunch. Damn!" Tristam looked at his watch.

"What?"

"It's after two. Come to think of it, I never gave you breakfast. Come on. I better feed you before you have a relapse. Doctor Monroe said I was to see that you got three squares, lots of tea breaks and plenty of sleep or you would likely flake out on me."

"Well, I like the sound of that," Karo answered, hoping he was kidding about the doctor's diagnosis. "I wouldn't want to start seeing ghosts again, or end up doing anything else to embarrass myself. Last night put me over my quota of dumb acts for the week."

"Last night wasn't all bad," Tristam replied cheerfully, tucking Valperga's portrait back against the wall, facing inward. "Let's take the main stair. I don't feel up to another run as a lab animal. This house has given me a true understanding of how rats must feel in a maze."

"It wasn't all bad, huh? I suppose you liked sleeping in the library."

"Of course not. But then, I didn't sleep in the

library." He pulled the door shut behind them. When Karo hung back, letting him take the lead, Tristam brushed by her and started down the steps. He added over his shoulder: "And I quite enjoyed carrying a beautiful, half-naked woman to bed—even if she did bite me."

Karo stopped in her tracks and watched her boss's lithe form disappear from view. So much for his being an indulgent uncle! None of her relatives had ever spoken to her like that. Neither had any of her employers.

"I'll never wear linen again," she muttered.

"That would be a shame." His voice floated up clearly. "And the bedroom chair was quite comfortable."

Karo was grateful that he didn't turn around and look at her. She knew she had blushed a shade of red to rival roses.

"You sound like something out of a bad romance novel!" she yelled.

"If I had a mustache I'd twirl it," he called in reply.

"You'd look hideous in a mustache!"

But he wouldn't. There wasn't much of anything that would make Tristam English look bad.

Over towering roast beef sandwiches stuffed with artichoke hearts and peppers, Tristam set about putting his wary nymph at ease. She had plainly been disturbed by his teasing and he was very curious about what would make her poker up so completely when she joined him downstairs. Had the thought of him watching her sleep been that unnerving? Surely she understood that he couldn't leave her alone last night after her accident.

Or, was there some exposed nerve that he'd accidentally trod upon? She had been rather anxious to vacate her last position, and he had been too happy at finding a qualified prospective employee to ask any questions.

"I know why I hired you," he said thoughtfully, pouring the rest of his Coke into a Star Wars glass. Karo had refused one, saying she preferred to drink straight from the can. "But why did you take this job?"

"Why does any woman throw over a career and move to the black hole of Calcutta?" she tossed back casually, breaking off a bite of sandwich for 'Stein. The big cat never seemed to leave the dining room if he could help it. And why would he? The food probably ended up there eventually, and it was free of dust and grabby antlers.

"A religious calling? Temporary insanity? Boredom with the Fife and Drum Corps that had you dying for the British yearly," Tristam suggested. "Or, the old stand-by—an affair of the heart gone disastrously awry."

The last was a guess, and he was slightly surprised when she blinked. "Well, let's just say that I liked the Fife and Drum Corps well enough. It was the usual reason," she admitted. "Anyway, the job wasn't really in my field. I just liked Williamstown and I was willing to stay in a comfortable rut until it became . . ."

"Uncomfortable? And your employer let you go without a struggle or two weeks' notice?"

"It would be truthful to say that my employer was ready to move on to another . . . project. And notice was definitely given."

"I see." And he thought that he did—at least the general outline. "Well, that does explain a few things. Care to mention who the fool was? I would like to send around a thank-you note."

She laughed. "Please do. And send it care of the Board of Trustees. I'm sure they'd like to hear that their money hired a man so very dedicated to his job that he'll do anything to keep a good assistant, even stealing her work and passing it off as his own. I bet they would even approve. They're sexist enough."

"Hm . . . That isn't the best of ways to ensure loyalty, is it? Not unless you're very generous with your compensation or willing to seduce your victim first. I expect that he hasn't had the proper training. Very few academic types do. We're all in the private sector, where there's usually money for bribes."

"What!" She laughed again and then choked on a bite of sandwich. "Maybe I should be glad for that impoverished budget you mentioned. Neither of us will be tempted to misbehave."

"I wouldn't insult you with money. I'm sure you would never take it."

"Money isn't insulting. Not when you're poor."

"He must have been clumsy to have shattered your loyalty so thoroughly," Tristam persisted. "I bet his idea of a proper bribe was a single red rose laid on top of a mountain of research notes that needed typing. Overnight."

"What are you, clairvoyant?" Karo chuckled and

her face relaxed. "You're absolutely right. One rose for typing. Six white daisies for research. He was under the impression that I like daisies. To be polite, I had to keep them in the office where they smelled up everything."

Tristam opened his eyes wide, playing to her sudden laughter. "Of course I'm clairvoyant. It's not such a stretch, after all. My dear, you've gone and left him flat. What else would drive you to it?"

"What indeed?"

Tristam spoke to the air. "You know, I've always felt that betraying an optimist is rather like starting a butterfly collection. It can be fun at the time, I suppose, but one nearly always regrets it later."

"You think that we have to excuse F. Christian because of his possible eventual regret? I doubt remorse has ever entered his head. He was getting desperate. It was publish or perish time. You know what that means in the world of academia." She sighed and then found herself confiding: "It wasn't just F. Christian stealing my work—though he is a patronizing, lecherous, thieving pain in the butt. I suppose this is dreary, but I really thought he liked me. As a woman. I—Pardon?"

"Nothing." Tristam coughed into his napkin. "Was there another woman as well? There must have been. This idiot would seem to leave no cliché unturned."

Karo eyed him. "Yes. As it turns out, there is a very blonde, very rich, very unknown—at least to me—fiancée. I'm afraid I wasn't what you would call mature or dignified about the proposed pajama party he offered after admitting he stole my research." She, with an effort, quit grinding her teeth. "What a deal, huh? I get F. Christian and his bride, a chance to write papers he can steal, and an underpaid job from eight to five. Except on Tuesdays and Thursdays, when I could have him 'til seven, though remain underpaid. And Miss Magnolia gets everything else. Including a chance to do the kind of work that that bastard was promising me for the last three years. He gave her the job I wanted!"

Tristam made a choking sound that turned into another unconvincing cough.

Karo pointed a finger at him and added direfully: "He should be darn grateful that we weren't sleeping together, because he'd have ended up worse off than he did. I believe in Old Testament vengeance. None of this 'Let mercy season justice' stuff."

"What did you do?" Tristam asked, genuinely curious.

"I shoved him into a buffet and dumped potato salad on his head. Had there been a carving knife, he might have ended up dead, but there were only spoons."

"I see. And that would be in lieu of two weeks' notice . . . ? Well, there's nothing like a bit of revenge to raise one's spirits." His tone was quite bracing and made her glower, but he raised an eyebrow at her expression. "Do I really need to point out the obvious—that you're better off without the bounder? I'm sure it was the wonder of the week back at the office, but you'll live. Embarrassment never actually killed anyone."

"I know. I'm here, aren't I?" she grumbled. "I figured it out. The job was a tontine, anyway. I

mean, I wasn't going to be promoted until someone died."

"That's the stuff," he said encouragingly.

"You know what burns me most? F. Christian
and Mint Julep will probably be very happy together, her writing all the papers and him getting
all the credit, while I go down in history as the
one responsible for ruining the Williamstown
Founders' Day Dinner." She added, "I sure hope I
get a real job before anyone hears about this little
side trip of mine. No offense, but I don't think
this job is going on my resume. I'm going to have
to gloss over this interlude, especially if word
about Vellacourt's activities gets out."

"Gloss it with what? Even marine varnish won't
make these things look shiny. But you'll manage.
You are creative and efficient and capable of
avenging the wrongs done you. In fact, you faced
down a hurricane. In other words, you may be
dusty but you remain unbowed." He smiled.

"Please, stop complimenting me. I can't take so
much undeserved praise. Driving in that storm
was idiocy. It was all idiocy."

Tristam laughed at her glum expression. "Cheer
up. The tragedy has ended and life goes on. I pre-
dict that great happiness and well-earned fame lay
ahead of you—but not in the field of museum
work. Talk of masochism! It's not for you, m'dear.
You've far too much energy and life to be working
in such a fossilized field. We can do better. This is
a low-class, boiler room operation, but it's fun and
will be profitable. Just give me a chance to win you
over to my way of life."

"Yeah, I know. I know I'll be fine—just as long

as I stay away from blond men and bosses," she said without thinking. "I have a bad history with blond men and bosses." She was feeding 'Stein another bite of sandwich, however, and missed Tristam's arrested expression.

"There's been more than one blond heart-breaker in your short life?"

"Yes." Karo lifted a finger. "The first was Randy Potter, in the third grade. He always talked me out of my potato chips at lunch." A second finger went up. "Then Barry Deaver in high school. He two-timed me with the phys-ed teacher. Not that I blame him. She was a real Barbie doll, and what eighteen-year-old hormone factory could resist? Hm. I guess the last one—before F. Christian— was Professor Kayle. Bob didn't play around with bimbos, he just stole research from me."

"Good God!"

"Yes, that's what I said, among other things. I asked him why he did it, of course. But Bob had kind of a limited imagination. He couldn't even think up a good sob story as an excuse." Her brow furrowed. "That may have been why he had to steal my paper. Lack of imagination isn't good in a profession that requires a certain amount of cre-ative speculation, and where you have to find some-thing new to say at least once a year. I mean, I'm not naïve and I'm willing to take one for the team. I know some professors who routinely use their stu-dents' work to pad their research, but since he used my paper verbatim, don't you think that at the very least he should have given me some credit in the footnotes—called it a collaboration or thanked his research assistant or something?"

"Good God," Tristam said again.

"And after all that, he had the nerve to give me an A minus for the class!" She bit into her sandwich with unusual force, jaws slamming together with ten thousand PSI. "And then, to make the same mistake with F. Christian? I need a keeper."

"Um, Karo?" Tristam cleared his throat. "What color hair would you say I have?"

"Oh. Gold," she said, after she had swallowed and chased the sourdough with a mouthful of Coke. "Maybe a touch of brindle."

"That's nothing like blond, is it?"

"Uh . . ." She stared at him, her expression suddenly thoughtful. "No. I don't think so. I certainly hope not."

"Oh, well. I suppose that will do. I wouldn't want you thinking that I was a subhuman, research-stealing bimbo chaser."

"I don't. But, Tristam?" she asked, setting her sandwich aside. "I've been wondering about something."

"Yes?"

"Does this job come with dental insurance?"

"No. Do you need a dentist?"

"Hopefully not. And I think we'll get along fine as long as I don't do any research for you."

They gave up work as the sun set and decided to change before tackling dinner. Tristam came to his erstwhile room to collect the rest of his clothing, and Karo, as a matter of form, again offered to retire to the guest cottage. He declined firmly, again, citing her health and the benefits of a water heater for the bath, however small in capacity.

Then, with a bland smile that she had learned usually preceded some outrageous remark, he suggested in his most mellifluous voice that they could always share the hot water if she was truly concerned about putting him out in the cold. Her stupid heart stuttered and then picked up its pace as the light scent of vanilla filled her brain.

Share the hot water? Karo blinked in amazement while she considered the notion and all the ways that phrase could be interpreted. She had absolutely no intention of taking Tristam up on it, whatever the offer was. She wasn't congenitally stupid! She fully comprehended that she was currently stranded on a very shaky professional archipelago with a handsome man, and already burdened with a lot of bad history with men. She sensed plainly that the potential for self-immolation was growing. And she knew that neither her ego— nor bank account—could withstand any further romantic mishaps.

But, Tristam wasn't like anyone she had ever met. He was a lot of fun and . . . harmless. Sweet. British.

Reassured by her admittedly facile analysis, Karo decided to try some light banter, just to show that she could be sophisticated. Hands on hips, she tipped her head to one side and appeared to give the matter some thought.

"Well, I might be willing to share the . . ." The rest of her sentence never got past her lips. One of Tristam's mobile eyebrows flew upward at the word *share*, and the gold gaze sharpened into something completely different in intent from the genial flirtation they had shared over lunch. The man who looked back at her was no longer wearing his avuncular mask; the smile that crossed his chiseled lips was anything but harmless.

"Yes . . . ?"

Karo dropped her arms but those gold eyes remained fixed, those lean muscles tensed and ready to pounce. She found, much to her surprise, that it was both disconcerting and flattering to finally be wanted for something other than her brain. It made the knees weak. The blood sparkled. Her heart raced. She could feel herself longing to swim out into a sea of desire where his lighthearted lust would surely take them—

But then, two weeks later, it would be a sea of debts where she would be floundering alone after he fired her and took up with a twenty-year-old cheerleader from Roanoke.

Karo sighed. The mood was spoiled. She wasn't good at this flirtation thing. Why couldn't she ever get a job working for a woman, or a really unattractive, dark-haired man?

But this present situation was her fault entirely. She shouldn't have teased him. Now she would have to shove the camel's nose back out of the tent—and be polite about it.

She said in a scolding tone: "Don't even think it! You would not enjoy an office romance. Take it from me. They're painful and ugly, so don't tease me, and I won't tease you either."

"But what if I'm not teasing?" That voice was warm. The smell of invisible coconut drifted her way.

"Of course you're teasing," she said briskly, trying not to inhale the yummy scent. "Is this some sort of peculiar British humor? Find an assistant, lure her to a haunted mansion, strike her with lightning, deprive her of breakfast, get her hot and filthy—and not in a good way—and then proposition her? It's an original line of seduction, I'll grant you. Though, it might be harassment. I'll have to consult the union. Anyway, isn't there a wannabe Mrs. English waiting for you somewhere? Would she approve of this?"

Karo told herself she was pleased when the golden gaze registered something that might be chagrin, and the long body relaxed against the wall in a comfortable slouch.

"Good God! You're right. It is bad form to tackle a girl before her bath." He turned away. "However, I think you should know that the last wannabe Mrs. English called things off before I left for the States. She said my barbed and rusty conversation had given her tetanus. She didn't approve of my line of work either."

"She must have been very witty," Karo suggested, though she was in no mood to joke about anyone's heartaches.

"Oh, very. But not particularly kind." He reached for his suitcase. "I find that I value that rather more highly these days. Kindness and integrity. They are both difficult to find."

Karo stretched out a grimy hand. "Don't . . ." She stopped, unsure what to say, unsure if she should apologize for bringing up something painful. "That was American humor," she said quickly.

"Aggressive irony and overstatement. Please don't think I was making light of your relationship ending, Tristam. You really are a very nice person. It's just that I have lots of evidence that my SOP for on-the-job romance doesn't work. And since this is just a filler job until the Smithsonian or the Louvre snaps me up, I'd rather not . . . get involved."

He looked up from his suitcase. Far from being crushed, she could see that he was struggling not to laugh.

"Trying to spare my feelings, Karo? That's sweet of you, but hardly wise," he said, echoing her own thoughts. "It might encourage me to pour you another brandy and proposition you over dinner just to see if I can get away with it—and that is British humor, m'dear, so don't look so shaken by the thought. You're perfectly safe for the next"—he looked at his watch—"eighteen hours, at the very least."

"Eighteen hours!" she exclaimed. Then, unwisely: "Why eighteen?"

Tristam opened the door before answering. Limned by a stray strand of sunlight bleeding in from the hallway, his hair gleamed like butterscotch. His profile pure Byronic hero, he was definite centerfold material, even if the obscenely decorated door behind him made Karo shift uncomfortably. "Because Doctor Monroe said to give you forty-eight hours for the shock to wear off completely. Until then, I can't believe anything you say."

"Oh." More British humor, she assured herself as he left the room. She went on to tell herself that Tristam probably had the very highest professional ethics, and he never got involved with his assistants. In fact, just what made her assume that she was so appealing? Especially covered in filth and sweating in a far from ladylike manner.

Well, hell. Had she sounded like a total fathead telling him she wouldn't fall into his arms? Probably. Probably he just meant that they could take turns using the shower. Karo groaned and wondered if there was any end to her bad karma.

As an unspoken apology, she took on KP duties that evening. It was a pleasure to work in the vast kitchen, even if the larder was a little bare of ingredients. She found rice, tomatoes and an abundance of green peppers, however. A little onion, some ground beef and she had the fixings for a Texas hash.

Tristam helped out, assembling a rather simple salad from what bits and pieces he found in the refrigerator; whoever had done the last shopping hadn't been real fond of the "green" food group, and the selection of edible leaves was commensurately small. Karo commented that in the old days of this place, their dinner would have been heavy with selections from the garden.

The lack of veggies was compensated for by a fair selection of wine—mostly local labels, but there were a few California whites tucked in among them, and a suddenly silent Tristam had chosen a Sonoma chardonnay to keep them company while they chopped and stirred.

"I'm glad you're not a rigid vegetarian, though some endive would be nice," Karo said wistfully.

"My ancestors didn't battle their way to the top of the food chain so they could subsist on nuts and berries."

"My family is all carnivore, too. Lots of chefs and gourmets. You wouldn't believe some of the food trivia I've heard. Someday I'll write a book."

"Are you a good cook, Karo? At least, an informed one?" Tristam asked as he sliced his way through a stalk of pallid celery. "You look quite competent with a spoon and knife."

"Worried about food poisoning?" she asked. "Or are you afraid of the peppers? I fear most traditional British cuisine is too bland for me. You'll have to adapt if I'm cooking."

"No problem. I like hot food. Curries, especially." He'd answered her teasing question seriously, indicating that his mind was largely elsewhere. "It was actually an indirect way of wondering aloud about the possibility of running a small restaurant or a tea room here. A lot of the other plantations do it, and they are marginally profitable. I'm just wondering if it's something I should suggest to Clarice for Belle Ange. This isn't *research*—just an idea that I would like to examine." Karo noticed his stress on the word and hid a smile.

"Clarice?" She'd meant to ask earlier when the name came up. That she sounded only gently curious made her quite proud of herself.

"Clarice Vellacourt, the current owner. She lives in Florida. Eccentric lady."

Florida. That probably meant a nice, little old retiree. Karo liked that idea much better than a wealthy young tobacco princess who might decide to drop in for an occasional fling with her handsome hired hand.

"Hm. I suppose you could have a small cafeteria," she admitted. "Uh . . . but you weren't thinking that I would be the cook, were you?"

"Perish the thought!"

"Okay, then. Were you thinking of sandwich type stuff?"

"Not really. People can get that anywhere. I was considering something more upscale, a little bit more unexpected. Perhaps something with a historical slant."

Karo considered the scheme for a moment and found some objections. "It's a good idea, but I don't know if people would go for seventeenth-century authentic, if that is what you had in mind," she warned. "It takes a refined palette and some adventuresome taste buds to try peanut soup or game pies. In fact, there might be some problems with offering any wild meats. They'd have to be inspected for parasites. And there's the on-premises health inspections to consider, permits—"

"But what about things like sweet potato muffins or stew? Maybe some meat pasties—made from USDA choice," he suggested, not entirely ignoring her practical objections, but unwilling to have the idea quashed before it was given complete birth.

"That might work. Corn cakes with honey would be good, too, and vegetables from the garden. But . . ." Karo paused, allowing herself to truly consider how to implement the idea.

"But what? Come along. Spit it out."

"I think what I would do is lay on a dinner once a week. Like every Sunday. Take advance reservations and so on. And perhaps offer holiday dinners for Thanksgiving and in December. If you let people eat off old china in the dining room and charged the earth for it, I bet they'd come in droves—and it would be something that would set Belle Ange apart from the other plantations. Just in case the defrocked priest doesn't pack 'em in."

She smiled a little as she said this, but Tristam didn't smile back. His brain was making calculations. "I like it. Work up a menu, would you? Make a list of swishy extras, and I'll see about what sort of permits are needed to run a kitchen. Then we'll get on to finding a chef. I have a chap in mind. He's up in Maine and absolutely hates the winters there." Tristam looked over when she made a small sound of protest. "What is it? You don't feel competent to work on a menu without the chef's approval? Or do you want to talk to the licensing board first?"

"Well . . . No, of course I'm competent." And she was a wiz at research—as they both knew. So what if she wasn't a restaurateur? Wasn't this exactly the kind of wild-hare action she loved to contemplate and lacked the real nerve to try on her own? She had to learn to wheel and deal now that she had left the slow-paced world of academia behind. Besides, she knew all about boards of every type from Williamstown. She could cope with this.

Karo had another thought. "If we could find some old cookbooks in the library, or better still, some handwritten recipes, we could have some commemorative cookbooks printed up—you know the kind, Historical Feasts at Belle Ange. I bet dinner guests would buy them like . . . well, like hotcakes."

Tristam laughed. "Excellent. That's the kind of stuff we need. Remember, royalties go on paying forever. And we can sell them online, too." He pulled a PDA from his shirt pocket and started writing with a stylus. All leafy greens were shoved aside.

"Royalties?" she asked, startled.

"Of course. Haven't you ever published?"

"Nothing popular." And rarely under her own name.

Tristam looked up and smiled slightly. "Well, this can be your first. What about postcards? We should have some made. Are you any good with a camera?" he asked hopefully.

"Not *that* good! But I know someone in Williamstown. He does a lot of those tintype antique photos. He's a bit of a diva, but he could give us something unique and very historic."

Karo was still reeling from the idea of royalties.

Tristam looked up again, and this time he smiled a killer smile. Karo felt a small frisson of excitement shudder through her. For the first time, she allowed herself to hope that there was some potential for this stop-gap job to become an actual career.

A career with Tristam? her brain asked. *As a partner? A lover?*

Karo paused for a mental ten-count as she reviewed that idea. Planning ahead was not her forte, and the very thought of taking the first step back onto the road to romantic ruin was terrifying.

An incentive plan to total breakdown. The classic bringer of the worst kind of buyer's remorse. There was probably a very good reason why he was still footloose and fancy-free, she reminded herself. And hadn't she already decided that on-the-job romance wasn't for her?

Of course, if she were always on the move, what chance would there be forming real attachments with someone not in the business? She could see herself as old and gray and still alone. She and Tristam would have spent decades with all the irritations of a long-term relationship but none of the recompense.

Karo gave herself a mental slap: one thing at a time. She had known Tristam for a matter of hours. Sheesh! She hadn't been herself since coming to Belle Ange, and that was a fact.

"Do you really trust me this much, Tristam? After my grand entrance yesterday?" she asked worriedly. "I mean, I don't think I would trust me so very soon. I might be a flake."

"Of course I trust you. My instincts are almost infallible. 'You stick with me, babe. We're goin' to the top!'"

His Bogart was terrible. Karo loved it anyway. Tristam made her feel terrific, that life was full of possibilities after all. So what if her other relationships had been dumb and futile and bad for her nervous system and career? Tristam was right. They made a great team. There was no reason that they couldn't go all the way to the top on this one. Belle Ange really could be a four-star hit in the guidebooks and a credit to her name and resume. And, editorial credit for a cookbook? Just imagine!

"Tristam, I—" The flicker of the overhead lights and the roll of heavenly drums interrupted the impulsive words that were ready to roll off of her tongue.

"Yes?" he asked after the reverberations died.

The power went out before she could answer. "Damn!" Tristam said, reaching into the cupboard for the matches and candles that the owner kept on nearly every flat surface in every room. "Looks like we're in for more rain."

"Rain?" Karo echoed. Or was it a sign from heaven? A divine, wagging finger sent to chastise one of his stupider creatures before she screwed up her life again. What would it take to convince her that she should be cautious about bosses, no matter what they offered—getting hit by lightning?

Actually, getting hit by lightning wasn't enough. She'd done that already and was still thinking of trusting Tristam.

GHOST, n. *The outward and visible sign of an inward fear.*
—Ambrose Bierce from *The Devil's Dictionary*

Chapter Five

"Fish," Karo said, setting down her coffee cup. Tristam had the knack for brewing perfect java: the coffee was vehement but not impolite. She needed it after her night spent tossing and turning and a morning up in the elm. The top tree branches were the only place she was able to get reception for her cell phone, and she'd figured that, after the hurricane, she really needed to reassure her parents that she was alive and well. During the call her mother had enthused about the cookbook idea, but her father was clearly still worried—he'd talked her through how to change the oil in her car.

"I'm sorry. Did you say *fish*?" Tristam looked up from his PDA, which he was never without and which he'd been buried in throughout their toast and coffee. There had been no B and E waiting for her this morning. Though Tristam was nominally in charge of producing such, it being his only culinary skill, she forgave him because of the coffee.

"Yes. Are there any in the stream out back?"

"I haven't the foggiest. Why do you ask?"

"Fishing!"

"You sound euphoric. Do you enjoy fishing?" He appeared surprised. She had to wonder sometimes what went on in the murky depths of his brain when he was communing with his PDA.

"Tristam, come up for air! I'm talking about tourists. I'm talking about money. We could sell day-use tickets. You know how fanatical fishermen are. They'll stand around for days and in any sort of weather if there's even the hope of a catch."

Her employer stabbed several times at the PDA with the plastic stylus. It was a sure sign that she had gained his attention. They had already discussed hosting mystery nights, a croquette tournament between the local seniors and a group from the college, musical events and candlelight ghost tours like they had in Jamestown. The last had made Karo uneasy, especially considering her introductory experience in the Vellacourt mansion, but she had to agree that they would draw people.

"Find out if there are any trout or bass," she instructed. "They're better than catfish. And if not, can we stock the stream?"

"Right ho," Tristam replied.

"And while you're still with me, have you found out about health permits yet? And have we selected a publisher and format? I'm dying to start the cookbook."

A pained look marred his face. "I haven't been standing about twiddling my thumbs and stammering dirty limericks to the 900 operator," he replied, with a hint of indignation. "Whilst you have been mucking about with the bric-a-brac, I have been consulting the powers that be. Barratry, you know. Permits are imminent."

"Sorry. I guess I was getting enthusiastic again," she apologized. "I've been going through the china. It's absolutely outrageous. Limoges. And there's enough to seat thirty. And there's Haviland for twenty. We just *have* to offer dinners here. And it would be a crime not to use pictures of the stuff in the cookbook. It's too photogenic for words."

"You sound like you're having multiple orgasms. I've warned you about that enthusiasm. . . ." The tone was stern, but there was a pronounced twinkle in his twenty-four carat eyes. It had been there ever since Dr. Monroe's forty-eight hours had passed and she'd had no relapse. "You'll get your cookbook—at least five hundred of them, since that is the minimum that the press will run—but there's to be no tearing off on cheerful, sentimental jags about ghastly china. The budget won't run to color snaps. And, no, you may not adopt the appalling glassware. It stays at Belle Ange. So drink your coffee and let me be. You know that I can't tolerate keenness before nine o'clock."

"It's almost ten. And, fishing could bring in a lot of money. Like the restaurant and cookbook."

"Well, thinking of money is fine. I encourage it. Keep your eye on the bottom line, though, and see that you don't start acting like a Victorian female—mooning enviously over someone else's silver."

He was being deliberately offensive, she realized. It was a compliment, since he had, as per her instructions, given up flirting with her and moved on to more guylike insults. He was trying to be buddies. Tristam's concept of the role was a little odd, but she played along.

"I *am* a female," she said, obligingly rising to the bait in the interest of preserving good working relations. She had to give him something to pick at once in awhile or he would get cranky. "What of it?"

"All the more reason to be more cautious. *Limoges!*" he mimicked, rolling his eyes. "Now, when can I burn those twice-damned antlers?"

"Well . . ."

"What?" He groaned and put down the PDA. "What now? Are they rare Tibetan antlers? Gifts from King Charles to his subjects in the New World? Artifacts from the lost continent of Atlantis? Speak up. I can brick up and push on, but put me out of my misery at once."

"Don't be silly." But she couldn't stop her smile. "I just had an idea."

"An idea? Oh, well, in *that* case."

"Have you ever heard of the Winchester Mystery House?"

"Of course I have heard of the Winchester Mystery House. It is the Holy Grail of tourist restorations, and Sarah Winchester is our guild's patron saint."

"Oh." Karo never could tell when he was kidding. "Er, then you're familiar with the concept of occult appeal. It can be done tastefully."

"My dear, haunted houses are very popular in Europe. You cannot be a first-class castle without at least one ghost in residence." When she sniffed at his tone, he laughed. "Go on. Occult appeal, you said?"

"Well, I was thinking again about those Capuchin monks in Italy and their ghastly skeletons with their various parts stacked like cord wood. They're awfully popular."

"Yes, yes."

"What if we took all the antlers and used them to line that back hall? That boring one on the second floor that's reasonably wide. We could even wire them overhead like a tunnel or a hedge row. Then . . . Um, this isn't strictly honest," she warned.

"I've never let that stop me from considering a good promotional wheeze," he assured her. "We're all going to have to lie our heads off anyway. Have no fear. Speak on."

"Okay. Then we just mention how the family always collected them and used them to build fortifications." She took a deep breath for courage, still unaccustomed to taking flights of fancy while on the job. Until now, she had never considered perpetrating a fraud on anyone other than her parents and that had been about going to a slumber party.

"Go on," Tristam encouraged. "Don't lose your daring now. What might they have been fortifying against?"

"Against the swamp devil," she said in a rush. "And if we could just tie that in to the cookbook . . ."

"My dear, in another century they'd have burned you for a witch. What swamp devil? Is there one in residence that they have failed to inform me of?"

No, but a demon perhaps. She was thinking again of her first night here, and the vision she'd seen, though there had been no recurrence. "I'm sorry," she apologized, feeling mildly ashamed of her suggested chicanery. "It just seemed like a neat solution. And there are so many antlers! We'll be having bonfires 'til New Year's. Besides, there almost always is a swamp devil in these parts."

"It is a neat solution. And there are a great many antlers," he agreed. "It might even be true about the swamp devil. Old Vellacourt's actually been on my mind all morning. Remember Valperga?"

Karo shuddered and said, "She of the many bad paintings who didn't read Newton?" Her words were flip, a defense with the commonplace against that which challenged reason—or at the very least challenged her comfort. Valperga's paintings had been almost as bad as Karo's arrival at Belle Ange and her brush with what felt like the paranormal. This sudden semibelief in otherworldly things was a newly discovered and unwanted character flaw. Karo had never been tainted with such fears before Belle Ange, and she didn't like it.

"Yes. I've been reading up in various library journals before sending them to Clarice. It seems that Valperga is the one responsible for all that ghastly paraphernalia in the entry hall—the thumbscrews and such. Old Vellacourt never used them in his torture chamber. His kink was purely sexual in nature. Hers . . . ? Something else."

"Really? I'm relieved to hear it—about Vellacourt." And Karo was. Another thought occurred:

"That's odd. She lived in the late seventeenth and early eighteenth century, right? Most of the witch hysteria was over by then. Where did this mania come from? Those sorts of ghastly things wouldn't have been hanging about in the parlor where company could see them. In fact, unless she had them made, I don't know where she would have made such purchases."

"Too right," Tristam said. "But you misunderstand. She wasn't after witches. She started collecting antlers on the advice of our defrocked priest, who by then was in his dotage and none too sane. She . . . she hoped that it would scare dear old granddad back into the grave." Tristam paused, and Karo couldn't help her eyes from going wide. "The antlers were part of her mystical cure: powdered bone to feed the spirit or something. Every generation since has added to the collection. It's a . . . shall we say 'talisman against ill-fortune'? It sounds so much better than 'a homegrown voodoo gris-gris to keep grandpa away.'"

"You're joshin'!"

"If by *joshin'* you mean *joking*, then never a bit. It's all written down. They'd send servants—well, in the beginning it was slaves—out to comb the woods after the seasonal molt—"

"I was referring to the part about the ghost. She meant her grandpa was a ghost, right? Not a zombie or a vampire? Though, any of those options is equally crazy, I suppose." Karo felt compelled to say this, though it wasn't true. She didn't believe in zombies and vampires.

But, did she believe in ghosts? She didn't want

to. It was one thing to accept the hypothetical idea of the existence of ghosts and another to stay in a place where people had actually seen them. Or to believe that she had seen one herself.

"Ah! Well, she truly believed that Vellacourt had become a specter of the night and that he walked these unhallowed halls. If she hadn't retained a staunch Calvinist's horror of the Church of Rome, I'm afraid old granddad would have been sent off to spiritual oblivion with the old exorcism rites. Good thing, too, that Father Basco was defrocked, or we wouldn't have a ghost left to our names."

He said this all blithely. Clearly he was untroubled by the notion of paranormal activity in the house. Did that mean he was a nonbeliever, or that he expected such uncanny happenings? Or was she just crazy?

"Why did she think that her grandfather was a ghost?" Karo asked, feeling truly nauseated for the first time since the afternoon of her arrival. This wasn't a topic she entirely wanted to discuss. Wasn't there a belief that using a ghost's name could conjure it?

She mopped at her brow. The room was suddenly rather warm, and Karo had the oddest impression they were being listened to with great interest, though the only other living thing near them was the cat. Karo wiggled her fingers at 'Stein, but since they were empty of food and permanently begrimed an unattractive shade of gray, the beast just sneered, contempt radiating from his every hair.

"Because he spent his days on earth having carnal relations with the devil's handmaiden, our very own Eustacie La Belle," Tristam was saying. "That, and a large collection of things on the third floor going bump in the night. These kept the lady—if that's the word for her—from any sleep of the righteous. She also had *dreams*. Naughty dreams which she blamed on her grandpa."

"Oh." Karo understood that. She'd had a couple of naughty dreams here about Tristam, dreams she would never have had anywhere else. In them, she'd stared. She'd coveted. She even had these thoughts during waking sometimes—even though she'd been sincere in her vow to never get romantically involved with her boss again.

Of course, Tristam wasn't her grandfather. That would be icky.

"Um, are we talking generic naughty, or incestuous naughty?" Collecting gossip and snooping, both socially indefensible habits to Karo's mind, could be cheerfully sanctioned when one was a historian. Or a detective. She sort of fancied herself both.

"Generic naughty, with Eustacie and Hugh in the leading roles. But modern psychiatry had not yet freed women from guilt about their libidos, and such visions were bad enough for Valperga," Tristam explained reasonably.

"Right. In the garret? She thought he was still cavorting up there, partying instead of going to hell liked damned spirits should. But . . . wouldn't that actually involve two ghosts?" Her voice sounded convincingly light, but the very idea was raising gooseflesh on her arms.

"Just so. And that's not the best of it. She claims

to have even gone so far as to purchase a copy of
The Witch's Hammer."

"The *Malleus Maleficarum*?"

"Yes, The Hammer of Witches, as it is also
called—in the hopes of ridding Belle Ange of
the vile, lecherous spirits. Unfortunately, though
thorough in describing the many efficacious
treatments of suspected witches, this very expensive book didn't tell her anything about lascivious
ghosts or methods of ridding oneself thereof. If
only she'd had the internet."

"Tristam!" Karo was horrified. It was irratio-
nal, but she lowered her voice against the listening walls. "If that book's here we have to find it. A
copy of the *Malleus Maleficarum* would be worth a
fortune!" But that wasn't the only reason why it
had to be found.

"I'm aware. That's why I would like you to help
me in the library today. It is our new priority. We'll
turn the room upside down if we must, but I want
that book. I can't imagine how I've overlooked it."

"It's a priority," Karo agreed. "That book
should be in a museum." Or, rather, in a vault—
deep underground and far, far away from anyone
who might want to use it. Karo didn't believe in
burning books, but in this case she might make
an exception. In her morbid youth she had done
a fair amount of research on the witch trials,
which had led her to witch hunts in Europe. Some
estimates were that nearly nine million people
had been put to death by the Spanish Inquisition
and other religious nut jobs. Almost eight million
of them had been women, most of them elderly
women with property and no heirs to defend

them. The whole subject was sickening. She wanted to believe that humans had evolved beyond that sort of cruelty and nonsense, but she didn't think it had happened yet.

"Never." It was Tristam's turn to be shocked.

"What!" She blinked at the strength of his refusal. "But, Tristam! We must. If we leave it here the mice will get it. Damp will rot it." And she just didn't want the damn thing in the house.

"We'll do whatever we must to make the library safe. Alarms. Helium filled bookcases, whatever. But I'm not letting the *Malleus Maleficarum* out of my sight. Clarice agrees with me. It is the ultimate drawing card for Belle Ange. Throw in the rumor of a ghost who might be a vampire, and we are a guaranteed success. Besides, Clarice won't part with it. Says it has to stay at the plantation, a family bequest or something. She was adamant. We have to keep the ghosts happy, remember."

But were they? Karo wondered.

"But," she expostulated weakly. "That book's so old." And *evil*, the distillation of man's inhumanity to man. But she didn't add that. It was an alien thought and not one that modern, rational people discussed over breakfast.

"Don't be dense, my dear. I told you from the first that we aren't running a museum. We are here to turn this plantation into a moneymaker. We can't cower and edge out now that we've come to a rough spot. We'll find money for the cost of the book's preservation."

"Couldn't we display a copy?" she asked desperately. "That would be safer. And, think of the insurance premiums! They'll be absolutely sky high if we leave the thing out where someone could snatch it. Or it could get burned!"

Tristam stared at her while he considered her argument. Or was he finally feeling it, too—that sense of being eavesdropped upon by the windows and doors of a house that wished this horrible and foreign thing, this book, purged from its bowels.

A good portion of his accent disappeared when he answered her. "You have a point. A sentimental one, I suspect, but a point. I'll talk to an agent. But the *Maleficarum* is not going to a museum. Clarice is firm on that, and since she holds the purse strings, I am solidly behind her. All we have to do is find the damned thing and make sure that it's still here."

It was good that Tristam wasn't blindly stubborn. Her last boss had been the kind to take a notion into his head and keep it forever, no matter what evidence was presented. One could give him a concussion trying to knock an idea loose, and it still wouldn't move an inch. He made concrete look flexible. But was this concession enough? Karo thought not. The book needed to leave here.

Karo stood up and carried her cup to the sink. She wanted a moment to think about the churning down in her gut that was getting worse instead of lessening. Something more than concern over a literary treasure was moving around down there among the liver and kidneys. But how did one say to one's boss of seven days that he was wrong in thinking that this book was nothing more than a vellum tourist attractant, that they might actually be in danger if they kept it in the house?

There was a sudden glint at the window. Refracted lighted momentarily blinded her, and Karo put up a hand to shield her face. As she squinted against the intense ray, a clear and preemptory idea popped into her head. It was clear to her that the *Malleus Maleficarum* was an evil thing and should be destroyed. Sending it away wasn't enough. It had been used by greedy men to justify the female holocaust of the Inquisition and should *never* be put on casual display for the titillation of tourists. It was a weapon, a symbol of oppression as great as slavery and as shameful. It should be buried deep in the ground or even burned in a ritual fire. Why, the book might even still be used to trap a poor spirit on the earthly plane by a vengeful woman, a spirit that longed to go free. And Karo could destroy it with very little effort when it was found.

She blinked and shook her head slowly from side to side, denying the idea. That wasn't right, was it? She didn't believe in burning books—any books. Not even the very worst Barbara Cartland novels her mother mailed to her. Karo shivered and then gave herself a mental clout on the nose. It took a moment for her to regain her sight, even after she looked away from the window.

". . . fine, Karo?" she heard Tristam ask.

"I'm sorry. What did you say?" She turned back to her employer. He had set his cup aside and risen to his feet. His gaze was intent. Watchful. Predatory.

Was he spying on her? Did he know what she

was thinking? He didn't seem to care about the house at all—not really. Everything was secrets and lies. For a moment, she looked at him and saw an enemy.

"I asked how you were feeling."

"Fine." The tone was a little too trenchant for good manners. She tried to make a joke. "I haven't been blasted by lightning in the last few days, so no worries."

"I'm ever so glad," he said. "So, where did your lovely brain go for the last four minutes?"

Four minutes? Had it been so long?

"Trinidad, Rio . . ." She waved an airy hand, knowing she had to lie. "Another century." She swallowed. "Tristam, can I ask you something? Just hypothetically."

"Ask away." He took a step closer, and her ganglia began to tingle. She could almost swear that there were eyes focused on her back and a hand poised to reach inside her skin and grab her heart, ready to turn her into a fleshy puppet.

She suddenly wondered where 'Stein had gone to. He hadn't been bothering them for breakfast. Did he know they weren't alone now and was choosing to avoid this room? Cats were supposed to be able to sense the presence of supernatural creatures.

She had to ask. "Do you think that there might *actually* be a ghost here?" She addressed the vee in Tristam's shirt, not daring to look her employer in the eye in case he started laughing at her.

"No. Unless you're from the press. Then I believe it absolutely." A small smile flashed past, and a splash of his mutant pheromones raced up her

nostrils. Her nerves began a different sort of tingling. Her body was trying to simultaneous go
tense and go limp. As an aerobic workout, it beat
the usual isometric exercises. She could feel herself beginning to sweat in the valley between her
breasts and in her tightly curled palms.

The last several days had been spent wearing a
government certified safety mask that was guaranteed to filter out spray paint, pollen, grain dust,
silica and asbestos as she sorted through the ac-
cumulations of the ages. Karo wondered if the #9
micron screen would offer any defense against
the very potent Tristam English musk. Alas, it
seemed unlikely that anything less than an en-
closed, environmental suit would do the trick—
and then only if she couldn't see him.

She pried her eyes up from his golden flesh.
They both tended to spend the days half unbuttoned with their sleeves rolled up, but she still
found the sight of his down-covered chest to be
disturbing. Normally she'd enjoy the distraction,
but not now. There was something more important that had to be done.

"Why do you ask? Seen any more ghosts? Are
you *hante*?" he asked, smiling slightly.

"No fair speaking French," she managed to
reply, though it felt like her heart was pressing
against the back of her teeth. The room had grown
very warm, the oxygen all being burned up. No
wonder 'Stein had given breakfast a pass. He'd
have had kitty heatstroke in two seconds flat.

But, the heat reminded her of something.

"You're being evasive." Tristam advanced another two feet. A shadow slipped over his face,

changing him; mild-mannered and meek had done a skip around the corner and left his evil twin behind. This bold doppelganger insisted, "Tell me what's worrying you. Let me help."

"I'm being cautious and thoughtful."

He was too close. She was burning up. The elastic in her bra was beginning to melt into her flesh right above her fourth rib, and she had the feeling that she was suffocating on moldering air.

"You're white as—forgive the cliché—a sheet. But you're also sweating. Are you certain that you are well?" Another yard of hard pine disappeared under a single, long-limbed step. This was what had happened the first night she met him, down in the library. The room could be measured in acres and she still felt that she was running out of safe kitchen space. If he took another step she would reach critical mass and combust all over the shiny floor. She had to get away. Had to get some air.

"Maybe. Maybe not," she hedged, stepping away from Tristam and nearer to the kitchen door. "What I am going to do is take a quick walk out to the guest cottage and have a look around. It should be dry by now."

"Karo!" His voice was hurt, but he halted his advance. "I thought you trusted me. I've been a lamb, haven't I? Why flee now?"

"Don't be stupid!" she flashed with sudden irritation. "I'm just interested in the old cookhouse. That's what it was in the old days, right?"

"And slave quarters." He came no closer. Perhaps he could see the flames licking at her ears. They felt on fire, sunburned. She felt something pressing in on her, like a blast wave that went on and on. "I wish that you would tell me what is troubling you, my dear. Is it the book? Does it truly frighten you?"

"Yes." She had been worried about the book, hadn't she? "And the fact that I don't know about the wisdom of promoting a ghost like a tourist attraction." Not when it was real. Was it real?

"A few minutes ago you were all for it," he pointed out.

Had she been? His words seemed to be eating up all the air in the kitchen. She was feeling light-headed. She had to get outside, but he kept her here talking!

"Think of the Cantervilles. Hamlet. Sleepy Hollow," he said. Karo couldn't think much of anything except the need for cool air, but she made an effort to stay coherent. It would be unwise to let him know that . . . What didn't she want him to know?

"A few minutes ago, I didn't know that someone else had seen Vellacourt's ghost," she managed. "And I didn't know about the book."

"Someone else? You mean Valperga? You still don't know she saw anything. The old bat was nuts. Absolutely whacko. The trick cyclists would have had a field day with her. She might have just had rats in the belfry."

"And in the garret. And that's hairsplitting. . . . What's a trick cyclist?" She scratched at a sudden itch in her palms. Her whole skin felt vaguely prickled. She was perspiring in the small of her back and soaking the waistband of her pants.

"An old time headshrinker," he translated.

"Look at it this way, Vellacourt was an exhibitionist. If his ectoplasm was really still hanging about, he would probably enjoy showing off for the gardeners and such. But no one has seen a thing. Other than you after being hit by lightning." Tristam sounded both calm and irritated. It was an interesting vocal trick, like two people both using his voice at the same time. "I know that the atmosphere here is unpleasant and a lot of the art suggestive of horrid things, but mightn't it just be that you had a bad start? Being hit by a million volts can do strange things to the mind."

"Condescension will get you nowhere," Karo snapped. "You're the boss. Do what you want. Now back off before I throw something heavy at your head. I want to go outside."

He laughed suddenly and the tension broke. He again looked like Tristam. Fresh air filled the overheated vacuum around her body and Karo could feel moisture condensing on her skin in heavy drops. Her muscles went limp and she almost staggered with relief. She wanted to lie down on the shiny wood floor and take a ten-hour nap.

"So. What's in the cookhouse, do you think? Have I missed something?" he asked, turning back for his coffee. He looked quite cool in his turned-up shirtsleeves, but there was a betraying sheen of dew on the back of his neck that said he had also been affected, if not to the degree that she had.

"Nothing, I hope. I'd like to move some of the household accouterments out there. It really is the best place for them." Karo took a furtive swipe at her brow.

"Good idea. Let me know what you find and I'll get whatever stuff you want moved out." His PDA was again consulted. The two of them were back to business, as if the previous odd exchange had never taken place.

"Are you going to get the gardeners to help? The cauldrons in particular are heavy," she added. A grounds crew had arrived two days after the storm and begun a cleanup and aesthetic transformation of Belle Ange's riotous gardens.

"No need. This body isn't all for show. I can bung that stuff about. Just shout me up when you're ready. I'll be in the library."

He did not again suggest that she join him.

"Okay. I won't be long," she promised.

"Take your time," he said agreeably. "It will be a help to clear out some working space instead of just shifting the masses around. And don't worry about that book. We can look for it this evening or even tomorrow. It's too stuffy to be doing intense poking around right now."

"Okay," she said again, and then headed for the door. She was bent on escape, but she still noticed his change of priorities concerning the *Malleus Maleficarum*. Was he trying to keep her away from the book? Did he know that for a moment she had thought about destroying it?

Tristam stared after Karo, wondering what had just happened. They had been having a pleasant breakfast conversation and then all of sudden the tension had been so thick he'd nearly had to swim through it. The moment he got halfway to Karo's side, she'd broken into a sweat and run away.

"Where are you running, my dear?" he asked whimsically. "Just away from the big bad wolf? Am I really so scary? Or was it just that book? Can you really be so frightened by an artifact?"

He poured out his cold coffee, frowning at the brown drops that ran down the sparkling porcelain sink. A sudden embarrassment had come over him. What had he been thinking, stalking her that way? He'd never chased a woman in his life—he'd never had to. At home, the English name had always been ample attraction for women, working for both him and his older brother, Jeremy. In the States, the women seemed to have a different outlook, and that had made it even easier! Being more aggressive than their European counterparts, American women skipped the usual catch-me-if-you-can bed races. They were also quite amenable to his lifestyle; they always understood that one or the other of them would eventually be moving on, and he'd always been content to have it that way.

Of course, he'd never had any of these women look at him like he was a roasted leg of lamb smothered in mint jelly before, a seven-course meal held just out of reach of the starving victim. And it wasn't his imagination indulging in a spot of wishful thinking. It actually happened sometimes: Karo would stare at him, and suddenly she would begin to breathe deeply, almost as if she was inhaling his scent and having an erotic daydream. Her eyes would go sort of blank and dreamy. At those times, her very readable face was an almost unbearable turn-on. It made him feel unusually hawkish and territorial.

He'd resisted her firmly for several days, but she kept doing it, so he'd finally given in and answered her silent siren call . . . only to see her turn away from him, to reject him completely—and apparently over some damn book.

A new, foreign instinct said to pounce quickly before she got away from him. He felt almost possessed, as if some entity compelled him to swoop down and take her, willing or not. But aberrant desires were no excuse for bad behavior, and he knew Karo's history with unscrupulous employers. Hadn't he already had a stern talking to with himself on that very subject? So, what ailed him all of a sudden?

His too tight slacks provided the readiest answer. The divine and insane matchmaker had been at it again. Only, this time the usual roles were reversed: it was a gold arrow for him, and apparently only a silver one for the object of his desire. He did not at all care for being on the other side of the coin.

"Bloody hell!" he said in disgust. "And it's only been a week. I'm probably going to die before we get this house in order."

Karo made her way across the shell drive. The sound was not cheerful. Every crunch reminded her of the last time she'd been out grinding across the sea's dead bones. Now, *there* was an unpleasant old phrase that people didn't use anymore. Dead bones. There was a cemetery full of human bones just behind the cookhouse, too. She had never previously been troubled by the thought of the dead being close at hand, but the thought of old Vellacourt perhaps hanging out in his family crypt was not a pleasant one. Of course, far better the crypt than the library. What had she seen that day?

Karo ignored her sniveling id as she pushed her reluctant limbs past an overgrown rhododendron and walked up the shadowed step of the first outbuilding she came to. Giving a businesslike shove of the narrow door—she could be Clint Eastwood when she had to—she nearly fell on her face. The hasp wasn't latched and someone had oiled the hinges. Surprising.

The inside of the old cookhouse was dark, and her graceless entrance had stirred up a smell of melancholy and disuse. The atmosphere was even less appealing than she expected, but that might have been doubled because she was half-prone on the packed earth floor and churning up a great deal of dust and droppings into an unhealthful miasma that made her wonder about the Hunta virus.

She had plenty of time while climbing back to her feet to be grateful that Tristam had convinced her to bunk in the main house. She hadn't taken up archaeology because she didn't like being in dirt or dealing with critters that had more than four legs or less than two. This bleak hole had both filth and a probable collection of creatures with improper leg counts. The dust was sticking to her sweaty body with aggravating persistence, and it itched fiercely. Finishing up her search as quickly as possible, she would rush back to the main house where she could have a wash in antiseptic conditions.

Upright, Karo surveyed the moldy room, letting her eyes grow accustomed to the new dusk. She grimaced at the dozen saucer-sized daddy longlegs hanging on the wall in a living wallpaper. Arachnids, her least favorite too-many-limbed creatures—it figured that they would be here in abundance. At least this kind wasn't dangerous since their fangs were too small to penetrate the skin. She was a bit prepared for rural perils. Of course, she had other things to deal with. Like, a ghost?

Bravely, she turned her back on the eight-legged abominations and considered the room with an artist's eye. The space would be marginally brighter when the one tiny window was scraped clean of what she had mistakenly thought were rotted curtains but in actuality were cobwebs and other filth grown dense from years of neglect. "Ugh." Nothing was going to make the place cheery. An electric light might help the gloom, but it smelled swampy and inhabited by unhealthful objects.

"What did you expect of the slaves' cookhouse—Bokhara rugs and skylights?" she muttered, taking another shallow breath and then following her nose to the far left corner where the floor had settled at the foundation. It was no great shock to find that there was a small pool of stagnant water beside the old hearth; it went without saying that the roof leaked.

Karo leaned over the squirming puddle. The brown water bulged with mosquito larva. Her insides dipped sharply and she was glad that she hadn't inhaled a large plate of Tristam's bacon and eggs before facing this. She would have to get the gardeners in here right away; none of them needed these bloodsuckers crawling out in the lingering autumn heat and plaguing their nights.

She straightened and turned her inspection to the scorched fireplace. It also seemed to be alive with scurrying insects. She nudged the ashes with a cautious toe and disturbed a pile of black beetles in the soot and char, though what they could be hunting for, she couldn't begin to imagine.

"Great. A roach motel," she muttered, wiping at her forehead with the back of her dirtied hands. The temperature was absolutely stifling. They would have to do something about the ventilation in the little building or people would be dropping like flies on a pest strip.

She saw a movement from the corner of her eye and turned reluctantly. Half of the room was very dark and filled with old pots. Could something be nesting here—an opossum or a baby squirrel? She hoped it wasn't a snake trapped inside after the storm. Next to spiders, the creatures she feared most were snakes.

"Okay, guy. Show yourself," she demanded bravely. "Slither for it now and you won't get exterminated. Oh, spit!"

Once again, the spiky shadow unfolded with inhuman speed. Old Vellacourt himself was soon hanging in the corner and turning the cookhouse into a coke blaster. Karo fell back against the wall, too frightened to care about the spiders.

Amazingly, through her terror, she found her voice. "Look. If it's about the book, there's nothing I can do," she whispered, wondering with half her brain if she was truly still sane, while the other half cataloged the ghost's seventeenth-century riding regalia. The black and gold was severely elegant and went well with his insect eyes. He was dressed as a cavalier and not a Roundhead. She tried not to think about the way his overcape billowed around him in the drafts of hot air rising up from the floor. It was much too evocative of watching sulfur clouds billow up from hell.

"And if it's about the ghost tours . . . well, I can't do much about that, either," she went on. "I'm not the one in charge. You'd do better to take this up with Tristam or your great-great-whatever niece. She's living in Florida."

Nothing. Not a twitch in that expressionless face to show that he could hear.

"Look, could you maybe just tell me what you want? Do you want to be left alone? Is that it?"

The mouth opened. The thin lips pulled back from pointy teeth, and when she saw their gleaming length, Karo wished that he had remained silent.

"No," a thin voice whispered. She had the feeling that the ghost was exerting great effort in order to speak.

"Then, you want us to bring people here?"

It was too hot to feel relief, but Karo was glad that this high-temperature spook wasn't upset with Tristam's plan. She had little desire to tell her employer that their deal was off and she was heading for the west coast on the first red-eye. If she walked out on this job because of a haunting, her career on the east coast was truly over.

"Yesss." The white head nodded, and the cob-weblike strands floated upward like they were rising on a thermal updraft. His cloak was spread out like bat wings, blocking the doorway.

Did he know that she wanted to run? The thought was annoying. So was the heat. Her clothes were beginning to squish with sweat. Static was dancing over her body, making her hair rise, and she was feeling faint. The only thing that kept her still was the fact that Vellacourt stood between her and the egress.

She didn't know if it was possible to outrun a ghost, but she was ready to give it a try. The moment he moved away from her escape route, she'd book. Somehow, she couldn't find enough courage to run *through* him.

"Okay. That's our plan. A few more weeks and they'll start coming. There'll be lots of tourists, God willing and the river don't rise."

The ghost said nothing.

"Look." Karo wiped her forehead again and set about bargaining. She needed a job, but there were limits. Either the spook respected her boundaries or she was out of there by sundown. She'd just have to find some way to make Tristam come with her, because in spite of her words, she didn't want Vellacourt plaguing him. "Look, in the meantime, I'd really appreciate it if you left me alone. I do not care to sweat, you see. It's not ladylike. I thought ghosts were supposed to be cold anyway," she grumbled. "What's wrong with you? Is it hellfire that's finally got you?"

The specter gave a laugh but the only sound that came out of that white face was a dry rustling like the beetles made while scrabbling over one another. It was unpleasant, but not terrifying. Karo's calm returned by slow degrees. "I mean it . . . Hugh. May I call you Hugh?"

She watched the head nod again and forced herself to step away from the wall. Cowering was so undignified.

"Look, I can't have you bothering me like this. Tristam is going to think I'm insane. The only reason he didn't fire me the first time you showed up is because he thinks that I was hit by lightning and that I just don't remember lighting that fire in the library."

"You were hit," the ghostly voice breathed. It was growing limber but still creaked like the wet moorings on a boat. "I arranged it so that we could talk."

"Don't say that!" she begged, thinking of that peculiar hole burned in her shoe and dreading that he was right. "My grip on reality is not real firm at the moment, and it wouldn't take much to tip me right over the edge. And you wouldn't want that to happen, would you? That might queer the tourist thing."

"You are safe here—as safe as you want," puffed the dry voice. He raised the whip in his hand— this was the first Karo had noticed it. "He wants you by his side. You want him, too. I can help you do everything you want. You can help me. We can all be free."

His gaze was hungry. Men! From the dumbest to the most brilliant, the enlightened to the brutal—and even the dead—they still all wanted one thing. Okay, two things, counting research.

"No! Don't help me with anything!" she said, looking at his riding crop and having a sudden premonition of his intent. "Don't you even think about it! People don't do that anymore. It objectifies women. It's disrespectful."

"*Oui?*" he asked. But the smile was knowing. "Sometimes *objectivity* is to be admired."

She watched as he flicked the crop against his boots. "Objectivity and objectifying are not the same things."

"But you want . . ."

The notion should have been repulsive. It *was* repulsive at an intellectual level, especially if participation wasn't voluntary. But wouldn't it be fun, just once, to be completely and utterly in control of one's partner? Or, okay, maybe to sometimes be relieved of the burdens of self-determination and guilt and all that twenty-first century politically correct garbage women were supposed to be masters of, to become more submissive than usual? Would it be so bad to be forced into doing what your mother and some feminists always said was wrong—to be compelled to give in and have orgasms that someone else was forcing upon you? And if that was naughty . . . well, you had already been punished for it! A spanking instead of five Hail Marys. Either way, no lingering guilt.

Free will was great. It was everything—almost. And while political and economic equality were to be striven for, did the battle for feminine equality have to come into the bedroom? She wanted to be in control sometimes but not thought unfeminine. She wanted to be overpowered sexually and

not thought weak. The chance to give up all that
responsibility in the bedroom once in a while . . .

No. No, absolutely not. Especially not now. Not
with a ghost. Not even with Tristam. Well, maybe—

No. No! This creature was confusing her, playing with her brain. This wasn't free will. Was it?

"We shall see, *ma belle.* I must warn you that
I know my own kind. Sometimes you must put
yourself in bondage so that you may be free." The
shade laughed again as Karo's mind raced, and
then he folded in on himself in the blink of an eye.
The heat went with him, sucked into some cosmic
vacuum along with that ghostly laughter.

"Hugh? Wait a minute! Are you going to leave
me alone?" Karo demanded of the dark place between the pots where he'd disappeared. "I really
have to insist on this . . . Hugh? Hugh Vellacourt!
I'm not kidding. I don't want you around me. And
no kinky stuff! I'm not that kind of girl."

At least, she hadn't been that kind of girl before.
Tristam probably didn't go for this stuff, either. In
fact, though she was sure he wanted her, he seemed
to be moving in on her with the ponderous slow-
ness of an arthritic pachyderm. Which was totally
okay with her.

Except, today he hadn't been slow. Had that
been Hugh? Had the ghost somehow warped
Tristam? The thought was distasteful and fright-
ening.

"Hugh?"

Nothing stirred.

"Miz Follett? Ma'am, are you in there?" A few
loud crunches and then a khakis-clad shape filled

the doorway, blocking out what little light there was.

"Yes. It's me." Karo peered at the dark corner where Hugh had vanished and kicked over a pot. Nothing moved. All that was left was twigs and ash and dead beetles. The ghost was truly gone.

She began to shiver. The room was suddenly quite cold, and her blouse was clinging to her like an icy rag.

"Were you talkin' to someone, ma'am?" The voice was polite but puzzled.

"Uh . . . yes. Myself." Karo forced a smile. Her lips felt stiff and bruised, and she wanted to get some moisturizer on her face. She felt like she'd spent the day roasting on the beach. "I think we have mosquitoes hatching and there are roaches or beetles in the fireplace. Could we do something about that today—a bug bomb or something? Mr. English would like to begin moving some of the kitchen stuff out here as soon as possible."

The tan shape came into the room and began to look around. She saw it was one of the siblings who were working as gardeners: the Campion brothers. "Where's the mosquitoes, ma'am? Got to get to them buggers right away. They'll be hatching quick in this heat."

"Over there." She pointed and then noticed that the puddle had been all but evaporated; there was only a brown crust on the floor to indicate where the larvae had lain. Her stomach rolled as she smelled the faint odor of swamp and boiled gumbo rising from the stone floor.

"Here, ma'am?" The worker was staring at the goo.

"Uh . . . yes. Somewhere over there. Maybe in one of the pots. Don't you hear them?" Actually, the rustling in the fireplace had stopped, too. She looked at the right wall. The spiders were gone—driven off by the heat? "Well, never mind. If you could just spray in here, that would be great. Thanks. I'd better be getting back to the house."

Karo didn't allow herself to bolt for the door, but she was sorely tempted. Her footsteps cracked like thunder as she hurried across the drive. Her hair was still wild with static waiting to discharge.

Holy spit! What did she do now—tell Tristam about the ghost and have him calling up Dr. Monroe to see about the symptoms of delayed shock? Or worse yet, what if he feared for her sanity and fired her before she got to finish her cookbook, never letting her see that Limoges again? Karo glared at the inoffensive branches that had been nearby piled into an eight foot mound, preparatory to being hauled away. She went to take a vindictive swipe with her sneaker and then remembered about some poison ivy the gardeners were clearing. With bare branches, it was hard to know what you were kicking. Stymied, she turned away.

Back at the cookhouse, she saw one of the Brothers Campion going inside to hunt the now-boiled mosquitoes. That gave her pause. Weren't ghosts supposed to be cold? And, why the vague smell of brimstone? Of course, how would she know brimstone? Lots of things had been cooking in that room. She'd have to watch her mystical thinking. There was no need to make the situation worse than it was.

Karo surveyed the grounds, turned toward

what had once been a boxwood hedge maze. Its days of tidy, geometric trimming were long gone. The maze remained, but it was a far gloomier and probably more dangerous affair than its designers ever intended. In many places, the two sides had interlocked overhead, creating a living vault, and like the mausoleum in the cemetery it had no living visitors. There was birdsong, but that was coming from the far side of the maze. Birds had tried to pass through though, she thought, looking down at her feet. Their bones and feathers were all over the place, blown in amongst the twigs and leaves and other detritus of the storm.

Karo wanted to believe that the remains were 'Stein's doing, but she couldn't make herself swallow the idea. There were just too many dead birds, and many of the leaves looked blistered and scorched, as if exposed to fire. Though she didn't want to think about it, the notion that Hugh had passed this way definitely suggested itself.

She exhaled slowly. She had never believed in ghosts, she reminded herself, though she had a close friend who did. As Annie explained it, sometimes when a life ended abruptly, when the soul was torn away before a person expected, a ragged edge was left behind. Sometimes this was the tender memory of a mourner. Sometimes it was a memory of the mourned. But whatever you called it—a haunting, a perseveration, a tear in the veil between worlds—it amounted to the same thing: the dead could rub up against the living. And sometimes they got trapped. It was something for which one should feel pity rather than fear.

Of course, Annie had been speaking of more passive perseverations. Hugh was both sentient and manipulative.

Karo picked up her pace again, turning back to the house and heading for the library. She knew what she had to do. She'd keep her mouth clam-tight on the subject of ghosts until Tristam or someone else saw old boy Vellacourt himself. It was bound to happen sooner or later, she hoped; Hugh was the most blatant ghost she could ever imagine. After that, they could have a round robin about what to do and maybe get some professional help. She wondered if they had a local chapter of ghost busters in the area.

Well, her boss was right about one thing. If Vellacourt got into the habit of showing off for the visitors, they'd have the hottest tourist stop in Virginia. And the most terrifying.

And maybe the most sexually deviant.

Tristam looked up from the desk and smiled politely. "All set?"

"Not quite. The gardeners are going to spray for bugs; then we can haul some of the kitchen things out." She stayed out of range of his phero-mones, as her nose got more sensitive with each passing day. It also occurred to her that maybe her attraction to Tristam was making the ghost bolder. Maybe he even used sexual energy to appear. How depressing.

"Bugs?"

"Beetles and mosquitoes. You about ready for some lunch?" she asked.

Tristam glanced at his watch and then back at

her face. "I could be. You look like you could use a bit of a break. In fact, you look like you've seen a ghost."

"I do?" She felt herself pale. "Well, it was really hot out there. Look, why don't you go ahead with . . . whatever you're doing, and I'll make us something to eat. We missed breakfast, you know."

"As you like." He didn't say anything about her remark, about her continued implication that they should share kitchen chores, though she had a right to complain about his failure to remember breakfast.

"I'm really hungry! I think I'll fix a large animal with a side of everything. You know, the basic four plus something extra from the high calorie, fat and sugar group."

"Sounds perfect. I adore 'large animal.' Do you need any help? I could—"

"Nope, got it covered. I may be a while, though," she warned. "I need to wash up." Ghosts stank. She had never known that before.

"No problem," he said, but he was tapping his stylus against his PDA and frowning slightly. The tapping and the frown reminded her of Hugh. "Karo . . ."

"Found any recipes yet?" she asked brightly, cutting him off and backing toward the door.

"Few. The mistresses of the house did very little cooking, and the slaves were illiterate. Still, every housewife had her specialties."

"Good. Can't wait to—Well, actually, I *can* wait. But I'll see them first thing after lunch." She continued to back toward the shortish doorway. Food and a shower were crucial, although not necessarily in that order. Maybe she'd head for the sunny, sane kitchen.

"By the way, I found a new painting. It's of Florence," Tristam said. He pointed toward the west wall. "Usually when one thinks of Florence one thinks of great artists like da Vinci, Michelangelo, Raphael—"

"Fra Angelico, Brunelleschi," Karo agreed, still backing up.

"But I don't think any of these masters had anything to do with *that*, did they?"

Karo made herself look. "Nope. I'll examine it more thoroughly after lunch," she promised then bolted.

"Well, hell," she muttered, retreating down the gloomy hall. "Girl, get a grip! Think of this as . . ." A close encounter of the spiritual kind? A chance to go where no man—or very few—had gone before? Shouldn't she be glad to have some proof that there was life after death instead of nothingness?

"Shut up," she told the voice speaking in her head, hoping it was her subconscious and not Hugh's thoughts. The words had sounded feminine, but who knew? Maybe he had found a way to haunt her from the inside out. What she didn't need were any glimpses into Hugh Vellacourt's brain.

"I don't need this right now. I am being re-oriented to accept this situation, but it is not going to happen without some help. Of course I can handle it—eventually. I've had worse problems. I think. Well, maybe not many. Geez! If we had to have a ghost in residence, why couldn't it be someone nice like the one in Canterville? Why'd I get stuck with the king of S and M who seems to bring hellfire with him when he appears? Like I don't sweat enough when Tristam is around, spraying me with his pheromones."

Tristam. According to Vellacourt, her new boss wanted her. She knew that for a fact. But *how* did he want her? Was he like Vellacourt? Could that be why the ghost had reappeared—because he had found two people here inclined toward . . . ?

No. It was likely some kind of overshadowing of the will. Not possession exactly, but some kind of persuasion. But as much as she hated the idea of seeing into the ghost's mind, she hated even worse the idea that he could see into hers. It was something that needed serious consideration. Hugh had a dirty mind. And whether what he said was true or not, he couldn't have meant anything good by his insinuation that Tristam wanted her in a certain, non-missionary position kind of way, a way with which Hugh could conveniently help.

"It's not like I'm ever going to be trysting with the dead!" she called out. "I do not—absolutely *do not*—have a thing for you, Hugh Vellacourt. Or anyone else who is dead." Except perhaps Heath Ledger. But that was a holdover crush from when he was alive.

Suddenly Karo wondered: could ghosts lie? Could they lie about who and what they were? The Devil could—everyone agreed about that. Well, everyone who believed in him. So, what if she was giving Hugh too much credit? What if he wasn't a victim of unfinished spiritual business but instead had done something really bad to ensure an afterlife?

So, so, break off this lamenting kiss,
Which sucks two souls, and vapours both away,
Turn, thou ghost, that way, and let me turn this,
And let ourselves benight our happiest day.
—John Donne

Chapter Six

"Mom! I'm losing you!" That was a lie, but Karo's butt was getting sore. The tree branch was only about six inches wide and, with the wind picking up, the swaying was really quite sickening.

"I'll call you next week," she promised. "Maybe I can e-mail you some pictures of the Limoges." That was about the only picture she would send. The rest of the house continued to be too dirty, both in a physical and moral sense. "Give my love to Dad. Bye."

She closed her phone and began considering how to get back down with the current atmospheric conditions. The roof looked fairly close, but it was wet and the tree was far from stable. Sighing, she decided there was nothing for it but to make the usual climb back down and hope she didn't lose her breakfast before she reached terra firma.

Glancing about carefully, she made sure she was alone. People continued to come and go from Belle Ange, but out of habit Karo avoided them. She had met an electrician named Lucas Fane and a termite inspector with the unbelievable name of Daryl Pettibone. Both of them had caught her up this tree and been amused at her explanation about cell phone reception. And of course the Campion brothers—mostly landscapers but really jacks of all trades—were usually working in the garden. But inside it was just her and Tristam. And maybe the ghost. She hadn't seen Vellacourt again, and she was okay with that.

Seeing no one about to witness her less than graceful descent, she made the climb down.

A short time later, she and Tristam stood shoulder to shoulder and admired the entry hall. They were covered in enough soot to pass as a charwoman and a rag picker, but even the itchy black sweat that rolled down their backs and faces was insufficient to dim their pleasure.

"Well, the old girl scrubs up quite nicely."

"Quite respectable," Karo agreed. "Thanks to lemon oil."

It was the truth. There was lots of carved wood and wrought leather that had been hidden by decades of dirt and clutter, all of it very handsome and tourist-friendly. The hanging armory was gone. After a week of work, the hall no longer looked like it was expecting a siege from infidels.

Of the witch prickers and thumbscrews that had littered the hall, there was likewise no sign. All mounted animals, moth-eaten or fresh, whole or in parts, those actually extinct or simply on the endangered species list, had been removed and packed for storage in some later-to-be-identified location. Tristam was voting for the bottom of the river, but it would probably be a storage locker or one of the outbuildings. The only remaining hostile piece was the suit of armor stolen from the same Moorish fortress that had supplied the mansion front door, and that was almost welcoming now that the battle axe had been replaced with a smallish pike with a red and gold standard wired on top; he might be a high school mascot, cheering on his team. Other banners and tapestries had been hung from the peculiar balconies whose function was yet to be fathomed.

Karo was especially pleased with the fireplace. It was unlikely that mandatory late seventeenth-century ox-roasting hearth had ever seen an ox over its thick flags, as the practice was given up at about the same time as jousting and holy quests went out of fashion, but she knew instinctively that it would look madly picturesque in the winter, when the marble overmantel was decked out in festive evergreens and gilded pineapples.

The last piece to be removed was a large painted armoire. It disfigured the room with its looming presence, its shape rather like double coffins nailed together and weighing at least as much. It was hard to say what one noticed more once the dust was wiped away: the alarming color or the obscene murals.

"I'm surprised Valperga didn't burn it," Karo huffed as they shoved it out of the chamber and down the back hall. But then she realized why the woman hadn't. "She was afraid of her grandfather, wasn't she? Of retribution? That's why she left all his stuff alone."

"She never said so specifically—not in the jour-

nals I've read—but I think that can be inferred."
Tristam wasn't puffing as hard as she, but he was
definitely working.

The thought of Valperga's fear wasn't comforting. Ghosts weren't supposed to actually hurt
people, were they? At least, in real life and not in
movies? Karo shoved the idea aside for later consideration and applied herself to the last of the
cleaning. It felt as good as an exorcism and was
probably a lot more practical. Tristam helped by
moving the armoire and providing sotto voce
obscenities. He had a gift for invective. It was
probably from being fluent in more than one language. Of course, he only had the energy to curse
because of the lovely plastic sleds they had found
to slip under the armoire's thick feet. Carrying
it would have been impossible, and dragging it
would have marred the floor.

"Maybe we should have burned the damned
thing," Tristam said, leaning down to pull Karo
to her feet when they had the thing in position.

"I'd sure like to see a fire on that hearth," Karo
agreed. The whole room was a definite photo op.
It should go in the cookbook along with the Limoges. But she would mention that later. Tristam
seemed to get a bit cranky whenever she mentioned the china.

"I never suspected that you had such hidden
depths," Tristam praised her. "Such pretty hands
for so much practical work. You must have been
wearing gloves."

"Are you kidding? Of course I wore gloves. Do
you know how many kinds of spiders were living
in that chimney?"

"I have a fair notion of how many kinds took up residence in our stuffed friends," he retorted. "I should have called the Discovery Channel. There were species there I've never seen before and hope to never see again."

"That probably would have been a good idea. I wish we'd thought of it sooner." Karo was getting the hang of notions to seize on free publicity to draw in tourists. "Just imagine if we did have some howlingly rare spiders here. They might do a special on us."

"Too late. They're gone now."

While Tristam had hauled away the racks of antlers and badger masks, Karo had commandeered the Campion brothers' tallest pruning ladder and, armed with a bucket of water and oil soap, had attacked the webbed ramparts with sponge and rag. She had found lots of web but very few spiders. She assumed they were catching rides with her boss, which suited her fine.

Tristam had protested that scrub work wasn't expected of her, but when she persisted in the filthy endeavor he'd cheerfully rolled up his sleeves and set about destroying another good shirt with lemon oil. His lack of skill with the polishing cloth suggested that he was not in the habit of doing menial work, so Karo was touched that he offered to help with a job so far beneath his dignity and job title. She took it as yet another hopeful sign that things were going to work out with this job.

Of course, the first and best indication of future happiness was the fact that Hugh had left her strictly alone since their meeting at the cookhouse.

This was a once in a lifetime opportunity—at least it seemed more and more that way to her. Maybe for Tristam this was common fare, but she couldn't imagine ever again having the complete run of a plantation, one not yet turned over to tourists and guardians of a historical society. It would have been a shame if the ghost had driven her away.

"You're looking pensive," Tristam said.

"Just reflecting upon my good fortune." Karo was even beginning to talk like Tristam. It seemed right for the environment.

"Yes?"

"I am very glad that my family has no ghosts. In fact, we don't have much ancestral baggage at all—no money or scandals. I got saddled with my grandmother's name, but that's about it."

"I hadn't thought of that," Tristam admitted.

"I mean, of course I have ancestors. Everyone does. We just kept moving around and lost track of them."

"That could be handy." Tristam smiled. "I should like to lose any number of the boring sticks and demagogues I am related to."

"Does your family home have a ghost?" Karo asked. She was wondering if he'd seen anything lately, and this seemed a nicely roundabout way to inquire.

"Alas, no. But there is one at the rectory next door—and a ghost horse has been heard trotting up the lane!" He didn't mention anything about Vellacourt, though, and nothing in the mansion.

"A horse ghost? That seems rather sad," Karo remarked. "Animals shouldn't be restless spirits."

Tristam frowned. "I suppose not. I think perhaps I've been immunized by my childhood. The idea of seeing any ghost is more annoying than scary. Or sad."

"That's probably why you're handling all the weirdness of this place so much better than I am. The very idea is outside my frame of reference. I don't know what to think or feel." That was an understatement if Karo had ever made one.

"You've coped magnificently."

Karo smiled and did not contradict him. She indeed thought that she had handled things fairly well.

"Is it tactless of me to mention that I'm so hungry I could eat a badger mask?" Tristam said after they had basked in the glow of accomplishment for a minute or two longer. "Any large animal would do. A pig or cow would be fine. Or one of the larger fowl."

"No, it's not tactless. Especially not if you're offering to slaughter it. And cook it." She was feeling a bit punch-drunk with victory. Dizzy, even.

Tristam groaned. "I haven't the strength for the hunt. But . . . perhaps I could cheat a bit and take you out. I know a place that does excellent cow."

"Well . . ." Karo looked down at her splotched blouse and wondered if it was worth any attempt to salvage. She supposed that she should make an effort; she was going through clothes at a phenomenal rate, and there was no clothing allowance in Clarice's budget. "I'll have to shower." She looked at Tristam. He was just as tattered and grubby. "And so will you. I think we've gone beyond mere housework and passed into the realm of Dumpster-diving. Nobody will have us if we don't clean up a bit."

"I'll be out in five and then Bob's your uncle," he assured her, starting for the stairs.

"In your dreams!" Karo remembered that her room possessed the only decent shower, and that the boiler capacity was modest. She bolted after him. "Me first! I need longer to wash and dry my hair."

Tristam, hearing her pursuit over the wood and marble floor, lunged for the first stair. "Never! The race is to the swift and daring."

Karo snaked out a hand and hauled on his belt, beginning to laugh at his look of outrage as she pulled him up short. If she tugged any harder, she'd give him a wedgie. "Take another step and you'll be the halt and the lame," she threatened between giggles, tugging on the waist of his pants.

"I suggest a compromise," he said, straightening. "We'll share. Two minutes of warm each and then a rinse in cool."

"Nope. Me first," she insisted.

A gleam entered his golden eyes. It did nothing to sober Karo's mood, but it did make her slightly wary. She dropped her hand and retreated a half step.

"Absolutely firm about that, are we? Fine. First you shall be." Then, with the ease that he had shown on the first night, Tristam turned, plucked her off her feet and hoisted her up into the air. Karo found herself hanging from his shoulder like a carelessly donned backpack. This time he didn't bother being a gentleman.

"Put me down," she demanded. It was obligatory.

He ignored her. That was also obligatory.

She tried squirming, but he simply threatened to drop her on her head if she persisted. With each long step, the bathroom got closer. Karo's mind filled with deep suspicion.

"Don't even think it," she warned, and smacked him once on the left flank that she was getting to know up close and personal.

An immediate, retaliatory smack answered her. "Consider carefully before you start that game, my dear," Tristam cautioned. "I've probably had more experience, and I'm a great deal larger than you. Besides, I'm only seeing that you get what you wanted."

"Where's a witch pricker when you need one?" Karo complained, but then ruined it by laughing. "A stick! A stick! My kingdom for a—Tristam!"

The ugly doors were kicked open. It was no great feat, as they were unlatched, but the crash was dramatic against the wall. Four strides and she and Tristam were into the bathroom. Karo began to flail her feet. She tried tickling him, too, but to no avail.

The water was turned on. All the way. She couldn't see which knob he'd grabbed, but she was betting on it being the one with the C.

"If you do this, you'll regret it," she warned, a last effort of delay. "I always get even."

"I'm a bit of a plunger. Can't win a packet without having a little flutter now and again." Tristam shrugged her off his shoulder and used the momentum to sling her into the shower stall. Her feet slipped on the porcelain and only his arms kept her upright under the deluge. After a count of three, she was pulled from under the spout and allowed to breathe. They were both sopping.

"The only thing that may save you is the fact that the water is warm," she spluttered through her hair. She could see the knob's H turned on its side.

"It is? Well, of all the rotten luck!" Tristam made sure that she was steady on her feet and then let her go. Black sludge was streaming off both of them. "Make haste, my dear, I am dripping all over the floor."

"So use a towel—Not a white one! And then disappear. If you're lucky, I won't use all the hot water." She shoved her sodden hair aside and pretended to glare at Tristam. "You look like a grease monkey."

"Hm. I won't return the compliment. Such exchanges never lead to anything good." He sounded amused. Perhaps he hadn't seen himself in the mirror yet. A fastidious creature, he would be appalled. Through the folds of a maroon towel he added, "I think I'll shower downstairs. I don't fancy the odds of my getting lucky."

"Neither do I. I've decided to condition my hair and shave my legs," she informed him, and then pulled the shower curtain shut. Even dripping soot he was capable of producing those dangerous pheromones, so she'd just make like a Victorian lady and bathe with her clothes on until they went away.

She heard the heavy tread of his feet as he made his escape. Finishing her shower, she checked the

...oom carefully before she ventured out in her towel. Her clothes were still soaking in the sink, though her first impulse had been to throw them in the trash.

Karo was once again struck by the architecture. The builders of this estate had clearly not been the kind of people for whom wealth was an abstract concept. The house aside—and that was a vast aside, since the mansion was an end to end example of conspicuous consumption in a rather more erotic vein than the norm—most of the furnishings, being European, were better pedigreed and at least as well traveled as she. Of course, their passage across the sea had probably involved a good deal more danger than any she had ever made. Karo could only hope to someday be as well dressed as the windows in her bedroom—albeit a little less colorfully. In the meantime, she was fortunate not to be allergic to rare woods, priceless antiques and gilt.

"So, where are you taking me?" Karo asked as the BMW whipped along the lane. She smoothed her uncrushable skirt and thanked the technologists who'd invented Lycra. She had spent an idiotic amount of time deciding whether or not to wear it. The decision might have taken longer, since she was uncharacteristically dithery that evening, but she was *really* hungry. The taupe dress had been wadded into the back corner of her suitcase, and it was the only thing she had that could be described by adjectives like "feminine" or "pretty." Finished off with a brass and bead belt, she felt quite ethnic and sophisticated.

Gold eyes turned her way. They were still smiling, smug at getting away with his prank. Obviously it took more than a cold shower to squelch his spirits. She felt pleased he wasn't a creep.

"I warn you now that 'artistic vegetables' are out," he told her. "We are not in Williamstown."

"I am not in the mood for 'artistic.' Just a small salad," she told him. "Then cow or pig—or fowl, if it's in large quantity, as you once said—some heavy starch and a bit of wine. Perhaps some fruit and cheese."

"I'm not fussy, and frankly I haven't the faintest idea where one would go to find artistic around here. This isn't exactly California Cuisine country."

"You're prejudiced, having been raised on mushy peas and overcooked Brussels sprouts." Karo looked at the bare birches whipping by alongside. They didn't lay so much as a dirty leaf on the perfect paint job. She had offered to drive, but Tristam had shuddered. She couldn't blame him. Her car was a mess, and her father was correct that at the very least it needed an oil change. She couldn't actually recall the last time she had taken it in for a tune-up.

"That's probably true. I rather avoid the entire *brassicaceae* family. The smell of cooking cabbage still brings me out in hives. They have decent vegetables in Williamstown," Tristam admitted, as if considering the food to which she was accustomed. "I've seen them there. I've even dined on them, though I prefer a good chop house. Still, the know me at the place we're headed, and I get goo service and adequate food—though generally n quite so early in the evening. We will be missing the usual redneck crowd that lends it such a wonderful local color."

"I think I've had enough color for the day."

Vegetables. Karo thought of the cafeteria at her old job and grimaced. They'd had good vegetables there, but she didn't know the next time she would dare show her face. The management there probably had her picture on file on a Least Wanted List, right behind the Madagascar Hissing Cockroaches that had invaded their kitchens back in '05. "Yes, they do have nice veggies . . . We're not going anywhere near Williamstown, though. Are we?" she asked, feeling sudden alarm. Would he drive them that far?

Tristam looked over. His expression was bland. "Scared? What have you been doing, Karo Follett?" He tut-tutted. "Of course I'd like nothing more than to round out the evening by watching you have a flaming row with your ex in a public place and then getting myself arrested and thrown in the stocks for blackening his eyes."

"Would you?" She chuckled. "Thanks. I'm touched by the show of support. I think you'd probably manage to take him out. I did. Nevertheless, an evening without bloodshed would suit me better."

Tristam glanced her way. He was smiling a bit. Maybe he thought she was kidding about assaulting F. Christian. Certainly none of her friends back home would believe it. She'd always been too ladylike.

"I should certainly hope I could 'take' him. It isn't as though he earns his living off honest toil."

"Just dishonest."

He nodded. "Since you're ravenous and don't require vegetables, I think the Mountain Lion Lodge will do. They specialize in barbecued large animal, and in pale tubers like turnips and potatoes."

"Sounds perfect," Karo said. "I can always take a vitamin supplement later if I feel scurvy coming on." She was more sanguine now that she was safe from bearding familiar faces. It wasn't that she was afraid, exactly, but she could wait an eternity before being involved in another brawl and it would still be too soon. "And you needn't worry about a flaming row. I've already done that—hurled wine, potato salad and accusations included—and I don't like to repeat myself."

"Did you really hurl the potato salad? I thought perhaps that was just an expression." He glanced at her.

"No, I threw it, bowl and all."

"What a vengeful creature it is! Are you going to hurl your wine at me for helping you shower?" He didn't sound worried, so she grinned. "Is that the planned revenge—food in my lap or face?"

"Oh, no. Been there. Done that. I'll think up something special just for you. Something appropriate and personal. Let the punishment fit the crime, I always say. Anyway, I'm hoping it's a good wine."

He laughed. "It's adequate."

The Lodge was charming, the ceiling low and timbered and they had a fireplace built of gray stone. There was also a small dance floor and a dais for a band, though there was no indication that anyone would be playing that night. As promised, they clearly knew Tristam, and his arrival caused a certain amount of fluttering amongst the mostly female staff. Karo and Tristam were the first ones in the door that evening and had everyone's undivided attention.

Sipping at a surprisingly good burgundy put out by Seven Witches, a label Tristam chose solely to tease her, Karo watched as her boss's charm sent the probably underage waitresses running to implement his every desire. He had the gift of genteel command. Also, they were quite willingly bidden.

Karo wondered why he'd never tried such charming orders on her. He'd probably taken her number right away and, in spite of her protests about getting involved, had decided that he didn't want to spend his days beating her off with a stick if he was too nice. Hence, the buddy-buddy treatment. Too bad he didn't know about his pheromone problem. Should she mention it? It wasn't like bad breath or body odor. She couldn't just slip some mouthwash into his bathroom. And would she even *want* to stop it?

"Do you get such sterling service everywhere you go?" she asked at last, trying to distract herself from the rich vanilla and coconut smell that surrounded him.

"Certainly. America has been most welcoming." His eyes twinkled. The arrogant so-and-so knew exactly what effect he had on women. That was dangerous knowledge for a man to have.

"It certainly looks that way," Karo agreed. "Even

the ones old enough to know better are all but wagging their tails."

Tristam just smiled and sipped his wine. "So, Mistress Follett, it occurs to me that we are—in the local parlance—on a first date. If I have the American ritual correctly, that means that we are supposed to cover some personal conversational ground between the cocktails and the first course." He looked politely inquiring, but Karo was getting to know the gleam in his eye: pure trouble. "Or is that off-limits, given our employer-employee relationship? I have to admit to a case of raging curiosity about what you've been doing all your life. It can't have all been spent hurling potato salad and climbing trees. I assume the latter is a matter of cell phone reception and not some kind of privacy fetish."

"Oh, you'd be surprised how many cads have deserved a potato salad bath," Karo said. She was trying to decide if she was going to let the supposition that they were on a first date stand unchallenged. In the end, she chose to let it go. Nor did she explain about her tree climbing.

"So . . . personal stuff, like family pedigrees, ex-spouses, illegitimate children—that sort of thing?" she asked him. Though she was ragingly curious about him as well, she added: "It sounds a little predictable, especially since I don't have any pedigree. Maybe we should discuss politics or semicurrent events. Though, I haven't actually read a newspaper in a couple of weeks."

Before Tristam could reply, one of the girls, a young blonde with delicate freckles and a blouse that was now unbuttoned to her lacy push-up bra, came bustling over and set the soup bowls down with a small flourish. She beamed at Tristam. Karo could almost hear the *voila* that went with the dramatic gesture, and his bowl was placed perfectly. Her own was off center and the soup sloshed over the edge.

"This is minestrone, but there's chicken if you'd rather. It wouldn't take but a minute to fetch it for you." The blonde sounded breathless.

"This looks delicious, thank you." Tristam nodded regally, and the girl backed away with shallow bows. She was practically shivering with delight.

"Go on. Ask for some crackers. She'll love it," Karo whispered, though she was beginning to get annoyed by all the hovering. She took her napkin and blotted up the soup edging for the lip of the table. "I bet she'll even roll over if you scratch her behind the ears."

"Jealousy ill becomes you, my dear." Tristam looked down his perfect, arrogant nose at her and smirked.

"'My dear,'" she mimicked his accent. "This isn't jealousy. It's amusement—the malicious kind. You know, à la Noel Coward. After all, she's young enough to be your daughter."

"Noel Coward, are you sure? But perhaps it suffers in translation. The American accent is so barbaric, and you tend to abridge everything—especially wit."

"Ha! If the rednecks were here, the shoe would be on the other foot. I am very attractive to drunk men." She stuck out her tongue.

He smiled blandly. "I'm sure you are, but we

have veered off course. Our topic tonight is personal." He took a taste of his soup and nodded, then picked up his wine. "America has some excellent vineyards. Ever been married?"

"No. You?" she shot back without blinking.

"No. Involved?"

"Always, but not always with men."

"Women, then?"

Karo glared. "No. With my work."

"Is it a good lover?"

"It's faithful." She reached for her wine, ignoring her own steaming bowl. She knew that this wasn't wise on an empty stomach, but she was feeling strangely irresponsible.

"Ah, but that's not the same thing! Predictability is no stand-in for passion. Eventually you'll want a lover again, someone or something to thrill you. Will you go seeking one?"

"Doubtful. I've given them up for the rest of the decade," she lied.

Her gaze shifted past him to the garish jukebox against the long kitchen wall. On impulse, she reached into her purse and pulled out two quarters. Rising, she went to use them.

Tristam's eyes followed her across the room. She scanned the titles in the machine and quickly selected two. The first was an old hit by Jon Secada; the second had her hiding a smile. She'd give him some really *original* English usage.

"Very sexy, but then I knew you could walk. Do you like to dance?" he asked as she returned to the table.

"Yes. But not here. We'd trip over someone." Karo jerked her head. Another girl was bearing down on them with a basket of bread. This one, a brunette, offered to fetch Tristam some crackers if he preferred. Or cheese toast. Or biscuits with gravy. Pancakes, waffles . . . really, he could have anything he wanted, she added eagerly, even if it wasn't on the menu.

Karo picked up her spoon and tried the broth while a slightly chagrined Tristam did his polite best to banish further offers of starches. And other things. And others. She tried not to grin as his aplomb slipped.

"Don't worry," she said. "They are just acting more territorial than usual because I'm here. I don't think they'll actually try to mark you or anything."

The girl didn't notice Karo's words, though Karo's voice was not particularly quiet. She swayed closer, and Karo could see that she had rolled her skirt over at the waistband to make it several inches shorter.

"Do you like living on the east coast, or are you inclined to move around? No more bread—thank you!" Tristam said to the brunette. He frowned at Karo, who giggled, and got rid of the hovering girl by nodding at her again. Then he resumed his list of questions.

Such were the benefits of a one-track mind, Karo supposed, uncertain whether to be glad that he'd let the matter of her looking for a lover pass as he pursued the rest of his list. Karo was very interested in *his* romantic inclinations, but she decided to let sleeping dogs lie. Geography was a safer topic for the nonce.

"It's alright." She tried a little more soup. "I'm not wedded to it, though."

Bad choice of words. She hoped he didn't see it the same.

"How about England?" he asked.

"How about it?"

"Oh . . . My turn, is it? Well, let's see." He wrinkled his brow so that she would know he was thinking. "The ancestral manse is in a mossy part of Lincolnshire—pretty from May seventh through June third, and at no other time of year. To be honest, I'm grateful that Brother Jeremy will inherit the mire. As the younger son I have to be content with the leavings—which are rather generous, all things considered."

"It's tacky to brag about money. Especially to people who don't have any," she pointed out. "Didn't your mother tell you that?"

He just grinned. "When I get to feeling homesick I pop over for a week or two, visit with Mum at the dower house—my sister-in-law is a bit much, so Mum keeps her own place—and then I head back stateside again. There is a great deal of comfort to be had in placing an ocean between me and my nearest and dearest."

"I can't tell when you're kidding," Karo complained.

He grinned at her some more but didn't offer any clarification. "Gives you something to mull over in the dark stretches of the night."

"When I lie awake and think about you?"

"Precisely. Now, where was I? Right. Women in my life—that's next, isn't it?" He lifted a brow. "I used to prefer the high-dollar type, but since I've been in the States I've come to enjoy slumming with the masses. Such pretty masses you have here! Have I ever mentioned that I maintain a preference for dark hair and gray eyes? The combination is rather rare."

"Uh, no, you haven't mentioned this. Don't tell the blonde. She'll be crushed. Is this a new obsession or—Oh, look, she's bringing us crackers after all. And biscuits! What a surprise. Are you certain you don't like slumming with busty blondes? This one looks more than willing if not so busty. And maybe they don't have statutory rape laws for immigrants."

Tristam gave her ankle a light kick under the table. The first waitress was back, still shivering. Karo smiled politely and, to make her point, complimented the soup. It was a pointless courtesy; the teen barely spared her a glance. And with the other waitress . . . Well, maybe Tristam *was* in danger of being territorially peed on as the two girls fought over him. The thought had Karo giggling, and she began to think that perhaps she'd had too much wine.

"Thanks, Mr. English. Would you like some more water? Or lemon? Or lime—we have lime, too."

"No, thank you, Miss . . . ?"

"Basco. Rebecca Basco, but please call me Becky."

The name made them both blink. But though the same question sprang to both their minds, neither asked the girl about her genealogical relationship to a defrocked priest. For a moment Becky looked excited by the attention, and her

hand fluttered for her blouse as though considering whether to undo another button.

"Thank you, Becky, but I think we're fine for
now." Tristam gave her another unsmiling nod
and she backed away again as if leaving a royal
presence. The kitchen door whooshed shut behind
her, and in the sudden dead space that followed
the pause between jukebox songs, they could hear
Becky talking to her friends.

"Isn't he to die for?" the piercing voice demanded. "I could just eat him up."

"But I saw him first!" the brunette waitress
complained. "And you're dating Rodney!"

Karo almost choked on her wine and even Tristam looked startled. His momentary expression
of shocked outrage sent her off into paroxysms of
laughter that ended in a genuine cough.

"It's your own fault." She found a clean spot on
her napkin and mopped her streaming eyes as
the jukebox spun her next selection, an offensive
little number by Nine Inch Nails. The sound of
static filled the air. It wasn't a malfunction. The
song had a background of hissing white noise.

"Men who are 'to die for' just shouldn't be polite
to horny teenagers. We'll probably be shadowed
the whole night through," Karo pointed out to
him. "Hey, maybe the fan club will follow us back
to Belle Ange to see where their idol lives. If you
asked nicely, maybe you could get them to paint
the place. They seem willing to do *anything*."

"Did your father ever beat you?" Tristam in-
quired coolly. It was hard to do while pitching his
voice over the loud hissing coming from the speak-
ers overhead, but he managed.

"Never," she shouted back cheerfully, finishing her wine. Karo knew she was drinking too much but didn't seem able to stop. "Daddy didn't believe in physical discipline."

"What a pity. Still, it's never too late to start. Vellacourt left a nice selection of whips upstairs."

"So what? You can't beat me. I have a doctor's excuse. But I suppose that I could always beat *you*. If you ask nicely." Her glance was mischievous. In the back of her mind she knew that she would never have said as much without first being lubricated with wine—and perhaps the visitation by Vellacourt. "That's what Englishmen like, isn't it? All those years at boarding school . . . ?"

Yes, the wine had made her bold.

"You little horror!" This time the indignation sounded real, but his gaze was . . . intent.

"Are you really upset? I'm sorry. No, truly I am. I shouldn't tease you." Karo stopped smiling. "That girl's affections . . . Well, it must get tedious having women mooning over you," she said a bit enviously.

Tristam leaned forward and covered her hand. His eyes were unblinking, almost soulful. "Does that mean you won't tease me anymore?"

She was certain that he had touched her for the very purpose of infusing her with more of his heart-fluttering musk. Despite that suspicion, her blood thickened enough to make her heart thud. Her mouth went dry. She had to resist the urge to turn her hand over and return the deliberate caress of his long fingers.

"Not over dinner. Afterward, I don't promise anything."

"So?" That mouth curved up and the hand withdrew. "Our game goes on. I'm so glad you're not a coward. It's no fun to win by surrender."

So, it was a game. He was still playing a game. Karo was relieved but also piqued. She wasn't looking for a lover—absolutely not—but the gender gauntlet had been thrown down between them. She might not pick it up, but she certainly wasn't going to go racing away from the challenge. A woman had her fair share of pride, and she might have any man she wanted. Probably. At least for one night.

"What in blazes is that revolting noise?" Tristam demanded in outrage, his accent stronger as horns began to blare from the jukebox. They were like sirens.

"Noise?" Karo asked innocently. "Oh, that's Trent Reznor. He's still very popular in some circles. Industrial music. It's got a good beat, hasn't it?"

"Can he actually *say* things like that? Aren't there decency laws in this country or something?"

"Careful. Your age is showing. This is very with it." Actually, it was almost passé. She had only chosen it to annoy him.

The second waitress materialized before Tristam could continue his harangue. She set their entrees on the table and beamed expectantly. Her skirt had gotten even shorter. Karo kept a straight face while Tristam thanked her once again and declined any more bread or soup or water or wine or cola or coffee.

"Don't say a word," he warned her, pointing a long finger in her direction. "I won't answer for the consequences."

"Who me? Wouldn't dream of it." Karo picked up a fork.

He stared at her for a moment and then picked up his own utensils.

"I'm glad you can manage the cutlery properly." She smiled at him. "I thought you might need a little help cutting up your meat, and dear Becky—"

"There are lots and lots of whips," he warned. "Whole racks of them. Not all of them velvet."

"Okay. *Pax*. But you have left the left-handed fork behind. I never quite gained the knack when we lived in Europe, though it looked quite practical."

"It's a working-class affectation. And when in Rome . . . You Americans do a ridiculous amount of switching knife and fork about. But that's typical, I guess, making the complicated out of the simple."

"I think that when you're on a date you're supposed to say *nice* things to the woman. Compliment her and stuff. Complaining about her countrymen's table manners is out."

"Very well. You're terribly pretty and very smart," he said easily. "Also a bit precocious and overeducated, but I'm a gentleman. I can live with that."

"Hm. Not bad. For a start. And it's mostly true."

He eyed her. "Be a lady and say something nice back. I want to see if your tongue cleaves to the roof of your mouth when you try."

"Well, it's a stretch for a nonpedigreed slum-dweller like me, but . . . I'm glad you're not boring. And I like men who have a sense of humor. There really are damned few of them around, especially in management."

"And you think I have nice hair."

"You can't hold that comment against me. I wasn't myself when I said that," she objected.

"But you do think that I have nice hair?"

"You have nice hair," she agreed reluctantly. "And eyes. They are unique." Except, that wasn't quite true, was it? She had recently seen someone else with gold eyes. Hugh. Hugh had gold eyes. The thought was almost enough to sober her. How had she not made the connection before?

"And nice hands. You said that you liked them, too. In fact, I believe you said that—"

"I take the Fifth and plead amnesia. I'd been hit by lightning," she reminded him as the blonde came bustling back with the dessert tray. They hadn't had two bites of their entree. "Look, Tristam, it's Becky. Again."

Her amusement was wearing thin at the constant interruptions, and Becky had her chest thrust out so far that Karo had to actually lean to the side to see Tristam. She began to wonder if she'd have to drag the girl into the ladies' room and slap her silly. Or silli*er*. It was probably a lost cause. She couldn't hit the waitress hard enough to knock out the stupid.

"Why don't you have some sponge cake? I think you could use a little sweetening, and maybe it would stick your lips together before you say something really outrageous," Tristam suggested to Karo, also leaning to the side.

"You said it first. Maybe you should have the

lemon meringue. I prefer my dates to be a little tart. They're more fun that way."

"On the subject of you becoming my sweet—" he continued.

"He and I are hanging together on this one," she warned, pointing at the jukebox. Trent was still singing about having a head like a hole and how he'd rather die than let someone else control him.

Tristam looked up at Becky, upon whom the entire exchange had been lost. "We'll have one strawberry shortcake—after dinner. Please unplug that ghastly machine and bring me a bar of soap. I want to wash out my date's mouth. And maybe my ears. Her taste in music is appalling."

"Uh . . . what kind of soap?" the ever-helpful Becky asked.

Tristam and Karo both began to laugh.

"Got any Irish Spring?" Karo asked through streaming eyes. She had guessed right: no amount of slapping would help this girl.

"No. Just Ivory or Dove. Or the stuff for the dishwasher." The girl still didn't get it and looked hurt by their continued laughter. They made an effort to stop.

"I think I'll settle for pie," Karo said. "Lemon will be fine." Taking another drink of wine she watched the girl retreat kitchenward. She shook her head in wonder. "Geez! I thought all those stories about blonde ditzes were nasty rumors. No wonder you like dark hair."

"With gray eyes," he reminded her, pouring her more wine.

She was having such a good time, Karo didn't even notice that Tristam was swamping her brain with dangerous vanilla pheromones just as much as he filled her glass with burgundy.

*"Would you tell me, please, which way I ought to go
from here?"*
*"That depends a good deal on where you want to get
to," said the Cat.*
—Lewis Carroll from *Alice's Adventures
in Wonderland*

Chapter Seven

Karo was fairly certain that she was awake, prodded out of dreams by an outside agent. It was hot and there was too much telltale static in her sheets and hair for it to be anyone but Hugh.

So, where was he? Hiding under the bed? And why was he here? Was it because she had been sensible and sent Tristam away without so much as a kiss at the bedroom door?

The bedroom was cast in darkest shadow, so she could not swear that she had actually wakened, but the darkness felt different on her open eyes than it had moments before, was a sort of electric gray instead of the usual India ink. And there was a damp smell of morning on the air that floated up from the garden and tickled her nose with dew and the distant scent of the river. The last moments of night were thick with the honey scent of blossoms, which made no sense, most of the flowers having bloomed earlier in the spring.

There was also an uncanny breeze that crept silently though the window that Karo had left open. It ran first one direction through the drapes and then reversed itself, as if the house were laboring to breathe. The curtains fluttered inward again and then stilled. The inappropriately warm zephyr moved silently to surround the giant bed and play with the satin dust ruffle.

That, or 'Stein was under the bed chasing dust bunnies.

Or Vellacourt was under the bed getting ready to chase her.

The latter thought had her sitting up straight and listening to the whispering cloth with great attention. Her hair began to crackle and heat danced along her skin.

In converse to the sudden warmth, it seemed that she could hear a storm coming, approaching like a train. She could feel a cold waiting just beyond her room, a chill that the house feared but could not flee, and having no ready defenses, its timbers contracted with arthritic creaks and soft exhalations of pain. The noises were unnerving. Unnatural.

Karo pushed back the covers and slowly stood, conscious of the weight of her body on the chilly wooden floor. A warm current played about her knees like invisible trade winds might a ship's sail, but the clear sensation of cold feet and bare legs negated the underlying dreaminess that filled her head and tried to drive out the growing alarm. She knew that she was awake, and she knew that she needed to shut the bedroom window before some creeping, crawling or flying critter—like

Vellacourt—blundered into her room and flung itself upon her. But an inner prompting, softer than any voice but absolute in its compulsion, moved her instead toward the mirror screwed into the wall over the bulk of the oak dresser to the right of the bed.

Mirror, Mirror on the wall.

She waited coolly, hands still, her eyes fixed on the tarnished glass. Gradually, her attention focused on a bright glow forming behind her, somewhere over her right shoulder. The room reflected in the mirror quickly filled with a gray motionlessness that pushed back the night until the very walls were shoved away by this bright void. It was like being in the eye of a silent storm, or lost inside a sheet of lightning. Someone was coming. Fast. She recognized the smell of ozone, the heat. Karo was certain that if she looked at the clock on the end table she would find that it had stopped. She was in a place between times.

With a courage she did not possess in waking hours, Karo waited to speak until she could see the soft outline of a tall, slender form resolve itself into a nearly human shape. This time, because she watched without flinching, she could see him unfold, limb by limb, unpacking himself from some other dimension. And, as expected, it was Hugh Vellacourt—but he was dressed in the strangest clothes. It looked like some kind of tartan knickers and a golf sweater!

So, there went the theory that she was actually awake. Unless . . . They had been playing golf in Europe for a very long time, especially in Scotland. Maybe this wasn't too weird. Why shouldn't an active ghost get out for the occasional round of golf?

A sudden white noise distracted her from her inward fashion commentary, whispering that he had been waiting for her all day, waiting for it to be night so that he could come back and see her in her dreams. But *who* had waited—Vellacourt?

Karo studied his reflection, this time without fear, noting the unnatural pallor of the spirit that was wholly manifest. He was not alive, could never be mistaken for a living man. His dreadful stillness was unremittingly corpselike. Yet, there was a suppleness and sturdiness to this ghost's skin, and the glitter in those metallic eyes belonged to a nocturnal hunter all too aware of his prey.

Hugh wasn't a mournful ghost like Jacob Marley, a poor soul who had gotten lost on the way to Calvary or Valhalla. Nor was he a confused remnant of life left behind when the body had gone. No, Hugh Vellacourt was wide-awake, and he wanted something on this earthly plane. He wanted it badly, if not badly enough to try reaching her during the day when she might betray herself to Tristam.

It was not a comfortable thought, that the ghost had desires. She had really hoped that they'd already covered his list of wants and that he'd agreed to stay away from her.

Karo's mouth was dry as she addressed her visitor, but she managed to sound both brave and sarcastic. "Don't you ever knock?"

Heated fingers danced over her shoulder as the ghost's arm stretched an impossible length and reached past her body, but Karo didn't turn from staring into the glass to confirm that spectral hands were actually brushing her shoulder. The mirror implied that he was still hanging by the window, tangled in the lace sheers, but the heat on her neck said Vellacourt was actually nearer. Objects in the rearview mirror were not as close as they appeared, right? Why push her nerves right over the edge of that cliff they were teetering on by turning about and confirming the theory that a spook was actually touching her? It seemed much safer to just stare into the glass and ignore the hand beside her cheek.

Vellacourt's long finger pointed into the darkness. His gesture was emphatic. Insistent. And the light behind her was getting warmer all the time, as if he couldn't quite control his personal thermostat, and it was rising with his agitation.

Karo bent slightly, stepping away from the spirit light. At first she saw nothing but Vellacourt shining in the glass; the dark surface was completely bare of reflection, except for the sporty ghost and his white hand hovering by where her ear would be if she had an image of her own.

The sudden realization that she couldn't see herself left Karo shaken. She was in a place where Vellacourt was real and she was not.

But Vellacourt insisted she look again, inching closer to her back, getting warmer as he crowded her against the dresser. Reluctantly she leaned over the vanity top and peered into the black well of the mirror that had become a window.

Something pushed on her back. She had a brief sensation of falling—or of being pulled through joinery, pegged post and beam—and then she was standing upright on a different floor of the house, looking down the length of the garret. She had fallen up, not down when she passed through the looking glass.

A young woman with very long black hair was standing beside a benchlike gallows, swaying and humming under her breath. Karo felt that she should know the tune and after a moment she had placed it. *"He is running for his dinner, I am running for my life. . . ."* She couldn't remember the rest of it. Something about a hare and a hound. Had she heard this the first night she arrived at Belle Ange?

Anxious, Karo stared hard at the almost familiar woman, willing her to turn so that her face might come into view. The only light in the garret came from a single candlestick set on the floor. The woman's hair covered her face like a veil. The shadows were thick in the room, and stare as she might, Karo could see only that the woman was small, pale skinned, and wearing a thin old-fashioned slip called a chemise over bare limbs. The woman had no shoes on her slim feet, but that did not suggest powerlessness, for she carried a whip in her hands. Long, delicate, flexible, it was held with an ease that proposed familiarity and even comfort.

It would be one of the velvet whips, Karo hoped, but the sight of it in the woman's hand made her nervous and itchy. She had a feeling that she knew why Hugh had brought her here and a part of her was fascinated—outraged, too, as any modern woman should be at being kidnapped and likely soon to be made to witness a pornographic act.

But how many people in the history of the world had been given the chance to actually watch history played out before them? How many people would ever see inside a sadist's bedroom?

A door opened behind Karo, making the candle flame waver. She froze, listening for footsteps. She heard the hinges creak and felt a current of air brush her body as someone entered the garret. She tried to turn her head and look behind her, even though her memory told her that there was no door at her back, just an open window and Vellacourt's ghost. She was having a vision—she hadn't actually left her bedroom! But Karo couldn't move more than her eyes to prove that this was so.   .

The dark-haired woman half turned and beckoned impatiently. A man with long, gold hair walked toward her. He was panting slightly, like he had been running. Karo could not see the man's face, only his long, limber back and legs. He wore no clothes at all upon his golden flesh, but again, this nudity did not suggest powerlessness. There was too much arrogance and grace in his stride to call the man subservient.

This was Vellacourt? He felt oddly familiar.

The blond man started to reach for the woman, but she brought up the whip and then pointed at the cuffs dangling from the wooden frame. The thin cane cut the air as it moved in a downward slash.

"If you want me, *cher*, this is how it must be." The woman's voice was a whisper. "You'll have me no other way."

The man stared and then shook his head once

in negation. The candlelight sparked gold in his hair.

"*Non*," he refused. Karo thought she knew the voice, but the strange accent and rough tone threw her.

"*Il est pas rigolo.*"

Karo had enough French to know that the woman was saying that the man was no fun.

"*Tu charries.*" *This is too much*, the man answered.

"*J'suis drolement emmerde,*" the woman said in a husky, caressing whisper.

Karo didn't speak French well, especially gutter French, and should not have understood the provocative words. But she did. They made her shiver.

The man stared a moment longer, clearly frustrated, his shoulders tense, his posture rejecting, and then he changed his mind. He complied with the woman's order by lifting his arms to the shackles. He might have surrendered to her wishes, but he had not relaxed, and Karo felt nervous as the woman moved toward him. This was a dangerous moment.

The dark-haired woman floated close. Still humming, she snapped the cuffs around the man's strong wrists, which were now crossed, bound together in front of him. Not cruelly tight, because of the fur that lined the shackles, but they were inescapable with the locking-pin dropped in place.

Karo began to mentally squirm. History or not, this was about to cross a line she hadn't ever planned on crossing—except maybe in her deepest, most private fantasies?

She made another attempt to move back from the two people but could not force her feet to obey. Was the ghostly Vellacourt and all his heat still standing behind her, waiting to burn her flesh if she retreated? Was he holding her there in some kind of thrall, and that's why her body wouldn't move? She couldn't tell. She had no sense of his presence anymore, or even of her own body beyond knowing that she was still pegged solidly to the tongue-and-groove floor, her muscles apparently locked in place by a will other than her own.

The dark-haired woman walked around in front of the man. Her hands were in his hair, hard, and she pulled his mouth to hers. Her kisses were aggressive, an attack. The man pulled on the shackles as though trying to break free, but he returned her kisses with fervor, running his tongue over her cheeks and even going so far as to bite her lightly on the chin. It was as if he tried to devour her.

"Enough!"

The woman reached out with her left hand and dealt a stinging slap to the man's right thigh. She backed away from her prisoner. Was she pouting? Karo couldn't see her face, but she *knew* that those lips were pouting. The woman looked almost fragile in her thin slip and bare feet, except for the whip in her right hand.

The spectral beauty walked around her prisoner until she was behind him. Now her back was to Karo. She stepped out of her chemise, leaving it to pool on the floor, but nothing of her body was revealed because her long hair covered her in a black cloak.

She began tormenting the man—kissing, suckling, tickling his neck with the end of her whip while he writhed and moaned in his shackles. Her laughter was low and smoldering, sexy as she rubbed against his back and between his flank and legs with hands and velvet cord. Karo could feel perspiration begin to collect between her breasts and inner thighs. She really wanted to blame the sudden heat on Vellacourt, but it seemed that he was keeping his distance from her. No, it was prurient interest alone that slicked her skin and let the hunger loose in her stomach. To be perfectly honest, she wanted to touch the man, too, while he was safely shackled. That was the wisest way for any woman to have a man.

The captive began to make angry, helpless noises that only increased as the woman stopped touching him and walked over to the rack on the wall to hang up her tiny whip. The man swiveled his head. Almost, Karo could see the side of his face. The bit of profile she could see through his tangled hair looked uncomfortably familiar. But it was Vellacourt she was seeing, wasn't it? It had to be. And Eustacie La Belle, his French concubine. Who else would have used this room in such a way?

The woman selected a stiffened leather paddle, examining it by the dim light. It was long and rather thin, perhaps only two inches wide. She brought it down hard, and it sliced the air with a whistle. The man made a sound of protest and threat that was lost under Karo's own exclamation.

Karo knew she should be repelled by what was

about to happen—she was an educated, liberal woman who believed in sexual equality and non-violence in such equal relations—but she wasn't *entirely* disgusted. This was consensual, she assured herself. She could feel the waves of desire coming off of the man as he stared at his mistress. She could feel the flashes of lust that had washed over the woman as she touched and kissed and teased the man she had chained before her.

Power was a real high, and mixing it with sex increased both exponentially. This struggle was about more than deciding who would be on top. It was id and ego at war. It was about trust and surrender . . . and the arousal of pleasure that came from submitting to pain. Yes, Karo understood what the woman was feeling, the symbolism of what the man did by placing himself in her care. He was making himself vulnerable. It was an almost unbearable turn-on.

"Enough," she whispered. "Let him go."

"Not yet, *cherie*," the white noise whispered behind her. "Admit the truth. You wouldn't want it to end now."

No, she wouldn't.

The woman walked back to the man. She kissed him tenderly on his cheek, smoothed his hair with a careful hand and then backed away a step. "I love thee," she whispered. "Dost thou love me, too? Dost thou agree?"

"I do," he assured her, but a blush spread up the back of his neck as he gave permission.

Her first blow was soft, just a tease, but the sound of leather on flesh was loud in the silent room. The man sighed. "Cruel-hearted bitch," he said. His words were crude, but his tone was not. "You've always brought me pain."

"Pain that you need. Pain that you want," the woman whispered back. "Power I need, power I want. And with the pain comes pleasure."

"Yes, damn you. So just do it." She smacked him again on the back of his long legs. Karo saw that the blows, though light, had to sting at least a little. She could all but feel them herself as the leather bit into the man's flesh, kissing up and down his legs and flanks and thighs. She could smell the heat and sweat pouring from their bodies. The scent was vanilla and coconut. It sizzled.

Shock at her own bloodlust, psychic disorientation and carnal appetite were all rising in Karo. She did not notice when the white light began to glow again behind her, heating her back. Her eyes and all other senses were given over to the two people in front of her.

The woman stopped the playful paddling. She pulled the pin from the man's shackles and backed away. It was a clear taunt.

He jerked his hands loose from the cuffs and was on her in a flash, flattening her upon her discarded chemise, belly to the floor. "It is my turn now." He bit her neck through her thick hair and then moved up over her body, pushing her legs apart. His muscles tensed and coiled as he began thrusting into her.

Both Karo and the woman cried out, but not in pain. No, it was pleasant fire burning through Karo's loins, making her shudder and gasp.

With a soft snarl, the man pulled back the woman's head by a handful of hair, forcing her to turn toward his mouth as he ravished her with his tongue.

"Exciting, isn't it?" asked the white noise. "Do you think he knows yet?"

Knows what? Karo was confused by the question. Then she felt a hand in her hair. Her head bent back in a parody of the spectral woman's, and for an instant she saw clearly both the woman and the man's faces. It was like looking in a fun-house mirror where reality was distorted.

"Tristam!" Karo cried. She went into shock as the white light came down over her and dropped her back into bed.

Tristam woke with a startled cry and sat up like a scalded cat.

Wait! he thought. He wasn't the scalded cat. That was 'Stein yowling indignantly from the foot of the bed where Tristam's foot had flung him.

He took three gulping breaths of air and then wiped the sweat from his face with a shaky hand. It did no appreciable good, because his palms were wet. In fact, his entire body was covered in perspiration. Bloody hell! He was too old for wet dreams. Especially ones so literally wet.

Okay, that *was* a wet dream. It had to have been. It absolutely could not have been anything else. Tristam glanced down at his body, which was bare except for a damp sheet twisted around his loins. His body had not yet settled down, and it caused quite a bulge.

He flopped back against his pillow and glared at the cat. 'Stein glared back, demanding with his glowing eyes that Tristam admit just who had woken whom.

"Oh, shut up. I apologize."

'Stein twitched a contemptuous tail and jumped off of the bed. Tristam watched his pale shadow stalk over to a wingback chair where the cat planted himself with an audible huff atop Tristam's slacks. He began kneading them with sharp claws.

"Hey! Hair but no claws," Tristam warned, but he wasn't paying much attention to the feline temper tantrum. To be honest, he was too distracted by his X-rated hallucination.

He must have been thinking about starting work in the garret as he fell asleep, because this sort of thing wasn't his usual style at all. Not a bit. Something must have prompted him to order up that kinky combo from his subconscious and ask to have it super-sized. In spite of Karo's teasing, he had never done the whole caning-in-the-classroom stuff that so much English porn was about.

The dream had started off all right and tight. He'd been at Saint Andrew's, on a beauty of a fairway, a slight breeze, mildly overcast, an adoring crowd gathered around. He was beating everyone on the leaderboard, was ahead of Tiger Woods—a sixty-four, the best game of his life, for pity's sake! It was the score of a lifetime. And who should appear but the old reprobate in the painting, Vellacourt himself, dressed in some damned weird tartan pants. He had showed up right in the middle of his swing and planted himself right in the fairway where the ball needed to go.

"I have a message from a lady," he'd said.

"What lady? And what message?" he'd said back, annoyed but also intrigued by the change in his dream's direction.

"A lady you want more than any other. She is waiting for you now in the garret. She's lonely and bored and wants to have a little match."

Nothing on earth would have lured Tristam away from such a round of golf. Nothing that is, except the message that Karo Follett was waiting in the garret for someone to come and play with her.

"Shall I stand in for you?" the old lecher had asked. When Tristam didn't answer, the ghost added speculatively, "I do kill the ladies, you know. And we look a lot alike. . . ."

"Like hell! Keep away from her!" Tristam exclaimed, throwing down his club and racing past Tiger Woods and a crowd of shocked faces. Vellacourt had just laughed and taken out a three wood.

Bon soir, mon ami," he called in pursuit.

Tristam did not consider himself a modest man, but his race for the garret—peeling off clothes and leaving them scattered all over the fairway while the media filmed and his fans stared in wonder—and also his willingness to let Karo play with him in Vellacourt's damned torture chamber, suggested that modesty had completely forsaken him. Indeed, the dream suggested that he had lost his mind and will. He'd even let her chain him to that bloody rack just so he could have her hands upon him!

So what if it was completely out of character? he argued when his conscience felt appalled. Yes, it was a bit of a jar for a right-thinking man. If he'd had any fantasies at all—okay, he'd had one or two—they'd involved laying his new assistant over the rack and pulling down those tight jeans. . . .

Tristam stopped himself and tossed away the damp sheet. Obviously, his libido was placing an express order with his subconscious. It wanted Karo Follett, and it would have her any way it could, even if this was at the expense of his sleep and nerves. Even if it had to submit to being tied down and tormented so that she would feel safe enough to venture near.

Of course, she hadn't been all that safe at the end, had she?

Tristam snorted in self-disgust that was mostly genuine. He had enjoyed turning the tables and ravishing his elf just a little too much. It wasn't civilized. Not that the dream Karo had minded. No, the little minx had driven him to it with great deliberation, even going so far as to speak French while swanking about with her little whip.

Did Karo speak French? She had never mentioned it. But surely she must if she had lived in Europe.

Tristam waved the stray thought away. It didn't matter what languages the wench spoke. What was he to do about this dashed problem—ask Karo to please trust him and have an affair with yet another boss? Ask her to be kind to a bowed-down heart before his fantasies killed him?

He didn't fancy many of her possible replies. Her lips said no way every time he got near enough to ask a question, even that night when she was weakened with wine. But her greedy eyes and tense, overheated body said something else entirely. She was conflicted—and given her past, he didn't blame her.

"So, what should I do? 'Stein, should I have a lash? Try a bit of the traditional wooing and flowers?" he asked the cat.

He'd prefer to listen to her body talk, to just . . . But he was supposedly a gentleman, a sober man and true! And also he was her employer—more rotten luck. That meant having to wait for a clear invitation from the woman before helping himself.

"Things are a bit thick, 'Stein." He scrubbed his face with an agitated hand. The cat didn't answer, just sat, shedding on his dark clothes.

But what if she never invited him? What if she was so put off by blond bosses that she never got around to making him an offer for anything? A brief fling, a bed for life, marriage—whatever she would spare, he'd take. But was she that scarred by the past bastards in her life? That heartless? That stubborn?

An odd and completely unexpected memory tickled the back of his brain. Hadn't Karo said that she would have revenge on him for the shower stunt? Something creative, she'd promised. Could she have somehow hoodooed his sleep? The minx in his dream certainly hadn't shown any signs of contrition for her torment, treating it like some kind of punishment.

No, that was crazy. This fantasy had nothing to do with Karo's possible revenge. It had been a dream. A strange one, admittedly. Powerful. But just a dream. He might just as well blame it on the late night movie or Karo's fire-lighting ghost as on some kind of ESP she might have.

He had to remember to keep it separate from reality, this dream. It hadn't really happened, no matter how real it felt.

Tristam groaned and draped an arm over his eyes. The dream had been a very effective punishment, if only Karo knew. Was he going to suffer this way every night from now until she put him out of his misery? *If* she put him out of his misery. Well, he'd be dashed if he was going to do any more gesture-making in his sleep. He just couldn't do it again. They had to take turns with this. If she invited his dream-self back to the garret, he'd just say no thank you.

Not that it had hurt, the concessions he'd made. No, actually, it had been—But he wasn't going to think about it! It was just too . . . too inflammatory. How was he going to face her over a plate of eggs without blushing? The image was going to stick in his head for a long time to come . . . and if she had even the smallest peep into his fevered mind, she'd most likely pack her bags and head for the west coast on the next flight from Richmond. Good girls didn't go for stuff like this.

And if she didn't head out, but instead kept peeping into his mind? He'd end up chaining her to a rack and biting little pieces out of her.

It was imperative that he cool down a tad before facing her again. They were supposed to start on clearing out the garret this morning, for pity sakes! No, this just wouldn't do at all. The two of them in the garret with these images in his head . . . ?

Tristam rubbed at his cricked up neck and began choosing his words for their next meeting. They needed the requisite amount of teasing, but nothing that would provoke any embarrassing memories and make him betray himself to her with stupid blushes—or, worse yet, a reaction a little further south. In the morning he would tell Karo that he needed to go down to Florida and have a little chin-wag with Clarice Vellacourt. While he was there he'd eat some great food, maybe look up an old friend or two and maybe try scratching this insane itch with one of them, just to get back in balance.

His groin throbbed in disappointment.

"You're joking," he said. But it stabbed him again in answer. "Swell."

At the moment, his body seemed pretty emphatic about wanting Karo Follett and no one else. No gray-eyed brunette substitute would do. He'd bet it might even roll over and play dead when approached by another woman. It could happen, the way his life was going. And why not? Wasn't Karo Follett what his brain wanted, not just his body? So, who was he fooling with this talk of itch scratching? No one.

But, it was so unfair. To be unmoved by all other women at the age of thirty-seven! It was all Karo Follett's fault.

Tristam sighed heavily and stared at the ceiling. It was beginning to pass from night black to dawn gray outside, and he could now see the outline of the decorative crown molding that ringed the room. He called up Karo's face, not as she had been in his dreams but staring at him over a cup of morning coffee as she enthused about some new project she had thought up, or some tacky treasure she had found to add to their growing display. She was lovely—so easy on the eyes, even in the morning—smashing company, brilliant with the tourist wheeze and . . .

Well, she was perfect, damn it! He'd found her; he'd keep her. She was *his*. It was sheer dog-in-the-manger stuff, the same territorial reaction that had sent him pounding off the golf course and up the stairs rather than let Vellacourt get there before him, but frankly he didn't much care if it wasn't properly twenty-first century thinking to feel this way. He just did.

He hadn't a clue where this attraction would eventually lead, but for the first time in his life he'd been shot by Cupid's gold-tipped arrow and he wasn't going anywhere—and neither was she—until they got together. He wasn't like the other unscrupulous men in her life, and she'd eventually admit that she was smitten, too.

Until then, if that meant nightly torment . . . well, he would take it like a man. For a while. Tristam punched his pillow into a new shape and rolled over on his stomach, squashing his remaining tumescence in the feather tick.

Surely she would succumb soon. On the marriageability scale—which had admittedly changed through the years—he still ranked right below a titled lord and well above a doctor, rock star or Hollywood actor, the last two having notoriously high divorce rates due to drug use and infidelity.

Even as a one-night stand he ranked pretty high—though probably below rock stars and actors, he admitted fairly.

"Please, woman," he muttered into his soggy pillow sham. "You've spoiled me for other females. Have a little mercy!"

*Then away out in the woods I heard that kind of a
sound that a ghost makes when it wants to tell about
something that's on its mind and can't make itself
understood, and so can't rest easy in its grave, and
has to go about that way every night grieving.*
—Mark Twain from *Huckleberry Finn*

Chapter Eight

Karo looked up from the myriad knobs on the
espresso machine and drew a deep, steadying
breath. Tristam was here. She could sense the
pheromones rushing up her nose as she inhaled
the delicate smell of vanilla that overlaid the pun-
gent coffee beans she had loaded in the grinder.
This was the real McCoy, the substance to last
night's sensual shadow. In the flesh, he was enough
to cause a heart attack. A lovely one.

"Morning." She turned and offered him a
smile, hoping that her cheeks didn't betray her
thoughts.

Tristam had checked himself abruptly in the
doorway when he saw her bent over the espresso
machine and momentarily considered the craven
course of running the other way before she spotted him, but once she looked up and offered a
tight smile of welcome, he stepped bravely into
the room and forced an answering grimace.

"Good morning. Will she go for you? Or would you like me to have a lash?"

"Be my guest." Karo raised a hand to her head. Her temples were softly throbbing and her stomach was a bit upset. "I only got as far as grinding the beans. I haven't been able to decide which knob to try next." She stepped back from the gleaming brass and cleared her throat. "Tristam? Are you set on going up to the . . . the garret today?"

She could see a red stain racing up the back of his neck. She recognized it from the night before—

But that was ridiculous! That had only been a dream. Hadn't it?

"Um . . . Well, actually . . . Why do you ask?" He didn't turn to face her, a strange lapse of manners on his part. Tristam as a habit preferred eye contact when speaking.

"No definite reason," she lied. "I have a bit of a headache and I wanted to do a little reading in the library."

"Reading?" He reached for the pitcher of milk she had filled and plunged in the thin, stainless steel nozzle. Steam began to hiss and spit as it frothed the cold beverage.

"Yes. In Vellacourt's journals."

"What?" The pitcher slipped but was recovered before the milk was upset. Tristam kept his back to her.

"If you don't mind," she allowed, watching him grope for the correct knob. His dexterous fingers were unusually clumsy. "I, uh, I had a dream last night."

"A dream?" Tristam's voice was constricted almost to the point of squeaking into an unfamiliar octave. His shoulders were taut enough to bounce quarters off them.

"Is something wrong?" Karo asked—reluctantly, but she did ask.

"Wrong?" he questioned, feeling craven but unwilling to rush upon his fate if it could possibly be avoided.

"Yes, wrong. As in, not right."

"Yes. Well . . . quite. I mean, why do you ask?"

"Because you've scalded the milk at least three times long as usual and it's dripping onto the floor."

"Oh." Tristam set the pitcher down and reached for a tea towel. He still hadn't turned around. If Karo didn't know better, she would think that he was embarrassed about her . . . well, her double's behavior last night. But that wasn't possible. The only way he could know about last night was if it had been real, if he had actually . . .

"Oh, no!" she blurted, too horrified to be discreet. "It wasn't a dream at all, was it? That horrid old letch! He went and got you, too! I told him not to. I told him . . . If he wasn't dead, I'd kill him."

Tristam whipped around and stared at her with horrified eyes. Steam boiled into the air. He was definitely flushed three shades beyond normal hue, and it wasn't the espresso machine's fault.

"Do you mean . . . ?" he wheezed, dropping the towel.

"Yes!" Karo buried her face in her hands and began to laugh as a vent to her hysteria. A heart attack was imminent. It would finally happen: she would actually die of embarrassment.

"Karo!" Tristam recovered his voice, and it was horrified. "Dear girl, you aren't crying, are you? I assure you, it was nothing! I am at your service completely. Really! I don't know when I've had a better time."

Karo lifted her head. "Liar. I don't know anyone more fastidious than you. The whole thing had to have been repugnant."

He was fastidious, but only an innocent could image that the experience was repugnant.

"No. No, *really*. Karo." He sighed, bending to retrieve the towel and turn off the steam. "Are you laughing at me, you wretched girl?"

"No. I'm sorry. I've always laughed when I get hysterical. It's no more helpful than crying, but less disconcerting to others."

Tristam stared at her. His hectic color began to subside. "I wouldn't say that. Inappropriate laughter is most disconcerting, let me assure you. And this is most highly inappropriate."

"Is it?" Karo put her hands back over her eyes. She added to herself, "But, then, you didn't think you were going crazy, seeing ghosts when none were there. Bad as this is, it's still a relief. I'm not crazy after all."

"It's not bad, it's . . . Uh, ghosts? Like . . . *ghosts*?" Tristam's voice rose as he finally processed her words.

"Yes, ghosts. You've heard of them? Popular in literature and lore? The Flying Dutchman. The Wild Hunt. Headless Horsemen. Banshees. Poltergeists, restless spirits . . ." she enumerated.

"But ghosts? Here? In this house?"

"No, in Burma! Of course here. Think it through. It wasn't just a random dream we shared, some kind of ESP or hallucination because of the underdone potato. Couldn't you tell it was Hugh? Who took you up there to the garret?"

"Er, a dream Vellacourt did rather suggest I go on up. Blighter interrupted a damn fine golf game, too," Tristam added indignantly.

Karo strangled some more laughter and took a grip on her fraying nerves.

Tristam frowned. "You aren't really suggesting . . . Karo! My dear, please say that you aren't suggesting what you're suggesting. Why can't this just be a shared dream? Or a bit of the extra-sensory stuff? You can't really mean that creature—"

"But I do, Tristam." She lowered her hands, all laughter dying. "I mean just that. I've talked to Hugh three times now. I've felt him hanging around more than that. We have a real live—or dead—ghost here at Belle Ange. You even recognized who he was when you saw him in your dream."

"But . . . do you mean that he was *actually there* last night?" Tristam was again horrified. "In the garret? The whole time!"

"I'm afraid so. He even said . . ." Karo trailed off.

"Said what?" Tristam's tone was ominous.

"Well, he suggested that . . . that, um . . . Never mind. It isn't important. The main thing is that we have a ghost here."

"I wouldn't say that that's the *main* thing."

Their two flushed faces stared at one another across the brass espresso engine as the steamed milk cooled between them.

"But it didn't really happen. To our bodies," Karo insisted. "It was an illusion."

Silence.

"Alright. First things first. A ghost," Tristam said at last, mercifully breaking the uncomfortable quiet. "Then, by all means, let us adjourn to the library and try to find out exactly what he wants. That was the first place you saw him, yes?"

"I know what he wants—and it isn't his diary." Karo stared bravely into her would-be love's annoyed golden eyes. "He's lonely and he wants tourists to play with."

"To *play* with?"

Karo flushed at Tristam's outraged tone. "Not that way! At least, I don't *think* . . . I hope . . . Good heavens! Do you believe he might . . . ? But he can't do anything if they're awake."

Her sentences were disconnecting at crucial, embarrassing points, but Tristam easily translated her incoherence. "I don't know, but we had better find out, hadn't we? I've only skimmed the other family members' journals. I think it may be time to look more closely at the family history."

"I have a headache and my stomach is jittery," Karo complained.

"Oh, sorry. I have just the thing." Tristam turned toward the cupboard and got down a small glass and a couple of bottles. Karo didn't see what he was mixing, but she wasn't surprised when he put a frothy pink drink in front of her. "Try this. It's a corpse-reviver. I had it off a publican in Dublin."

"It doesn't have yogurt, does it?" she asked. "I hate yogurt."

"No." He waited until she swallowed a mouthful before adding, "It's an antacid and a splash of bourbon."

"Ew! Tristam!" But she stopped there. The drink was ghastly, but her stomach was beginning to feel healthier.

"Better? Then let us go exploring." He reached out and took her arm in a firm grip, propelling her toward the library. The touch was not exactly sweet, but Karo enjoyed it anyway.

"Um, Tristam?" she asked as he hustled her down the dark hall. "Did you mean what you just said—about never having had a better time? Because it was great in a really strange way, but that just isn't my normal . . ."

"I should hope not," he said, blushing. "Let's drop it for now."

"But—"

"Don't tempt me, Karo Follett. I am trying to do what's right, but you are skating on very thin ice. We have to think about this. More than that, I suspect that we're going to . . . well, we're going to have to *do* something about this." He shook his head and changed the subject. "Let's see. I've heard iron is supposed to keep ghosts in their graves. And you can pour salt on the thresholds and paint the doors blue to confuse the spirits," he mumbled to himself. "And then there's always exorcism."

"Exorcism? But, Tristam! You're not thinking clearly—"

"I've had a shock. I expect I'll be more coherent in a moment or so." He thrust open the library door, ducked under the low arch and marched inside at a dignified crouch. "Damn doorway! I'll just get on the horn to my old chum, Liam McDonnel. I believe his family has a hereditary ghost. He'll have some ideas about what to do with Vellacourt."

"But Tristam," she tried again. "Why do we have to do anything to him?"

"What?" He stared at her.

"Look. Hugh does a lot more than just wander the corridors at night dragging clanking chains—"

"He certainly does! The cheeky bastard."

"But he's not some trigger of disaster. He's not an omen, like a death coach or a baying hound or a banshee."

"How do you know? I think he's one of the Riders of the Apocalypse."

He wasn't taking this the way she'd expected. Now that it was out in the open and she knew she wasn't insane, Karo was beginning to think quite differently. "Nonsense!" she expostulated. "Tristam, where's your sense of avarice? You're not thinking. We . . . we have a ghost. One that can *do* things." She spaced out her words and enunciated clearly. "Like Mrs. Muir's ghost. Like Sleepy Hollow."

"Not exactly. Vellacourt is a reprobate Peeping Tom who would spend his time hanging about the ladies' loo peeking up women's skirts."

"Well, I know that. But nobody else does. As far as the rest of the world is concerned, he'd just be a regular old Southern haunt."

"But last night," he objected.

"Last night he was just trying to be helpful. He thought we needed a romantic nudge. He won't do it again." It was more hope than promise, but Karo made her voice firm. And loud. With any luck, Hugh would heed her warning. If he didn't, he might well end up spending eternity in the great spiritual void—assuming exorcism could truly work.

"Helpful! Romantic nudge!" Tristam tottered a few steps and collapsed into a chair. He laid a hand over his eyes. The gesture was pure theater, and Karo knew that everything was going to be fine after all. Tristam went on in a hollow voice: "I suppose that *you* could call it so. You were in control. Of course, you found my presence so disturbing that you set me on a perch and hooded me like some blasted bird of prey . . . !"

"Oh, stop it. You're embarrassing me. And I— the *real* me—didn't do it. Even if it had been, it wasn't odious. Not like I thought it would be. It was . . ."

"Kinky." Tristam's fingers parted, and a golden eye looked her way. Karo stared at the ceiling and willed herself to fight off a blush, and he seemed to read her mind: "You *should* blush, my girl. That was very strange, and you obviously enjoyed it entirely too much."

She defended herself. "I already have blushed— several times. But that is neither here nor there. We were discussing Vellacourt and the tourist trade. We can talk about the other business later."

"Oh, can we? I think that we should talk about it now."

"Absolutely not." Karo was emphatic. "We have work to do—you have a deadline, remember—and I can't concentrate when I'm . . ." She swallowed.

"And so?"

She huffed. "And so we can't be having a—"

"Tête-à-tête on our sexual preferences and hang-ups? But why not?" he asked wistfully, even though her logic made perfect sense. His desire was overwhelming his practicality. He was thinking of everything he wanted from Karo and trying to forget Vellacourt's involvement. "It's bound to be more fun than anything in these blasted journals. . . ."

She didn't seem willing to play along. *"Because,"* she spluttered. "I already told you. I don't do on-the-job romances. It's a rule for me. Besides . . . there's Hugh. I'm not an exhibitionist. Two's company but three's an orgy."

Tristam stared at her flushed face and agitated hands as she avoided both his touch and gaze. "If I fired you, would you run away with me?"

"If you fire me, I'll end up in debtors' prison—or worse yet, back at home with my parents. Besides, you'll never get all this work done without me." Modesty was a virtue but not when overdone, and Karo couldn't afford any false modesty. Neither could Tristam. Not if they were going to keep things safe and balanced.

"Perish the thought." Her employer stood suddenly and squared his shoulders. "Very well, then. As our cup overfloweth with woe anyway, let's get down to business. I just want you to keep in mind that we don't know Hugh can't follow us when we leave. What if we are never rid of him?"

Hugh wouldn't follow them. Why would he? She shook her head. "He won't. He likes it here. Maybe he has to stay here. So, yes, let's get to work. Let's go back to normal," she said, relieved to finally be able to leave the subject of last night.

"Are we ready to send something off to the printer? We've only four weeks left." Tristam's voice was calm but he strafed the walls and ceiling with his gaze. She knew who he was looking for. Karo was just glad that he'd never looked at her that way.

"Uh . . ." She pulled her wits together. "We're ready—or we will be by next week. Except for photos."

"No photographs!" he commanded. "Unless Vellacourt agrees to pose with the china."

"I could ask," Karo offered.

Tristam goggled, momentarily startled out of his erect posture. "What!"

"I said that I could ask Hugh to pose."

"Good God! That was a jest. Don't even speak of that devil. I don't want to encourage him. Or any ghost-hunting nuts."

Karo wasn't certain if she should take Tristam seriously. "I have a photo of him on my cell phone. It isn't real clear, but we could use it. Want to see?"

"No. At least, not right now." He continued to stare at her.

"Well, it's an idea. Ghost-hunting nuts would pay money to see him," she pointed out. Her thinking had evolved over time and she was no longer worrying about what the academics would say.

"It's a terrible idea! We want a tourist attraction not a freak show. If we offer proof positive of a ghost, every nut-job from both sides of the Atlantic would show up here for séances and spirit-raisings. There'd be animal sacrifices," he went on, warming to his Cassandraic theme. "Soon the National Enquirer will be camped on our doorstep, and the historical societies and the DAR will demand that we close our doors or be run out of town on a rail. We'd never make it into Frommer's or Michelin, and—"

"Okay! Okay! I get the point," she interrupted. "Don't be so melodramatic. We'll be a little subtler about cashing in." Karo took Tristam's abandoned chair and reached for a pad of paper. "Do we mention anything about him in our cookbook—throw in a recipe for ghost punch or something?"

"No. We handle all this"—he waved a hand, indicating both the architecture and the graveyard that lay just beyond the north wall—"by word of mouth. If I can't get rid of him first," Tristam added under his breath.

"Okay." Karo scribbled a note. "When is that cleaning crew coming back? The floors need waxing."

"Next week. We need to have the garret empty by then. We have a termite inspection on the thirtieth." Tristam walked behind the desk and consulted his calendar. "The roofers have their inspection the next day—Halloween. And then the plasterers will be back to finish the repairs in the west wing. Also, I've called in a firm to deal with the largest of the chandeliers. The rigging has rusted. I put up a ladder and took a few swipes at the thing but even WD40 didn't knock those things loose. I decided that it would be best to call in a professional before I fell off the ladder and became an example of Newtonian physics in action."

"That's best. Falling apples are one things, falling bodies another. Shall I schedule Miles?"

"Miles?" Tristam looked up.   ·

"The photographer. For the postcards," she reminded him. "Not the brochure."

"Oh, yes. He can come anytime after the exterior work is done." Tristam nodded, but continued to stare at her.

"What is it?" she asked, laying down her pen.

"We really have only one job left, excepting a tour of the lower basements."

"Yeah? What's that?" But she had a feeling she knew what he would say. Their plan to avoid it just wasn't going to work.

"The garret."

"Oh." Karo looked away.

"We could do it separately. Want to toss a coin to see who gets stuck with it? Or . . ."

Karo could hear the laughter in Tristam's voice and allowed herself to glance back at him. His eyes were gleaming. "Or?" she asked warily.

"Or do you think that you can keep your hands off of me for an entire afternoon?"

In response, Karo threw her pen at him.

They tackled the room together. In spite of their concern, Vellacourt tactfully made no appearance. They were only hampered in their task by their own memories and febrile imaginations, which they wisely kept to themselves.

After much debate, they decided to leave the room as it was, save for some cleaning. Vellacourt's toys had to go somewhere, seeing as Clarice didn't want any of it destroyed, and this was as good a spot as any. The garret would be straightened—it was surprisingly clean, and Karo wondered if it was Vellacourt's ghost having kept it tidy or something else—and then they would install a sturdy lock to discourage visitors from the tour. They would bring up Vellacourt's more eclectic journals and inventions and put the whole lot under lock and key. Everything would remain safe and sound.

Karo hoped the plan would please the ghost. She didn't put much stock in Tristam's suggestion that Vellacourt would like to be sent to an eternal rest; their overly friendly haunt wasn't spending his semicorporeal moments leading them after his moldering bones or toward lost gold, nor was he spinning tales of murder and vengeance. Nor was he trying to drive them off with clanking chains or ghostly moans. As spirits went, he was a very quiet soul. The only way she ever knew he was watching her was when her body temperature took an unexpected rise. When she explained the phenomenon, Tristam was dismayed. That he was hot instead of cold seemed suggestive of bad things.

The moments of feeling the ghost's presence were uncomfortable for Karo, both because of the betraying heat washing through her body and because of Tristam's silent anger when he noticed. Jealousy, she could tell. It was weird, in her opinion, his annoyance, and it was making her uncomfortable. She explained that she thought it was the lightning strike that had done this to her, opening her to seeing Hugh's spirit, but that only made Tristam more suspicious. He suggested Hugh had arranged for her to be struck. Karo didn't mention that the ghost had said something to this effect.

One thing that was gone from the room were the candles. There were candles all through the house, in bottles, in saucers, in candelabras and sticks. They all scared Karo, who could too easily imagine accidentally setting the old house ablaze. *Flameless candles for the rest of the house*, she wrote in her notebook, planning more things to buy. Better a fortune spent on batteries than a fire.

She also found a cedar chest shoved into the darkest corner of the room. Mothballs—the odor of things past, perfume to the historian—wafted out of the chest when Karo lifted the lid. Inside she found a scrap of yellowed linen that she was certain had belonged to Eustacie, and that was the very one featured in the previous night's X-rated experience. Karo decided not to show it to Tristam.

They took a break around five and stepped outside for a breath of air while they surveyed the Campion brothers' recent work. The grounds were greatly improved over the jungle they'd been on the day of Karo's arrival; the overgrown plants were slapped back from the house, and the red stony soil was buried under acres of new green sod that rolled on, smooth as a velvet croquet green. Which in fact it was. The first scheduled tournament would be played the last week in November.

Filtered sunlight filled up the mansion's usually shady hollow like pale wine and gilded everything with an autumnal touch. It made a nice change from the dusty daylight on the third floor.

Karo and Tristam strolled out to the center courtyard where the laborers were currently working at restoring the formal gardens. A mighty winged gryphon at the center of a rediscovered fountain, carved of stone, had been scraped clean of its undignified bird droppings, and the small, cascading pools had been emptied of a decade's clutter to again run quiet and clear over his stony toenails.

They took a seat on a stone bench held aloft by two pairs of scantily clad nymphs that looked to Karo like a quartet of cross-dressing Mr. Universes doing the clean and jerk. While the ugly cherubs were far too muscular for modern taste, all that concerned Karo was that they were quite capable of supporting the combined weight of any four humans on their fat ankles and bulky arms.

She inhaled deeply of the perfumed air. It was as potent and intoxicating as modeler's glue. There were roses still blooming in the dappled shade. Autumn Damasks, the shrub roses of ancient Rome. Rosa Gallica, emblem of the Persians some three thousand years before. Moss roses from China, their thick pink blossoms drenched in scent. Albas, Bourbons, Musks, Rugosas, and arching sprays of the red ramblers that had attached themselves to the south side of the house.

"I'm glad they didn't spoil it," Karo said softly, so as to not disturb several nearby droning bees.

Tristam's arm settled casually around her waist.

It was the first touch he had allowed himself since that morning. "It is a bit like the Secret Garden isn't it?"

"Yes. Or some other fairy tale." Despite her best intentions, she allowed her head to rest lightly against Tristam's dusty shoulder. Her eyes closed. Her tired brain went to lunch.

"Better, I think." His neck bent, and his soft lips brushed over her mouth. "Sweet."

"Vanilla," she agreed before returning his delicate kiss.

It was their first real kiss, and everything felt exactly right to Karo. Her ambivalence faded. The arms that had been so rough the night before, dream or not, were now as gentle as the afternoon sun. They coaxed her closer, and his mouth continued its light, magical seduction.

Tristam's golden hair felt like silk beneath her fingers, and he was warmer than the late afternoon light reflecting off the marble bench. The knot of tension that had been clenched tight against the memory of their dream released its clutch and Karo relaxed completely into his embrace; the rich scent of vanilla and rose musk overcame any objection her brain might have raised.

There was a soft breeze that followed Tristam's fingertips as they walked the length of her arms with a butterfly touch. Karo shivered and moved deeper into his arms. Her own hands stayed buried in his golden hair as she returned his kisses with growing fervor.

Heat was blossoming inside of her, a slow unfolding of red desire that was new and yet strangely familiar. It made her skin prickle. She wanted to put her hands inside his shirt and touch his golden flesh, which flexed beneath her fingers. She wanted to press an open mouth against the pulse in his throat and taste his skin as she had the night before. She wanted to . . .

He stopped. Slowly he pulled away from her lips. Only an inch of space separated them, yet Karo felt like her skin had been peeled back, leaving her body naked and chilled in the failing light. The lovely heat that had flooded her body folded back in on itself and disappeared with an inaudible whimper. She moaned in soft protest and leaned forward. Tristam's arms tightened briefly in comfort but again he set her away from him.

"Why?" she asked, shivering.

"It's getting late, and the mosquitoes are out."

"I don't care."

"You would in the morning." Tristam stood and helped her to her feet. "Anyway, it's for the best that we stop this now."

"It is? I don't think it is," she grumbled.

Tristam put his arm around her and guided their steps toward the house. Karo resisted the urge to sneak a hand under his shirt and play with the downy hair covering the small of his back, but it was hard to do so—much harder than she liked to admit.

"No? Well, perhaps I am thinking more clearly than you. There are two very good reasons for being sensible."

"I can't think of a one."

He chuckled. "That is indeed flattery."

"If you turn into a typical male pig I'll belt you," Karo warned.

"I believe you, love, and I wouldn't dream of being a typical male anything. For that reason, I am going to respect your wish about an on-the-job romance for a while longer."

"You are?" Karo could hear the dismay in her voice and made an effort to pull herself out the sensual miasma that had coated her brain. Was all this heat from arousal, or was there another cause? She was distressed to find that she couldn't tell. She just knew she was acting different than usual.

"Yes," he admitted unhappily. "Much as I'll suffer for it."

Karo sighed and mentally chided herself. It wasn't fair to make Tristam be the sole guardian of her rules. Still . . . "Well! What a time to decide to do things my way. Why weren't you this agreeable about my suggestions about the Limoges?" she demanded as they started walking and her higher brain functions returned.

That struck just the right chord and made them both laugh.

As soon as the house was in sight, Tristam dropped his arm from her shoulders. He scanned the windows, as though expecting to find someone watching them.

"Respect of my request—is that the only reason for this newfound nobility?" she asked. She had her own suspicions about his sudden reluctance to make love and could understand them. Telling Tristam over the course of the morning about Vellacourt's several appearances since her arrival had made the incidents sound appalling, and now that the specter had taken an interest in their love life . . .

"No," he admitted, proving her correct. "It's that damned ghoul."

"Ghost," she corrected. "Let's not make him any worse than he is."

"He's a bloody albatross. I can practically feel him peeking through the bushes and licking his chops."

Karo knew what he meant. She felt the ghost's presence far more keenly than she imagined Tristam did. The only difference was, while Tristam was kissing her, she'd been far too wrapped up in the moment to know if her feelings were pure lust or some manifestation of Hugh and his will. Tristam had obviously been less distracted by the experience.

She tried not to scowl at the unwelcome thought. When a man kissed her, she preferred to be the only thing on his mind.

"In fact . . ." Tristam continued, making a sudden hard right. His right arm flew out to tug her along in his wake, pulling her like a string at the end of a high-performance kite.

"Where are we going?" Karo asked, but it was a pointless question. She could guess where they were headed. The only thing at this end of the property was the family graveyard. There was a slave's cemetery somewhere else, but it had boasted only wooden crosses that had rotted away, and now the location was forgotten.

"To find the old reprobate's mausoleum," Tristam answered. "I want to leave some garlic on his tomb."

"Hawthorne," she corrected him again. "Garlic is for vampires."

Tristam thrust open the iron gate that separated the living and the dead. It should have squealed but the Campions had been busy in there as well. The old stones and Gothic temples no longer looked eerie now that the creepers had been shorn back and the headstones pushed straight. Things looked better, but there was yet some proof that weeds had been at work for decades, pushing their way into every crack in every headstone and marker. Karo chose not to dwell on the fact that plants in the cemetery were better fed than the rest of the garden—except in one corner.

"Where is he?" Tristam growled, prowling among the stones.

Karo called his name worriedly, looking about for snakes and spiders before following. "You aren't really thinking of doing anything, are you? I mean, we can't go around desecrating graves or anything like that."

"Who said anything about desecration? I just want to give the pervert a taste of his own medicine. Maybe it'll teach him some respect if we take a peek at his naked bones. Maybe I'll take them hostage as an assurance of good behavior."

"Don't say that!" she pleaded, hurrying after him. "That's a horrible thought."

"Well, at the very least I want to see that he actually has some bones to peek at. That's the main cause of classical hauntings, don't you know. Missing bones."

"You have a point, I suppose," she conceded unhappily. His explanation felt correct on a visceral level. "But let's not do anything drastic. We don't want to piss him off."

"Speak for yourself," Tristam retorted. "But maybe he wants his bones back. We could be doing him a favor. There's Valperga." Her employer pointed. "What a hideous angel! It looks just like the pilaster on the second floor. Is it crying because it's stuck on her grave until kingdom come?"

Karo stared at the ill-favored cherub. It did bare a strong resemblance to the gargoyles clinging to the parapets of Notre Dame, only not so noble of brow. She remarked, "Bad taste should be carried to the grave but no further. I wouldn't want that squatting on my grave for all eternity."

They walked on slowly. They were running out of possible sites where Hugh's remains could be resting, and Karo found herself growing every bit as anxious as Tristam to find Vellacourt's tomb and make sure his bones were where they ought to be. The thought of Hugh's remains going astray made her uncomfortable.

They reached the end of the wrought-iron enclosure and a grim-faced Tristam slowly turned her way. He pointed to a heap of white rubble that had collapsed in an untidy pile. There was a great deal of it, enough to build a wall. Or a mausoleum. And nothing grew there. It was as though the earth had been sewn with salt. It did not cheer Karo to find that the ground around it was laced with cypress roots and rocks and was obviously unseeded by any subterranean graves: Hugh had been buried aboveground.

"He's not here. Maybe his marker was here. . . ."

"No. There isn't so much as a trace of a name on this stone." Tristam added to himself, "This has to be it, though. Why isn't he here anymore? This is where they buried him, I'm certain. Where else could he be?"

"Maybe the grave was moved when the mausoleum collapsed. It was over three hundred years old."

"This is most irregular, though. I have no notes of his being moved from his mausoleum—or of its collapse. Some mention should be made in some document."

"Uh-oh. It kind of looks like lightning hit the grave." Karo stared at the pile of shattered stone and felt the small hairs on the back of her neck rising. She had seen similar scorch marks on the road after the lightning strike. She spun around and began reviewing headstones. "Where's Eustacie's grave? Shouldn't she be here, too?"

"Eustacie La Belle?"

"Maybe that's what Hugh wants," Karo continued. "Eustacie. Remember that story of the lovers' graves parted by the mother-in-law tree? Maybe they only moved his bones."

The two of them stared at each other. It was a famous ghost story of the Tidewater region. According to it, parted lovers could sometimes lead to hauntings.

"I don't have any records of her being buried here. She was a lot younger than Vellacourt. She might have married after he was gone."

"But he'd have wanted her here, wouldn't he? In spite of some mere husband or his own children's objections. He would have made arrangements for her burial."

"Would Valperga have respected them? I confess to skepticism," Tristam pointed out.

"She's isn't here. Tristam, I've been having a—"

"Maybe she's in the slave cemetery. Frankly, I'm a lot more worried about Hugh's remains. If he has gone missing . . . This is Valperga's doing, I'll bet. She really hated the old man. She'd have gladly booted them both out of the family crypt."

"And separated them."

"And maybe knocked the whole thing down." Tristam kicked at a white stone. It didn't budge. The fallen blocks were too heavy to move casually. No, Valperga couldn't have done this. Only a tornado or a tractor could have. Or maybe repeated lightning strikes, if they were very, very powerful. Could Hugh, in the midst of a temper tantrum, have done it himself?

"Not to sound melodramatic, but do you suppose she had the slaves rebury him at a crossroads or dump him in unhallowed ground?" Karo shivered with sudden cold.

"Very likely. That or quicklime. Damn and blast! Now what the devil are we going to do? If we can't find his bones, we'll never be rid of him!"

"No," Karo agreed. "And I wouldn't count on Hugh being so obliging as to show us where he's buried. I think he's quite happy as he is and not anxious to see the hereafter."

"We'll just see about that. There are ways to compel spirits to talk. . . ." Tristam's jaw thrust out belligerently. "Come on. Back to the library. We are going to take that room apart. I want to know exactly what the old bat was up to. There must be records somewhere."

"The *Malleus Maleficarum*," Karo reminded him. "We haven't found that yet, and I bet you it's at fault one way or another. It probably gave Valperga the idea of moving him. It might be key to figuring this whole thing out. In fact, I've heard of spirits being bound to objects rather than houses. Maybe she decided to try her hand at magic."

"I suspect you are correct. There must be a clause in the will about keeping the book here at Belle Ange—perpetual torture. I should have seen it before. There has to be a good reason why Clarice won't let that book out of the house if we find it. She's usually as avaricious and unsentimental as I am. If she could, she'd sell it in a minute."

"I notice that she doesn't live here. Did she ever? Do you think she knows about him?" A locust began to chirp. Other night sounds were beginning, too.

He paused, thinking. "I'm certain she does. But it's nice to think that we might be able to escape the old ghoul by moving to Florida."

"Would *she* conspire to do something so cruel, keep a spirit from its rest?"

"Maybe," he mused. "Clarice likes money. If it was a condition of inheritance, sure, she might very well go along with it. And she might not know that there's anything she could do to lay a ghost. It isn't a normal kind of pest control problem."

Tristam's words were reasonable, but Karo was suddenly pretty sure that she didn't like Clarice Vellacourt. "Maybe the *Maleficarum* is the only thing holding Hugh to this part of the world. Maybe the book has to stay or he escapes." Karo was appalled at the suppositions that were popping into her brain—and what it meant if she were right and someone removed the tome. The vision of eternal pursuit by a bored Hugh Vellacourt was all too easy to imagine.

Tristam seemed to feel the same. "Hell and damnation, you've got the pitch. Without it he might be able travel without let or hindrance. Irish banshees certainly do, at least in repute. They can supposedly even visit the New World by traveling over the land bridge."

Karo had a sudden thought. "I wonder if we're misjudging Valperga. Maybe it was some kind of affection that made her keep him around. They were family after all." Karo slapped at a mosquito. They were growing in number as the light died.

"If it was her idea," Tristam said, as he again took her arm, "I think we can count on it being something else entirely than affection. Self-defense. Revenge, even. I can just see her chortling over a gory plan to imprison Vellacourt at Belle Ange for all eternity. She's probably still laughing somewhere in the beyond."

"Maybe. I just wish I knew if Hugh has a plan of his own."

"What?"

"A plan. For us. For himself."

"Can ghosts have plans?" Tristam looked appalled but Karo didn't notice. She was busy taking a long look around the wooded estate and remembered the way she had felt on the day of her arrival. There had been a great deal of anticipation in the air before the lightning strike, and a feeling of guidance, of being lured. Had she been enticed from her car for a specific reason? Hugh said he wanted to talk to her, but why? "I just wonder who's really having the last laugh here," Karo added softly. "Valperga might have thought chaining a spirit was punishment, but I don't think Hugh minds. Maybe, if she didn't do it out of affection . . . I wonder if he manipulated her into doing it."

"I'm going to pray to every god in every pantheon that you are wrong. If he's that clever, we're in terrible trouble."

We shall die in darkness and be buried in the rain.
—Edna St. Vincent Millay from
"Justice Denied in Massachusetts"

Chapter Nine

"We must find that book, and the only place we haven't looked is the basement," Tristam said as Karo set the grocery bag on the counter. In need of comfort, she had borrowed his car and immediately gone to the local market. It was small by most grocer standards, but they stocked all the legal perversions. Karo had returned with wine, donuts and potato chips.

"But . . ." She glanced at the window. The light was nearly gone. Her reasons for not wanting to search for the book at night would sound silly, given that Hugh had manifested more often during the day, but she was very reluctant to attempt anything once the sun was down. The dream had been one heck of a big manifestation.

"No, we won't do it tonight," Tristam assured her, sensing her fear. "The basement goes on forever and it hasn't much in the way of light. The Campions have been setting up some outdoor lights along the driveway. We'll get them to run something external down into the basement."

"I suppose we'll have to gloss over all of the

reasons," Karo said unhappily, thinking of the outside world's response to Hugh.

"Gloss? Not even marine varnish would make this look shiny. No, this is something we keep to ourselves to our dying day. Every bloody bit of it. We'll just tell the Campions that we're looking for old wine bottles or something. They are fairly incurious as a rule."

Thinking specifically of what her parents might say about her brush with ghosts and witchcraft, Karo could only agree that silence was the best option.

Though it called for some willpower, Tristam and Karo went to their separate beds just after ten o'clock and stayed apart that night. Hugh did not trouble them with dreams, perhaps because neither of them slept much.

They rose early the next morning and, after coffee and toast, Tristam went down to the basement with the Campions to ascertain what might be done to shed some light in that heretofore unilluminated netherworld. Karo did the dishes while the men talked wiring, and then she tried her best to find Hugh by wandering through the house and waiting for a hot flash that never came. Was the ghost evading her? Maybe they actually were on the right track. Or perhaps—and this was a horrible thought—he was hiding in her shadow, a shade within a shade. Watching but not helping.

Time limped slowly and then dropped to its knees and began to crawl. Still Tristam didn't appear. Hugh remained invisible, too, and Karo began to feel guilty about their proposed endeavor.

She returned to the kitchen because it was the sanest room in the house. Her sudden three-sixty, her internal defense of Hugh Vellacourt was impossible to explain, especially as she didn't understand her own feelings. The whole thing, from beginning to end, sounded like the silliest gothic romance, which no one would believe—assuming she ever breathed a word of it to anyone, which wasn't likely. So, didn't she want this ghost out of her life? Why was she flip-flopping every time she thought of him?

Karo's brain worked in secret, her internal logic a language no one else spoke. Until Tristam. He did have the knack for following her unspoken thoughts. Great minds and all that.

But not this time. Hugh had clearly crossed a line with Tristam, and her boss was not going to be deterred from attempting to rid himself of the ghost. What was the last thing he'd said before they'd gone to bed? *I don't approve of you and Hugh.*

"There is no 'Hugh and I,' and don't couple our names please," she had answered with a shudder. But she was lying. Just a little, she did actually feel some kind of a connection to the ghost.

Would using the book work? Assuming they lit up the basement like the surface of the sun and actually found the *Malleus Maleficarum* in one piece, could it really be used to banish Hugh? Vellacourt was no fragile ghost to be run off by light, however bright. Nor did remorse seem to be his weakness. He had lived his life as he wanted and the world be damned. He might not even believe in God. She didn't see how a book would help, unless there was really some sort of connection to his remains.

"Karo?" Tristam interrupted her thoughts. She saw at once that he had a small digital camera in his hands; he was enough of a historian to want to keep a record of what they were doing. "The lights are up, but look, there's no need for you to go down there. It's pretty foul. One of the Campions already threw up because of the stench."

"I don't care. You don't really think I would leave you to face this alone, do you?" Also, this could be history in the making. She had to be there.

"Okay. But I hope you aren't attached to those shoes. They'll be ruined."

"They're my grubbies," Karo answered.

The basement might have had an egress from within the house at one time, but they had not discovered it in their search. Likely the door had been plastered over at some point. The only known entrance was through an outside bulkhead, which had been overgrown with thorny vines whose sap bled a strange brownish red and smelled a bit like rotten meat and raised blisters on the skin.

Piled near the door were a sledgehammer, crowbar, shovel and a claw-foot hammer. And two familiar masks. They wouldn't keep out odors, but they would help with dust and mold.

"Give me the camera," Karo said. "I have deep pockets on these pants. It'll be safe."

Tristam went first. It took a surprising amount of will to enter the basement, even with the Campions' spotlights illuminating the old stair and the space beyond. The darkness soon returned after that. The spots might have been adequate to fight off night along the drive, but they were no match for the miasma beneath the mansion.

Karo paused to take a picture of the opening. There was no sign saying ABANDON ALL HOPE, but there didn't need to be. This wasn't a basement. It was more like a dungeon. No one in their sane mind would go inside with hope.

The ground was slimy with some kind of algae and the air was unpleasantly cold and filled with a smell she was reluctant to take into her lungs despite it being filtered through a mask. She also saw, almost immediately, that to call the place a basement was to use massive understatement. This was not a basement in the singular. It was actually a series of subterranean rooms, half a cellar and half a swamp, and completely unhealthy for humans.

The stairs were steep and slippery. There was a railing but—

"Don't depend on it to save you," Tristam said without turning. "The wood is rotten, as soft as a sponge."

Thirteen steps, deep ones. Karo counted, her heart pounding all the way. Then the horrible stair with its uneven treads finally came to an end.

Tristam handed her the shovel as they reached the floor and took the rest of the tools himself. The ground continued to be slimy, but the sludge was thicker now and deeper. It came up over the toes of her shoes. It was also gritty with what Karo realized was plaster and crumbled mortar, which was peeling off the walls.

"Is there a sump pump?" she asked.

"Yes, but it doesn't work. I think the basement settled and has breached the water table. It is below the water line now. And it floods. Look at the walls." They were wet to the ceiling and growing mold.

"Ugh."

"Indeed. Let's get started."

They were methodical in their search at the beginning. They began at the left wall and traveled in a clockwise direction. The basement had been compartmentalized. Some walls were unmortared stone, some brick. Near the doorway of the first room were rotten shelves whose brackets had rusted and pulled away from the wall. The shelves had held some kind of jars that were mostly broken, though there was one that seemed to be intact. Karo photographed it. The flash showed the glass to be purpled. That suggested great age. They should retrieve it later.

"Best to be thorough," Tristam agreed as she took a second picture. His voice was muffled, perhaps by the mask but also by the still air that ate all sound. The acoustics were odd, allowing no normal reverberation, and Karo wondered with growing paranoia if the pillars and walls had been placed deliberately to cause this effect.

"I think the Campions cleared out all the snakes," Tristam said, "but have a care where you step—and keep that shovel handy."

The warning was unnecessary. Alarm and paranoia had Karo's eyes opened to their widest.

They skirted a wall made of brick, which had clearly been added at a later time. The rest of the foundation and support pillars in that part of the basement were built from stone that had been plastered and painted, though little of either remained on the damp walls.

The stench on the far side of the brick wall was greater and reached out to them even before they ducked through the low arch and entered what might have been a wine cellar. There were no bottles left, only some scraps of rotten wood, but along with the smell of rot there remained the trace odor of something rather vinegary. Again, Karo fished out the camera and photographed the room. The camera's flash briefly drove back the thick shadows, but it showed them nothing except the bones of a giant rat and more spiders than Karo cared to count.

What the hell were these spiders eating? Each other?

Another arch, another room. By Karo's reckoning, they had traveled almost a hundred feet now. They would have passed beyond the foundation of the present house. Had there perhaps been some older building? The floor was angling down and the sludge was getting thicker. Karo began using the shovel as a walking stick.

The third room held the remains of a wooden staircase, and with the aid of the camera flash they could see where a door had been bricked in high up the wall. It barely looked large enough to accommodate a child and Karo pitied whoever had been forced to use it. At the fourth area, the Campions' light was conquered completely, and Tristam fished a flashlight out of his pocket. It was a strong light but did little to drive back the gloom and growing cold gathering around them.

"I am not an imaginative man, but this feels like a very bad place," he said.

"This is it," Karo whispered. Her words were all but swallowed by the stench and darkness.

"Look at the walls," Tristam remarked, ducking under the low arch. He paused almost at once as something—perhaps some loosened plaster—fell from the wall and splashed into the mud. The sludge burped, sounding almost human.

"Is it safe?" Karo asked, forcing herself to go on. Her gorge was rising along with fear and the tiny blonde hairs on her arms.

"I think so." But Tristam sounded dubious. How did one judge safety when their potential attackers were ghosts and mold spores that might evade their simple masks?

This part of the basement was older; the stone walls had not been plastered except in one area where a closet-sized enclosure had been built out. The stone was as wet as it was everywhere else in the basement, but in this room it supported a strange gray-green lichen that seemed to glow whenever the flashlight left it. The patches appeared suggestively body-sized.

Karo noticed this unusual phenomenon but was immediately taken with the thing that Tristam had captured in the flashlight beam. Ugly mushrooms and mold were doing their best to obscure the mural painted on the coffin-sized cyst protruding from the wall, but the image was still clear enough to cause hesitation: A dark angel—probably a fallen one—spread its somber wings over the enclosure and out along the wall. The painting was crude, perhaps done in charcoal.

And blood. That was the usual fixative.

This was a sinner's grave if ever there was one.

Simple it might have been in terms of execution, but the image still had the power to repel. Karo found it hard to breathe, and her hands were clumsy as she took out the camera and took several shots of the disintegrating mural. More of the rotting plaster dropped from the wall as she worked, suggesting to her lurid imagination that something was trying to get out.

"We'll have to destroy it to get inside," Tristam said. There wasn't much regret in his voice.

"I know." And she did, but she didn't like it. The plaster wasn't just keeping them out—it was also keeping something in. "I just hope the book isn't rotten."

Tristam looked back at her. In the poor light with his face half covered, she couldn't read his expression. "Take the flashlight," he said. "And stand back."

Karo did as asked. The light wavered a bit because her hands were shaking. She would have liked to brace herself against the wall, but the lichen was repulsive. Not just unhealthy but actually evil. She didn't want it on her sweater or in her hair. As it was, she was going to have to throw away her shoes and pants.

Tristam's hand curled around the sledge's handle. In the wavering light his long fingers looked like something on a marble statue. He swung the sledge with shocking force, and suddenly the room was full of sound and heat. There was also a fearful clap of thunder, and behind them the Campions's string of lights went out. Nature—or something more sinister—had pulled the plug.

Left only with the flashlight, it was difficult to see what happened to the wall. One moment the plaster and its sinister angel were there and then both were gone, shattered like a mirror. Tristam said something obscene as he stepped back from the cyst, and Karo fumbled for the camera with her right hand. She let the shovel fall against the wall.

The electronic strobe showed more clearly what was fixed in the wall. She was allowed time for one flash and then the skeleton embedded in the decaying plaster freed itself and fell to the floor where it started to submerge in the sludge.

"Get the bones! Don't let them sink," she ordered, pulling off her sweater. This was difficult to do while holding the flashlight. "Put them in here."

Tristam had already pulled out two handfuls of what were probably leg bones. The ribs came next. They were not intact. This was not some classroom specimen that had been wired together.

Karo didn't offer to help. One of them had to keep their hands clean to operate the camera. Also, it was beyond her capability to actually reach into that horrible goo and touch those browned bones. It was all she could go not to retch.

The room remained hot while they worked, but Hugh did not appear.

"Shine the light on the wall," Tristam ordered. "Do you see the book anywhere?"

"No. Nothing. Just . . . just the imprint from the skeleton." The plaster retained the marks where the bones had been placed, but it wouldn't for long. As Tristam worked, more of the rotting plaster slid off the wall. Some of it fell in his hair and he shook like a dog to remove it.

Karo took another photo, and just in time. The flash hadn't died away when the whole thing slithered to the floor revealing bare rock wall. There was also a square package of leather resting just above the sludge on a pile of displaced stone.

"Look!" Karo rushed forward and snatched up the parcel. She was careful not to step on the bones or to drop the light; being down there in the dark would be unendurable.

"She must have had lizards in her brain," Karo said. "How could she do this to him? How long did it take her to wall him up, down here in this horrible place?"

"I don't know. Maybe she ordered a slave to help. Don't open that package down here," Tristam cautioned.

"I won't." Karo didn't add that she wouldn't willingly open it ever. The book repulsed her as much as anything in the entire world. "She must have had help. That wasn't an intact body she bricked up." Karo swallowed. "She had to wait until the flesh had . . ." She trailed off, unable to discuss the logistics of the crime.

"Well, at least we know what happened to Hugh's grave. She must have somehow destroyed the stone when she had him disinterred." Tristam stood. The bundle he lifted was awkward, and not all the longer bones were fully contained by the sweater.

"I don't blame him for haunting her. What a horrible thing to do."

Tristam nodded. Sweat ran down his brow.

"You go first," he said. "And go nice and slow. Don't drop the book. I think we're going to need it."

Karo didn't rush, since she had no desire to fall in the horrible mud that clutched at her feet like rubber cement, but she did not stop to take any pictures of their retreat. If more photos were needed, then they would come back at another time. It was a huge relief to finally reach the bulkhead and see daylight beyond. A part of her had feared that she would be trapped in the Stygian darkness forever.

"Wait by the door. I don't want to leave the bones unattended," Tristam said, lowering his burden to the ground at the base of the stairs. Her sweater sank an inch into the mud. "We'll get the tools later."

Karo started to protest the abuse of her clothing, but her sweater was ruined anyway. There was no way that she would ever wear it again.

"I need to go get a box to put these in. We can't just . . ." Tristam shrugged.

"No." She could only imagine the Campions' reaction if they came out of the basement carrying slimy bones. At the very least they would gossip in town, and it was far more likely that they would call the police.

Of course there was no question of either Tristam or herself being accused of murder if that happened, the bones were clearly old and eventually the police would call in archaeologists and discover that the skeleton was ancient; but who knew what would happen with the ghost in the meantime? Hugh deserved a decent burial.

And there was the matter of the media that would cover such a sensational story. It might be good for Belle Ange, but it would likely destroy what was left of Karo's professional credibility. Who knew what it would do to Tristam's business. People paid for discretion as much as anything.

"We'll have the funeral this afternoon after the Campions leave," Tristam decided. He went to pat Karo on the shoulder, but then seeing the filthy state of his hand he let it drop. Both of them were dripping with sweat. The heat had dissipated a bit, but it was still unbearably hot and the smell of ozone was thick in the air. There would be a storm soon.

"I'll cut some flowers later." Karo pulled off her mask as she reached the top of the stairs and stepped into the light. The clean air and sun felt like a benediction. "Shall we put him back in the same place as before?"

"As close as we can get. I don't want to shift those stones."

"Do you think . . . Did she put Eustacie down there, too?"

"I don't think so. I looked around on the way out but didn't see any other oddities." Tristam's expression was wry. "I'll look when I go back for the tools, but I think we have to accept that she is buried somewhere else. Maybe in the slave cemetery."

Karo nodded. "Take the book," she said, thrusting it at Tristam. "I don't want the damned thing."

"My hands are filthy," he protested. "Hang on to it for a moment more. In fact, open it up and see what we have. If you can, take a picture. Whatever is left of it, I doubt it's intact."

"So, you think we should bury it with Hugh?"

"Yes. I know that thing is worth a fortune but . . ." He shuddered. Obviously he had also sensed the pure evil of that place.

"Yeah."

Tristam went to collect a box. Karo delayed a moment and then scolded herself for being cowardly. She set the parcel on the ground and went about unwrapping it. The task was not easy. The leather had hardened, and it cracked when opened. The book beneath was likewise in horrible shape. She picked up a stick and prodded. The vellum pages had fused into a solid block that refused to open. If the leather cover had been illustrated, no trace of it remained. There was no way to prove what the thing was. It could have been a Bible, though she doubted it.

She took a photograph anyway.

Tristam returned with a large Tupperware storage tub. As a casket it lacked dignity, but it was the right size and the sides were opaque so nothing could be seen from the outside.

"The book looks bad," he said after they loaded the bones.

"It is. May as well put it in there with him—but give me my sweater first."

"It won't come clean," Tristam warned as he

pulled it free. He shook it to be sure than none of the smaller bones had tangled in the yarn. "I owe you a new one."

"I know it won't wash up. I just don't want anything of mine in there with him. I'll burn it later."

He nodded and then snapped shut the lid. Karo appreciated that he didn't make fun of her for her statement. She *would* burn the sweater later, along with all her other current clothing. And Tristam's, too. Even if she could get her clothes clean to the eye, she feared some kind of spiritual contagion would always cling to the garments. This was silly perhaps, but many cultures through time had agreed with her on this. Touching someone's shroud could cause sickness, death and even hauntings. Fire was the universal purifier.

"The Campions have gone to lunch and to pick up some more silver polish and floor wax. They will also stop at the nursery and pick up a rose bush I ordered. It is some kind of cane rose that grows twenty feet a year."

Karo was sure that they didn't need more polish or wax. "Why the rose bush? More delay?"

"No. For the grave. I want something thorny to discourage exploration in that corner of the graveyard."

"Oh," Karo said. The rose was more tasteful than quickthorn but perhaps less effective.

"Let's start digging a hole. Then we'll have lunch. We'll need our strength."

She nodded, though eating seemed beyond her at that moment. "I left the shovel down there," she admitted, looking back at the bulkhead doors and shivering.

"It's okay, they have others. And it won't be necessary anyway. We're going to need a pickax to get through those tree roots."

It came as no shock to Karo that it began to drizzle the moment that they laid the plastic crate in the hole Tristam had dug. A look at the afternoon sky had warned that rain was imminent. It pretty much guaranteed that she wouldn't be speaking to her parents that day, though they would be expecting a call. A tall tree in a storm was no place to be, and she wasn't sure she was in the right frame of mind for it anyway.

What they dug wasn't deep as graves went, perhaps only about four feet. But they had been four exhausting feet, and Tristam looked fatigued. Time was running out, so they didn't change clothes for the ceremony. She hadn't come here prepared with funeral attire anyway.

Tristam opened an old Book of Common Prayer, and Karo opened an umbrella which she used to shelter the tome that he had brought from the library. It made some sense to use the prayers of the Church of England, seeing as that had been Hugh's origin, though she doubted he was faithful to its teachings at any time in his wicked life. She hoped that if the ghost was near that he could smell the roses they had waiting to place on the grave, and that he would appreciate that the sky was shedding the tears that neither she nor Tristam could manage to provide.

Tristam's voice was mellow, but Karo caught only part of what he read. Her own mind was caught up in a dirge by Emily Brontë.

Then did I check the tears of useless passion—
Weaned my young soul from yearning after thine;
Sternly denied its burning wish to hasten
Down to that tomb already more than mine.

" 'Wash away, O Lord, the sins of all those here commemorated, by Thy Precious Blood, through the prayers of all thy saints,' " she heard Tristam say. Karo was glad that she didn't need to make any response, since she didn't know the liturgy.

Tristam closed the book and then his eyes. He began to recite. He didn't seem to notice that the cemetery was suddenly full of frogs, which looked on in silence. And Karo couldn't help but shiver as she watched a variety of spiders scramble up the tombs and mausoleums looking for higher ground. Frogs and spiders—these were not the witnesses she would want attending her own funeral.

" 'O Christ our God, who on this all-perfect and saving Feast, art graciously pleased to accept propitiatory prayers for those who are imprisoned in Hades, promising unto us who are held in bondage great hope of release from the vileness that doth hinder us and did hinder them—' "

Karo looked at him in surprise. This seemed to her a somewhat provocative choice of prayers and wondered if he was making it up as he went along.

" '—send down Thy consolation and establish their souls in the mansions of the Just; and graciously vouchsafe unto them peace and pardon; for not the dead shall praise thee, O Lord, neither shall they who are in Hell make bold to offer unto thee confession. But we who are living will

bless thee, and will pray, and offer unto thee propitiatory prayers and sacrifices for their souls.'"
Tristam opened his eyes. "Do you want to say anything?"

Feeling irreverent, but also knowing that Hugh
would approve, instead of saying a prayer she
quoted from "Dirge Without Music" by Edna St.
Vincent Millay:

> *Down, down, down into the darkness of the grave*
> *Gently they go, the beautiful, the tender, the kind;*

It was Tristam's turn to stare in consternation.

> *Quietly they go, the intelligent, the witty, the*
> * brave.*
> *I know. But I do not approve. And I am not*
> * resigned.*

Karo reached over for a handful of earth and
threw it on the tub. The sound was every bit as
hollow as dirt falling on a coffin. Taking this for a
sign that the end was truly nigh, the gauntlet
thrown, rain began in earnest, and the wind
started to whip them with leaves and sticks as it
lashed itself into a frenzy.

"'Earth to earth, ashes to ashes, dust to dust—'"
Tristam shouted above the rising storm. He and
Karo worked quickly to fill the hole and to place
the rose bush on top and pack earth about its
roots. They didn't bother watering it; the rain
would take care of that chore soon enough.

The trees were in torment, and the green wood
moaned piteously. Karo wanted to moan, too. As

the last shovelful of dirt was tamped down, a sheet of lightning split the earth from the sky and hail began to fall inside the cemetery walls. If it was Hugh's final farewell, she supposed, it reeked of disapproval and anger at his banishment from the world.

"I'm sorry," Karo whispered at the grave and then ran for the house.

Where'er we tread, 'tis haunted, holy ground.
—Lord Byron

Chapter Ten

Storm clouds engulfed the estate. The pyrotechnics display that followed the hail could have rivaled the Washington D.C. fireworks at the bicentennial celebration. It seemed an indecent paean of joy for a funeral.

Karo found it suspicious that the hail stopped the moment they reached shelter, but she didn't voice her nervous supposition to Tristam. It was probably just paranoia, and it seemed a shame to make both of them worry.

Reeooowww.

"Poor kitty. Come sit by the fire," she suggested, only to be ignored.

'Stein was wet and grumpy. He blamed the humans for his discomfort and indicated with many yowls that they should make the thunder and rain go away. At once. And when they didn't do as he demanded, 'Stein stalked out of the room in a big, orange huff, leaving a wet trail behind him on the newly cleaned floor.

Karo sighed. She wished that she could oblige the cat. The sudden storm's uncanny fury was disconcerting, especially coming upon them when it had. All she could do was take hope from 'Stein's willingness to go off alone. He was annoyed but not frightened. Perhaps that meant their simplistic bromide had worked, and Hugh's ghost was truly gone from the house.

Tristam finished lighting the fire in the small hearth of a modest back drawing room and flung himself down on the settee beside her. His dirty shirt had been tossed into the grate when he discovered that it was covered with bits of fungus.

"Blast!" He screwed up his face in an expression of pain. "I keep forgetting how bloody uncomfortable this old furniture is. I say we invest in something modern with lots and lots of man-made fibers."

"Okay . . . When?"

"Tomorrow," he said promptly. "My battered body can stand no more. I'll write it off as a business expense."

Karo reached for his dirty hand with exaggerated care. There were blisters. "The sofa didn't do this."

"No, but let's chalk the wound up to defending your honor and let it go at that."

"Okay by me. But eventually we're going to have to talk about some stuff." It seemed inevitable.

She touched a finger to one of the deeper scratches on his lower arms and frowned at the wound. "The rose?"

His eyes danced. "Want to kiss it and make it better?"

"Not really. You're covered in ash and mud. So much for showering after the basement." Mud from the burial, ash from the fireplace they had needed to sweep clean before they had burned the clothes they'd worn in the basement.

"Oh. Well, then I guess we can talk instead." He flexed his fingers and moaned in a show of further suffering. "You won't reconsider the kiss? I'm in pain. Really."

"Go wash." She yawned. "I hope the power doesn't go out."

"I say, this storm came rather pat, didn't it? Thank heavens there was no ancient oak outside the door or it would doubtlessly have been blasted by lightning—and us with it."

"Yes, we might well have been. Even without the oak. I guess we shouldn't have expected Hugh to go quietly." *If he went at all*. It was a continued sobering line of thought. Karo let go of Tristam's dirty hand.

"I'm not ready to wash. So, on what topic shall we discourse?" Tristam asked, settling back into the corner of the sofa and laying his arm along the camel back. He found a strand of her wet hair and tugged it.

"It just doesn't seem real, does it? None of it." Karo leaned forward. "People would laugh at us if we ever told them. Frankly, I'm still amazed that you believed me about him. Even after the dream."

"Frankly, dear girl, so am I." His tone was earnest. "I've been in the most haunted houses in Europe and never bumped into a single specter. I'm too dull and unimaginative, I guess, to see actual supernatural portents."

"So, why did you believe me? It could have been just a dream we shared."

"I believed because I had to."

"Why?" she persisted, even as he rolled his eyes. "Well, I could hardly contemplate spending my time with an insane woman, could I? Believe me, Karo Follett, when I say that a sudden belief in restless spirits is easier to face than the prospect of losing you because I can't believe in your ghost."

Karo had a hard time meeting his gaze. The frank stare and blunt declaration had tied her tongue, even though she really wanted to know precisely what he meant. It all sounded like a romantic declaration, but he might only mean it in a business sense. No matter their attraction, there were no promises she could trust blindly. Hadn't her past taught her that?

He continued. "Once I did believe you . . . Well, obviously I had to go along—even at the loss of wealth and my fifteen minutes of fame that a ghost would have brought. The idea of him following you around, haunting you, *watching* you . . ." His words were light but they didn't hide a ruthless sincerity underneath.

"So, it was jealousy that moved you."

"That was one factor. There were others. In fact, we've many things to talk about, my dear . . . but can't they wait?" He pulled her close. Their noses were almost touching.

"Wait? Why?" she breathed.

"Because the only important question this evening is whether we should partake of the warrior's recreation. What do you think, Karo Follett? Will you chance your professional scruples one more time? Or do I have to fire you first and then follow the usual courtship rites while you slip into penury?"

This was what she wanted, wasn't it? His hand tightened around her hair as he waited for her answer. Karo stretched out her mental feelers, trying in vain to sense if Hugh was watching. Nothing. Maybe he really and truly was gone. She looked into Tristam's eyes and nodded.

The hallway was a long dark tunnel that echoed hollowly as they neared the master suite. They didn't bother with the lights but relied on the violent atmospheric flares outside the casements to show them the way.

The doors were standing open. Filtered light bleached the world of color and gave the illusion that they were bathing in silver air. Even the garish canopy above her bed was drained of color and made into a soft, bridal veil.

"Let me," Tristam said.

Karo's wet clothing was stripped away by impatient hands that only slowed when he reached bare flesh. Yet that pleasurable touch again hurried as they shucked the rest of their clothing and rushed for the warmth of the bed.

Their skin was dark against the pale sheets. Tristam raised up on one elbow to take in the sight of his flesh-and-blood fantasy laid out on the sleek satin, and he groaned at the sight. His torture was almost at an end. He ran a reverent hand over the fullness of her breasts, over her flat stomach as it fell away from her ribs, and then he tangled his fingers in the thicket of dark hair between her legs. Traces of soot marred her delicate curves.

"Beautiful," he said, burying his face in her hair and cradling her close as he nibbled her ears. "You've no idea how much I've wanted you."

"Tristam," she sighed. Heat and arousal was rising off of her in waves. His pheromones were the most powerful of aphrodisiacs, and he smelled like . . . "Vanilla," she whispered, turning her face into his throat where she licked at his skin.

"Coconut," he muttered, searching for her mouth as he rolled atop her. It was a devouring, erotic kiss that left Karo gasping as he slid those clever lips down her body, exploring his treasure with his tongue.

He stopped at her breasts. He could see the dark of her nipples and found them irresistible. He worried them with lips and teeth and tongue, flattening them against the roof of his mouth as he suckled. The heat rising up from between her legs was incredible. He had to shift away from her undulating thighs or risk disgracing himself like an inexperienced adolescent. His hands trembled.

He didn't make it much farther down her torso before Karo's arms were twined about him and pulling him back. He wanted to continue exploring but his control was slipping fast. Later, he promised himself. He'd do it all again.

He didn't resist when she pressured him onto his back and took a turn at touching and tasting his body. Her soft lips tickling his throat were driving him insane. Fevered hands stroked his chest, and the smooth legs that straddled his hips were urging with rhythmic strokes for him to come inside and lose himself in her heat. A lingering moment of reason reminded him of his vow to behave himself if this blessed moment ever came to pass, but he didn't feel like behaving. He was all animal. Victorious. Conquering. Male. He wanted in *right now*.

It was a hard battle, but the man of reason won the argument. With a moan he rolled back into the position of ascendancy and tried for a little control. His body was a beast that was raging with desire.

"Karo?" He smoothed the tangled hair back from her forehead and looked at her face. Her lips were parted and a bit swollen, her eyes no more than languid slits. The sight didn't help his self-control in the slightest. His mind had suffered days of foreplay and his body was starved for her.

"Yes, *now*," she whispered, running her hands down his flank and pulling him close.

He agreed. It had to be now. He felt impossibly hard, like he was going to explode. His heart would break from his chest and he would spill his seed and spill it until there was no more life in his body. It was the perfect way to die.

He slid into her wet heat and braced himself against the siren call of her sex. His mouth closed over hers as she cried out. He was going to die, but he wanted it to be a slow death.

Karo didn't cooperate. She writhed under him, twisting, pulling, demanding that he end the tormenting heat that was building between them. Every sliding thrust pushed a culmination that was torture to resist, especially with her hands running over his fevered flesh and her soft words urging him on. He finally captured her wrists and pinned them beside her head. He covered her mouth with his own.

But, it was too late. Climax rushed through him in a boiling torrent. He heard her small outcry and felt her go taut beneath him, and then his own cries drowned out all other sound, even the thunder that shook the house in one final luminous display.

The storm had been violent but short-lived. It calmed even as their pulses did. Soon the moon was riding naked in the sky and the stars crept out, one by one, to add their tiny lights to the October sky visible through the window. Karo stirred beneath Tristam and he politely moved over. She turned in toward his body and burrowed into his side with a small shiver. Belatedly he realized the room was actually quite cold and they had forgotten to get under the covers.

"Half a tick," he said, reaching for the comforter and pulling it over them.

Karo's mumble was unclear.

"Sleepy?" he asked.

"No," she denied—and then spoiled it with a yawn.

Tristam laughed softly. He hadn't felt so wonderful since . . . since ever. He was euphoric. He'd beaten back the supernatural; Karo was his; God was presumably in heaven and all was right with the world. All he needed was a little nap.

"Should we talk now?" Karo's voice was slurred.

"No. It might ruin the mood. Have a rest, my dear. We'll sort it all out later."

"Okay," she agreed and relaxed into a coma.

Tristam touched her lightly, enjoying the curve of hip and waist. She was sweet as any dessert he could think of. Most of the heavy perfume of vanilla and arousal had subsided, but it was still with them, clinging to the skin and to the sheets. He tucked the bedding around her and then allowed his eyes to follow their inclination. Thirty seconds later, he joined her in the arms of Morpheus.

Karo woke with the first penciling of rose-colored light that sneaked into her window through the sheer lace and scattered raindrops that clung to the glass casement in the east wall. She was momentarily confused and alarmed about the weight of the blanket that covered her, and she struggled against it until she realized who was with her in the monstrous bed: Tristam.

A whole range of emotions skated through her body when she looked down and saw the telltale marks on her breasts. Ashen fingerprints were there for anyone to see.

"Well, hell," she said quietly. She did not want to wake Tristam up until she had come to some conclusions about what emotions she was feeling zoom around in her gut. Regret? Elation? Terror? Joy?

Karo swallowed. Why couldn't she relax in the afterglow and not worry about what would happen next? Couldn't she just shut her eyes and ignore the handprints that decorated her flesh? Or maybe enjoy them? The previous twenty-four hours had been enough of a battery on her nerves,

Karo decided. She deserved a coffee booster before confronting her folly, and it was best to finish sinning before beginning one's penance.

"Tristam?" she whispered, rolling over to study his face. Even relaxed in sleep, it was chiseled and refined. His golden hair hadn't a single lock gone askew. It seemed unfair that he should be so controlled when she was so . . .

Reminded of her own state of dishabille and mussiness, Karo thrust a hand into her dark mop and tried to restore some order. It didn't work any better than the million other times she had tried, and she soon gave it up as a lost cause. Besides, the milk was spilt, and it was far more fun to let her fingers explore the golden fur that covered Tristam's chest in a T from nipples to navel.

Desire rose up very quickly and repressed the butterflies beating at her insides: it was an excellent if temporary panacea. She let it come welling up until it was double what she had felt the night before.

Ignoring the chill, Karo tugged the comforter away from Tristam's hips and allowed her eyes to gorge themselves on his nakedness. She understood for the first time why lust was so often described with the same words used for gluttony; they were very similar sensations of mouthwatering hunger, and both inspired in her a huge desire for animalistic wallowing.

She cast a quick look at Tristam's face. His eyes were still closed and his muscles relaxed. Feeling adventuresome, Karo leaned down and pressed a soft kiss to his flat stomach, inhaling deeply. The scent was faint, but she could still detect a mixture of vanilla and coconut.

Karo kissed her way down his abdomen, sucking lightly on the taut flesh. She smiled when she found his sex stirring to life. It also received a small kiss. And then a rather deeper one as it stretched for her mouth. A moment later she heard Tristam draw in his breath and felt his muscles tighten under her cheek.

She turned her head and stared up fully into her lover's golden eyes. A few wisps of sleep remained to cloud them, but they were alert enough to follow what she was doing.

"Good morning." She was quite proud of her nonchalance in the face of such daring.

"Good morning." His voice was rough with either sleep or arousal. "Don't let me interrupt you. Please, carry on."

"I plan to."

They were awakened for the second time that morning by a cannonade of blows on the front door knocker.

"Good God!" Tristam groaned. "That doesn't sound like Opportunity. Could the Campions be here this early?"

"I think it must be the voice of Doom. Do we have to answer?" she asked plaintively as he rolled from bed and paced over to the window.

He pulled the sheers aside and then swore with profane vehemence as he began hunting for his lost clothes. "It's Clarice." He found his pants and began to dress. "What the devil can she want? Sorry, love, but I'm afraid that I'll have to go and be civil to my fellow human being. My *employer*. Why don't you stay here and rest? There's no need for you to deal with this."

"Clarice Vellacourt? Why on earth is she here? She didn't say she was coming, did she?" Karo also went to the window, but all she could see was a cream-colored Lincoln parked in the middle of the drive. "Good Lord! Do you think she knows about what we did with Hugh? Maybe she sensed something?"

She heard a low whistle and turned back to find that Tristam had stopped dressing and was instead ogling her smudge-marked nakedness with an appreciative leer. She accused, "You look like Douglas Fairbanks on the bridge of a galleon getting ready to abscond with a fiery heroine and some sacks of stolen gold."

"Fair maiden, thou art—" he began.

Another fusillade of knocking battered the still air with its painful percussion, and this time a cat's plaintive bellow could also be heard. Tristam rolled his eyes and swore. "Damn. I've got to find a shirt." Keeping to her image of a corsair, he leapt over the bed, bussed her with the briefest of kisses, and hurried from the room. She could hear him humming *Rule, Britannia* under his breath as he rummaged through the armoire in his new bedroom at the end of the hall.

Karo longed for a shower, but duty called. Instead of a leisurely bath in three inches of fairly warm water, she settled for a cold washcloth. She stuffed her sore-muscled flesh into a pair of jeans and a clean blouse and was just slipping on her shoes when she heard the screech of bolts being pulled back from the front door.

"Tristam!" came a breathless voice that couldn't possibly belong to the octogenarian Karo had taken to imagining. "Darling, I was ready to call the rescue squad. What took you so long to get to the door?"

"It's seven in the morning, Clarice. I wasn't dressed yet."

"Well, hell!" Karo muttered. And feeling suddenly suspicious and alarmed, she yanked on her laces and galloped downstairs to referee the meeting between Tristam and the breathless voice. She was torn equally between fear of Clarice's true nature being exactly what she suspected, and trying to think up reasonable explanations for what they had done to her ancestor, just in case Hugh had made a bedside appearance and handed out an indictment before retiring to the Great Beyond.

The voice was a tip-off, but Karo's first look at Clarice Vellacourt was still a bit of a facer. She was glad that her ego had already passed through the crucible of envy and come out hard as brick, because Clarice's well-groomed appearance would have stunted it in embryo had it still been vulnerable to such petty comparisons. As it was, it still lost a little mortar around the edges. How could the woman have traveled any distance by car and not have a single wrinkle in her linen skirt?

Her shoes were immaculate, too. Karo looked down at her own footwear. Her once white sneakers were now an unattractive shade of dusty gray, and there was a tiny tear in the left toe where she had snagged it on an antler. Still, she had no choice but to carry on. There wasn't time to take a bath, repair the hair and apply makeup, let alone shop for new clothes and get a manicure.

Tristam and his employer both turned at the sound of her hurried steps, and Clarice's charming smile disappeared as if Karo was mephitic. Karo wasn't sorry to see that dentistry go into hiding. Teeth that white and bright could only be porcelain caps buffed with a professional strength floor wax, and it was inconsiderate of the woman to flash them around when neither Karo nor Tristam had been given a crack at a toothbrush.

She was prepared for Clarice to gather herself into the insincere but polite conversational greetings that happen when two strangers don't care for one another, but perhaps Clarice had been gone from Virginia long enough for this custom to have worn off. Or it might be that the Vellacourts had never bothered with good manners and she wasn't about to start with the hired help.

"Clarice." Tristam's voice was pleasant but firm as he drew his employer's attention. "This is my assistant, Karo Follett. I lured her away from Williamstown for this project. She's the one responsible for keeping your treasures safe, and for designing the Belle Ange cookbook. And . . . Karo, this is Clarice Vellacourt."

Clarice should have been pleased with the professional laurel Tristam had lowered onto Karo's brow, considering how cheaply her experience was being gotten for this dirty job, but the woman did not seem impressed. Her quivering nose and icy stare seemed to relegate Karo to the ranks of the smelly slaves and ugly Neanderthals she wouldn't hire to clean her bathroom.

"How do you do?" Karo asked the blaze of red hair that was presented to her as Clarice swung around to confront Tristam, eyes full of accusation.

The head turned back. Its expression was back under control. "Well! Hello. Did I also drag you out of bed, dear?" There came a sharklike smile. "How thoughtless."

"Yes, but perhaps your flight was early." Karo smiled with equal insincerity. She would be polite and accommodating, but she would not allow herself to be emotionally bullied by another man-trap, southern belle in a pink sweater and a fur coat; that had happened enough this lifetime. "I'm afraid we put in a rather late night. The library is still a disaster area. I hope that isn't why you've come."

Tristam cleared his throat and took Clarice by the arm. "Perhaps some coffee," he suggested, pulling her gently in the direction of the kitchen. He grimaced at Karo in a way that was probably fraught with meaning, but she chose not to understand.

"Why, thank you, darling! I could certainly enjoy a cup of your espresso." Clarice turned to Karo and added, "I won't take you away from your library, dear. And feel free to take a moment to comb your hair."

"You won't keep me away," Karo answered cheerfully, following them. "Tristam and I have an agreement. I don't work or comb my hair until

I get an infusion of caffeine, and I'm afraid that these days there's only one kitchen for both masters and slaves."

"It's best to let her have it, Clarice," Tristam told their guest, while shaking his head at Karo and frowning direfully. "The troops have a right to be fed. We'll have a quiet chin-wag later and you can tell me why you're here ahead of schedule. In the meantime, let me catch you up on what we've done."

He guided Clarice down the narrow hall, leaving Karo to trail behind. She tried not to be hurt by this admonishment and near dismissal by her lover of less than twelve hours. It was only what was to be expected, wasn't it? This was, after all, why she avoided getting involved on the job. When one did something stupid like she had, one ended up on the morning after having to sort out one's professional life from personal emotions. She was supposed to just white them out like they didn't exist and behave like an obedient dog, even when the object of her adoration was paying way too much attention to another woman.

This clutching sensation in the depths of her chest was a new symptom, but she recognized it for what it was: lust plus a little something extra. Then she was able to identify the biggest of the uncomfortable new emotions that were buffeting her insides, and it turned out to be huge. It dwarfed all the other feelings, and was very likely going to break her foolish heart when it left her stomach and went for her soft head.

Karo looked down at 'Stein, who had materialized underfoot. The cat had failed to follow Tristam to the kitchen and was instead twining himself about her ankles and stropping his furry face on her sneakers in what she chose to think was a gesture of comfort and support, not a need to get rid of some cobweb he'd walked through.

"It's nice to know that somebody loves me," she told him while bending to scoop him up into her arms. She returned his caress with her hairless cheeks. 'Stein purred his approval at her display of affection. Unfortunately, his pumpkin-colored fur was the final coffin nail in her ailing ensemble. Her sneakers looked like they had grown hair.

"Okay." Karo took a deep breath and stared into his pleasure-slitted eyes. "Let's go get some coffee and see how deep that hussy has her hooks into him. I'm going to be really sorry if I have to get another job before Halloween, but it wouldn't be the first time I've blown it, would it?"

Her persecution complex only grew as the day wore on. The air outside was still and moisture laden when they went into the gardens to see the sights, but the gauzy fog had lifted with the temperatures, and it looked like it was going to be a perfect fall day. Karo ignored Clarice's hints that she should make herself scarce and followed the two out to the marble bathhouse that the Campions had discovered the week before.

The house was located next to the Roman-style fountain chipped out of the inferior, local stone, and it was the most unattractive building she had ever seen. As yet, they had not uncovered either the Parthenon or the Great Pyramid, but they were bound to be out here somewhere. Hugh had been fond of mimicking the fashionable architecture of the old world, with varying degrees of failure. It was just a matter of finding the Coliseum in the shrubbery now, which was still thick enough at the perimeter to be hiding the entire Lost City of Atlantis—and maybe the Tower of London, too.

What a pity that Clarice didn't get lost in the bushes or fall in a well. Not a deep one. Just a real smelly, slimy hole.

Tristam's fluid voice intruded on Karo's sulking— that is, on her *study*—and Karo looked up from leprous granite to see Clarice was again batting her lashes at him, pretending to hang on his every word. She was up to no good. Did Tristam realize?

"No one could be that dumb," she muttered under her breath. "He won't fall for it."

"Roman ruins were all the rage, and it was a great way of tarting up the well," her lover said, helping his employer over a broken step. She laughed softly and clung to his arm. Karo was left to help herself.

"I just adore Roman sculpture," Clarice cooed. "So classically romantic."

Karo looked at the caryatids holding up the vaulted roof and sneered. They were done by the same artist that had carved the stubby winged cherubs on the bench in the rose garden. There must have been a shortage of stonecutters in the New World for Vellacourt to have continued patronizing this particular artisan.

"Vellacourt wasn't married to any one architectural style." Tristam went on with his lecture by quoting directly from the visitors pamphlet Karo had whipped up, which clearly Clarice had never read. "The house itself is a handsome example of Gothic Revival, but almost Victorian in its elaborate decoration. For example, the flying buttresses . . ."

He looked good in the sun, all Errol Flynn with golden muscles and Lord Peter Wimsey melodious piffle. Karo could smell the vanilla from where she stood, and her recently oversexed body displayed its usual sorry symptoms at his presence. Karo snorted at herself in disgust. What was she doing out here? Trailing along like the kid sister and pestering the adults? She should be ashamed. Had she no pride? No faith? No better things to do?

Tristam wasn't a shallow twit, she reminded herself. He had to be polite to his employer, and that was just what he was doing. The woman might even get around to telling him what she was doing in Virginia. And really, Clarice didn't seem like the kind of female interested in much of anything beyond her own fascinating self. Of course, what little bit of interest she did have seemed directed at Tristam, but he was a big boy. He could handle a man-eater. Couldn't he? Karo chewed her lip and lingered indecisively.

'Stein, who had stuck with the humans, even to the point of wading through wet grass with his tender, house-raised paws, made a rather well-timed meow and came to sit on Karo's feet. She had to admit that he made a valid point: her thoughts had been more than a bit catty, and she was disgracing herself with such immature behavior. Karo had a last wistful and immodest wish that Clarice might have caught them in the act on a blanket in the rose garden.

In her fantasy, her makeup was in place, her hair completely detangled and she was wearing a wispy little something in virginal white. Cruel circumstance had left Karo with the reality of facing her rival with post-coital hair and clothes, and too little sleep. Life just wasn't fair.

She pulled her eyes away from Tristam's heroic form. It was a nice fantasy, showing that polished-toothed homewrecker in the clearest possible way about the transcendental relationship that Karo and Tristam shared, but it was only a fantasy. Besides, who even said they shared a transcendental relationship? Tristam certainly hadn't. Not in any clear, declarative terms.

Karo sighed, dislodged the cat from her feet and turned smartly in the wet weeds. She started back for the house at a brisk pace, keeping her face forward and her shoulders back. She might not have neat hair, but she did have her dignity. Now.

"Peace at last!" cooed the hated voice. "Tristam, darling, now that we're alone, I really must speak to you about a personal matter."

Karo didn't pause to eavesdrop on their conversation, even when she reached the deep cover of the boxwood hedge where she could linger unseen. She just had to trust that Tristam would keep his head and remember to pump Clarice for information about Eustacie's misplaced bones—and for nothing else.

Would she have time to shelve all the books and still pack up her suitcase before dark? Maybe she should call her friend Diane to see if there was room for a guest tonight. The Honda was in

no shape to travel any farther than Williamstown.
Her poor car. She should probably shoot it and
put it out of its misery. It would be the kindest
thing to do since her father wasn't around to work
any mechanical voodoo.

Not that she was planning to leave Belle Ange
without a fight. And of course Tristam would resist
all advances from this hussy. But a careful woman
was ready for all eventualities, and she would prepare just in case this turned out to be the new
worst day of her life. After all, she who fights and
runs away . . . Only, if she ran there would be no
coming back to fight again.

"Is it a legitimate business expense?" Karo
mumbled, staring at the phone on the kitchen
wall. She made all her personal calls on her cell,
but this one felt like Tristam's fault. Therefore, it
was job related.

Lost in her reverie, Karo paused just inside the
kitchen door. 'Stein checked her pulse and then
began to revive her by licking her ankles. The
cat's tongue was rough enough to finally rouse her
to reluctant action.

One need not be a chamber to be haunted,
One need not be a house;
The brain has corridors surpassing
Material place.
—Emily Dickinson

Chapter Eleven

Tristam found her later that afternoon, weight-lifting her way to fashionable thinness in the stuffy atmosphere of the library. Karo was almost finished shelving the classics, D through H. She had a fondness for Restoration era poets, and for some Victorian novelists, but she had never acquired a taste for Defoe or Hawthorne. It seemed on par for the day that there would be lots of both to be shelved.

She had warning of his approach, first by the heaviness of his tread—it was more of a stomp, really—and then, secondarily, by the manner in which he opened the dwarf door with unnecessary force and allowed it to bang against the wall. If there was any doubt lingering in her mind about Tristam's mood, it vanished when he closed the door with equal strength and failed to make a cheery salutation.

Karo gave him a brief glance as he leaned his long, lean frame against the nearby wall and stared at her with what he imagined to be enigmatic eyes. The doorway was the classic place for such a pose, but it was far too short for him. He was stuck with the dusty wall.

No, Karo wasn't fooled by the cool expression. She had come to know him well during the last few weeks. He might be trying for lordly calm, but Tristam was annoyed enough to rip the pockets out of his slacks with his balled fists.

"Did you have a nice, private chin-wag?" she asked.

"We did. It was quite tactful of you to give us time alone," he replied, unclenching his jaw.

Karo turned her back on him and stuffed one of the last Defoes back on its shelf with an unintentionally brusque hand. She didn't trust herself to answer equally politely.

"Half an hour would have sufficed, though," he continued. "There was no need to abandon me to the hydra for the entire morning."

"Really? I couldn't tell. If you wanted me, you could have said something." Karo paused to see if she could hear his teeth grind. Maybe this would lead him to reconsider his thoughts on dental insurance.

"I might have . . . if I could have found you. You weren't here earlier. I looked. Several times," he said pointedly.

"No. I was in the garret, shelving some of the books we decided against displaying to the public." She brushed her sleeve, cleaning some imaginary dust. "You'll be relieved to hear that Hugh was nowhere around. I think the funeral worked. Oh, and I found another Valperga masterpiece. It's by the fireplace. In fact, it was only by a supreme act of will that I didn't put the painting *in* it."

"I was in your room just now," Tristam went on, ignoring her alternative conversational offering.

"Hm?" That seemed safer than any other reply that came to mind.

"I notice that you've wasted no time in packing."

"I'm trying to plan ahead these days," she answered, making an effort not to quail at the arctic drop in temperature that followed her glib words. Part of her could not believe that they were actually having this fight. It was so stupid. But the part of her that had been hurt before was in no mood to be reasonable or forgiving.

"Aren't you rather hasty to race to a conclusion? And a wrong one, I might add."

"Am I?" she asked. She began rearranging books on the desk. Her heart was thudding.

"You know, I truly prefer when you show some rudiments of intelligence," he growled nastily. "I've had quite enough of stupid women for one afternoon. I would take it as a great personal favor if you controlled your paranoia for the remainder of the day. And you can go unpack your bloody bags while you're at it."

She heard Tristam push himself away from the wall and start in her direction. Turning quickly, she pointed a finger at the middle of his oncoming chest but it didn't seem to do any good.

"You can just stop right there," she snapped. "Don't lay a hand or lip on me. I want to talk."

"Talk? Talk is for reasonable people. You want to run away, and I'll be damned if I'll let you."

He was right, so Karo picked up a second volume of collected Defoe and heaved it at his head. Tristam dodged it easily and kept advancing.

"I'd been having an emotional red letter day, in spite of Clarice's interruption. Until about five minutes ago." He added furiously, "How dare you lump me in with every other weak mind you've ever met! Let me warn you now that in future I will expect a little more faith from the woman I love. And I *do* love you. Someday I will even tell you why." He reached for her with quick hands, and Karo found herself blinking up at him as he hauled her close enough for them to touch noses.

"You might have mentioned that you loved me this morning," she said with reproach, pulling back a more comfortable six inches that let her eyes focus on his face without crossing. "You babbled on about everything else under the sun. Why not tell me what you were feeling?"

"I might have thrown out a trite phrase or two, if I could have thought of something sufficiently poetic, but it just didn't seem the sort of thing to blurt out for the first time with Clarice pounding on the door and you looking like you'd seen a gho—"

Tristam clamped down on the forbidden word and rolled his eyes heavenward. Karo wondered if he was beseeching the Lord for patience or having some sort of fit.

He continued speaking. "I should have guessed that you'd be indulging in an orgy of self-flagellation for giving in and making us both happy, and busily leaping to all the wrong conclusions. Maugham was right! Give a woman an opportunity and she'll martyr herself. Where would we be if *I* was so self-indulgent?" he demanded indignantly of the room at large and then grabbed her by the wrists and forced her against the wall where he gave a fair performance of a pirate ravaging a maiden. Unwilling to be completely dominated, she pushed him backward until he encountered the desk and sat abruptly. He let her wild kiss rock them back onto the piles of paper, scattering them on the floor. He pretended to be overpowered.

He was a bigger drama queen than she was! Karo felt her lips twitch against his as she fought unsuccessfully to hold back a smile. She finally gave up and laughed. "You know something? I really hate you when you're right."

"Oh? And what about the rest of the time?" he asked, beginning to relax as his better nature reasserted itself. His hands went from shoulders to waist and began to caress her.

"I don't think I should tell you." Karo buried her face in his shirt and inhaled deeply. "You're already far too cocky."

"Now isn't the time to be reticent," he informed her with a small shake and then sat up. He was careful not to spill her onto the floor as they regained their feet. "I'm feeling fragile. I need an immediate declaration of intent from you—and if it's not the right one, I'm going to drag you up to the garret and find a pair of Hugh's handcuffs."

"You, *fragile*? That'll be the day. I know rhinos that don't have hides as thick as yours."

"You wound me!" Tristam dropped to his knees and clasped his hands to his chest. "My heart bleeds from your cruel barbs. My life is shattered. You are *la belle dame sans merci*—"

"Okay. Enough with the theatrics. You look ridiculous." But Karo had to take a deep breath before she could say the words he wanted. Fortunately, a lungful of vanilla pheromones helped steady her nerves long enough to do so. "I love you, too, Tristam. I . . . I have for quite a while now. Maybe even from the very beginning, and against my better judgment."

"Good. It's a relief to have that settled." His wringing hands unclasped themselves. He rose to his feet and dusted off his knees with a grimace of distaste. He was himself again.

"The cleanup crew comes tomorrow," she consoled him.

"That will be extremely pleasant. I have grown quite weary of living in decades of squalor. In the meanwhile, come away with me while I set some things to right now that we are alone again."

"The hydra's left?"

"Yes, thank all the gods."

She was curious. "Okay. What did you have in mind?"

"Let's go fetch a blanket," he said, abandoning his poetic fancy in favor of plain English. "The Campions are gone for the day. It's too early for mosquitoes, and I've been having a fantasy about you and the rose garden."

Karo laughed. "I guess great minds think alike. I've been fantasizing about the garden, too."

"What are you doing in the library?" Tristam asked, finally picking up Valperga's painting. He grimaced and then quoted from *Richard III*: " 'I've lately had two spiders/crawling upon my startled hopes—/Now though thy friendly hand has brushed 'em from me,/Yet still they crawl offensive to mine eyes:/I would have some kind friend to tread upon 'em.'"

"Oh, dusting, looking." Sulking, but she would never admit it.

"Looking for what?"

"A satanic contract signed in blood," she muttered. Then, at Tristam's horrified look she added: "I'm kidding. I was just enjoying being around the books."

"Don't kid," he said and then kissed her. He put the painting down and muttered, "Horrid woman. Fearing God can have a revolting effect on some people."

"Not fearing God can do the same."

"So what did Clarice really want?" Karo asked a while later, as they strolled hand in hand in the direction of a cascading Himalayan rose bush that still had enough blooms to make a bower. Tristam carried a quilt on his other arm, and she simply had a bottle of sweet Zinfandel in her right hand. Tristam had said that they were going to reenact some of *The Rubiayat of Omar Kayam*, and in the spirit of the passages about "a loaf of bread, a jug of wine and thou" Karo didn't think that their particular jug of wine required any fancy stemware.

"Nothing," he said in disgust. "She was just fishing for details about our ghost. She didn't come out and ask if we'd been having any particular trouble, just made vague references to unpleasant atmospheres and colorful histories and so on."

"So, did you give her a prize for her trouble?"

"I made not so much as a nibble. I am quite vexed with her. Not only did she fail to warn me about the old Peeping Tom, she quite ruined the best morning of my life."

"Well, live and let live." Karo was prepared to forgive Clarice now that the woman was on her way back to Florida. After the way Tristam made it up to her, she quite believed there was nothing between them—and never would be. "You can't blame her for holding out about the family haunt. I mean, who would believe her if she came clean? They'd just think she was another Vellacourt loony tunes. There have obviously been others. No one has lived here for years. Decades, right?"

Tristam nodded. "I suppose you have a point. I just haven't achieved sufficient distance that I can be magnanimous about the situation."

"I'll forgive for you. You can owe me." She smiled. "I just wish we'd found out where Eustacie was buried. I still think it would have been nice to put the old guy and his lover together." Karo was a bit embarrassed, because she knew she sounded wistful, but she was a bit grateful to her time here: she had found her beloved, and had opened herself up to better things. Old Vellacourt deserved some credit for that.

Tristam's reply didn't help her self-consciousness. "Why? That has to be one of romance's more idiotic themes: Let us die together and be buried in a single grave!"

"You don't want to be buried with me?" she demanded.

"Oh, certainly!" he sneered. "I'll prepare the

ancestral tomb at once. You don't mind being shipped to England, do you? I'm afraid that's the only vault I own. Of course, it is rather roomy by American standards—and immediately available."

Karo pretended to glare. "I don't know why I love you. You have no poetry in your soul. You don't even like the Limoges."

"Here we are, man and woman, clasped in the bosom of a sensual Eden, but if you start in about that damned china, I'm leaving! What are the oddest fantasies you have, anyway? They must be kinkier than anything Hugh dreamed up—and anything you and I have tried—if they involve fine china."

"You need to broaden your horizons. You can do lots of things with fine china." Karo pointed at a shady spot overhung with crimson blossoms. "How about over there? Check for ants first."

He gave her a look. "And you say *I* have no poetry in my soul. What of the nobility of Nature? Don't you read Emerson?"

"Not if I can help it. And I bet Emerson checked for ants, too."

Tristam shook his head sadly at her alleged lack of spontaneity and then spread out their blanket on the new sod. He tugged the corners smooth and flung himself at the dead center. He patted the quilt invitingly. The bright pink fabric looked cheerful on the living green velvet, and so did Tristam.

"Join me. I'll whisper some sweet nothings in your shell-like ears." He didn't wait for her to agree. His hand pulled her to her knees and her body onto his chest. The Zinfandel was set aside for later. Much later. "Ah! This is much better."

Karo looked at her smudged hands. Plain soap and water hadn't rid them of the previous day's stains. Oh, well. Love looked not with the eyes but with the heart, or something like that.

"I was supposed to be clean and wearing white chiffon when we did this again," she murmured into his neck. The rest matched her fantasy rather closely. Well, she didn't really need Clarice to walk in on them.

"I beg your pardon? I didn't quite catch that."

"Never mind." Karo pushed his collar aside and kissed the pulse point beneath his chin. "Tristam?"

"Mmhm?"

"If we're going to share the same grave, does that mean that we're going to get married?"

He laughed. "Oh, you're taking me up on that? All right then—and I sincerely hope so. There'd be such a scandal at the churchyard otherwise. My family is very traditional."

"Can we do it here? In the rose garden?"

"Certainly. As long as we do it soon." He rolled onto his side so that he could see her face. "We have a new job lined up for December."

"We do?" She stopped nibbling on his chin. "Where? When?"

"California. It seems that we're finally going to open up the Youngbird Mansion in Humboldt County. DeWitt Youngbird has decided that it's time to share his Native American art collection with the world."

"Oh, my!" Karo's eyes began to shine. "That's a great house."

"We should have just enough time to pop over to the isle and see Mum and Jeremy. They are dying to meet you."

"They are? Why? I mean . . . why would they be?" she asked, surprised into partial incoherence.

"I told them days ago that I had finally met the girl of my dreams." He rubbed at a small streak of dust on her nose with delicate fingers.

"Really?" Karo could feel an idiot grin spreading over her face.

"Really." Tristam was also smiling. "They had some doubts as did I that there existed any woman with the right blend of intelligence, beauty and sense of adventure."

"What is your mom like?" Karo asked, nervously picturing a woman with a bust like the prow of a ship and a tiara perched in her iron gray hair.

"She collects stray animals, knits endless jumpers I refuse to wear, skis Saint Moritz in January and likes Farrelley Brothers films."

Karo blinked. "My parents will love her for her work with animals." She added hurriedly: "I will, too."

Tristam grinned. "So, when do I get to meet your parents? I've been absolutely dying to ask your father for a ride in his biplane."

"Ah-ha!" Karo shook her head in mock annoyance. "I knew you had ulterior motives for seducing me."

"You get to play with the Vellacourt family china, I get to ride in your father's plane." Tristam laughed even as he rolled her under him and distracted her with a long kiss. "I have to admit, you're the best-tasting dust bunny I've ever met. The loveliest, too."

"I wonder if my hands will be gray forever."

"It adds distinction," he assured her and kissed her again.

"Actually," she told him some blissful minutes later, panting in pleasure. "You might get your wish. Dad will probably fly one of his death traps out for the wedding, if Mom can't talk her way out of it."

"Excellent. Then we needn't wait for them to book a commercial flight. Let's call Reverend Tibbetts in the morning and see how quickly we can get this matter in hand. Now that we've made up our minds, I'm ready to drop into the depths and swim for the beautiful shore."

She was surprised but not displeased. "Fine. But I get to use the Limoges for the wedding brunch."

"Brunch? You're thinking of a morning wedding? How about Saturday after next, then? Is that too soon? What about *this* Saturday? I think we could be ready by then. I've talked to my uncle at the embassy and there are no legal difficulties. Actually, I'm ready now. Are you? Are you ready to—as you Yanks say—put your money where your mouth is?" His eyes glowed with cheerful lust. Karo knew that all time for rational discussion was running out.

"Saturday morning, week after next," she decided. "Our parents need time to get here. There'll be fewer mosquitoes. And . . . damn. I hope it doesn't rain. This red mud would never come out of a dress and veil. And I have to get one. . . ."

"How long does it take to get a dress and fripperies?" His tone was uneasy as he considered this potential new bar to his happiness.

"Not very," she assured him. "Mom will scare up something. She's big on planning my social life, and right now, I have to say I don't mind. She probably has had a wedding dress all put away for me since I graduated college. If not, I'll do without."

"Good. I want you to have your heart's every desire, of course, and to have a wedding befitting my greatest treasure. But I also want to do this deed as soon as possible. Now, the reverend is an early riser. We can make an *early* morning of it."

Karo informed him, more or less politely, that he was again mistaken. She had plans for a late night and then sleeping in. Since it wouldn't exactly be a white wedding, no matter her dress. She had *lots* of plans for them.

"I won't change my mind," she promised. "There are lots of things I have yet to try. And I wonder if you don't, too." It was the last thing she said before their lips reconnected and her brain went temporarily blank. She would climb the tree and call her parents later. Right now she had an agenda that was much more important.

Hence, babbling dreams! you threaten here in vain!
—Colley Cibber from *Richard III*

Epilogue

The afternoon sun was glinting off the third-floor windows way up in the trees. Neither Karo nor Tristam could see the house from the shelter of their bower, even if they had been inclined to look up at it, but it was probably best for their peace of mind. They didn't see the slight movement of the shutter in the garret, or hear the soft laughter of Hugh Vellacourt and Eustacie La Belle who looked down and watched the lovers in the garden. It was also doubtful that Tristam or Karo would have shared the spirits' amusement at the recent reburial of Old Father Basco's bones under the bush in the graveyard.

"Should we let it rain on them, *ma cher*?" Eustacie asked, looking at the bank of clouds gathering in the east. She cherished Hugh as much now as the day they met, though she had to admit his ever-changing appearance remained a bit of an oddity.

"*Non.* We shall make this storm pass away. They have, after all, done us a great service by removing that hateful book from the house. And it is sweet that she wished to bury our bones together." The two specters smiled at each other. Centuries had not dimmed their love, and their bones *were* buried together—in the armoire that Tristam had complained about moving to the garret. Reuniting them had been a herculean effort by a different Vellacourt, another attempt to expel Hugh's ghost.

"It will be wonderful to have guests at Belle Ange again," Eustacie said. "Shall we attend this nuptial feast? We shall have to keep our distance if we do. You make Karo so very hot, and I chill her to the bone." Eustacie went over to the bookshelf and selected a volume of Japanese erotica. The illustrations were beautiful. "Hm . . . This is new to the collection and very interesting. I am glad they discovered it and brought it up here. Such thoughtful children. Maybe we can show them some for their honeymoon."

Hugh looked back at his lover and chuckled. "*Bien entendu.* But of course we shall attend the feast! It is to *our* credit that they wed. Without a gentle nudge, they would still be circling and scratching at one another like wary cats."

"*Bien.* Then come away, *cher*, and let them make their plans and love in peace. It is only for a few days more. And we should also decide if we wish to see this home in California."

"Very well." The shutter closed slowly, and Hugh Vellacourt waved a lackadaisical hand at the two bodies twisted pleasurably in the garden. "*Adieu, mes enfants.* Until Saturday."

ELISABETH
NAUGHTON

ZANDER—*The most feared of all the Eternal Guardians. It's rumored he can't be killed, and he always fights like he has nothing to lose. But as a descendant of the famed hero Achilles, he's got to have a vulnerability . . . somewhere.*

Forces of daemons are gathering and have broken through the barriers of the Underworld. Now more than ever the Eternal Guardians are needed to protect both their own realm and the human world. Zander can't afford to think about what might have been with the bewitching physician he once regarded as his soul mate. But with eternity stretching before him, he also can't fathom spending his life without the one woman who makes him feel most alive. Perhaps he's found his weakness, after all . . .

ENTWINED

Eternal Guardians Series

ISBN 13: 978-0-505-52823-0

✂ ❑ **YES!**

Sign me up for the Love Spell Book Club and send my FREE BOOKS! If I choose to stay in the club, I will pay only $8.50* each month, a savings of $6.48!

NAME: _____

ADDRESS: _____

TELEPHONE: _____

EMAIL: _____

❑ I want to pay by credit card.

❑ **VISA**   ❑ MasterCard   ❑ DISCOVER

ACCOUNT #: _____

EXPIRATION DATE: _____

SIGNATURE: _____

Mail this page along with $2.00 shipping and handling to:
Love Spell Book Club
PO Box 6640
Wayne, PA 19087
Or fax (must include credit card information) to:
610-995-9274
You can also sign up online at **www.dorchesterpub.com**.
*Plus $2.00 for shipping. Offer open to residents of the U.S. and Canada only.
Canadian residents please call 1-800-481-9191 for pricing information.
If under 18, a parent or guardian must sign. Terms, prices and conditions subject to change. Subscription subject to acceptance. Dorchester Publishing reserves the right to reject any order or cancel any subscription.